D1505431

MORE PRAISE FOR *MATASHA*

"*Matasha's* brave and original heroine reminds me of *Harriet the Spy* and *Blubber*, her perspective captivating and inimitable. It's a joy to watch Matasha grow up, making meaning of everything. This novel has tremendous sweep and scope, with all the joys, sorrows, and revelations of a real girlhood."—RACHEL DEWOSKIN, author of *Big Girl Small*, *Blind*, and *Someday We Will Fly*

"The narrator of *Matasha* may be small for her age, but she is years ahead of her peers in how she faces a growing series of challenges. Matasha has to deal with the casual cruelty of her classmates, her growing alienation from her longtime best friend, her increasing awareness of her mother's dissatisfaction, and her own health issues, handling them all with a thoughtfulness that feels realistic (especially when interrupted by the occasional spectacular temper tantrum). Readers of all ages will enjoy seeing 1970s Chicago from her vantage point."—MICHELLE FALKOFF, author of *Playlist for the Dead* and *How to Pack for the End of the World*

"Tender, funny, and endlessly surprising, *Matasha* perfectly captures the confusion of being an eleven-year-old girl and trying to solve all of life's mysteries, big and small. This wonderful book—and the wonderful girl at its center—will stay with me for a very long time."
—ROBIN WASSERMAN, author of *Girls on Fire*, *The Book of Blood and Shadow*, and *Hacking Harvard*

MATASHA

MATASHA

Pamela Erens

NEW YORK, NY

For information, contact:
Ig Publishing
Box 2547
New York, NY 10163

ISBN: 978-163246-125-4 (hardcover)
ISBN: 978-163246-200-8 (paperback)

PART ONE

1.

Matasha Wax was eleven and in the sixth grade at the Margaret E. Marvin Elementary School in Chicago, but she was no bigger than many of the third graders at the school. She'd been the shortest in her class ever since kindergarten, and for a long time it was not something she thought much about, but in the past year some of her classmates had shot way up and she found, standing beside them, that she came up only to their armpits or—in the case of some of the girls—their breasts. The doctor she saw every May for a checkup said that if she did not reach four feet five inches by her half birthday in early November, they would talk about "treatment." Matasha didn't know what "treatment" consisted of, and the word frightened her. Would it involve needles? Matasha was terrified of needles. Whenever she had to have a regular shot—the tetanus booster, for instance— she ran from the doctor screaming and sobbing until her mother and the doctor had to trap her in a corner and hold her there, writhing, to meet her doom.

Matasha didn't know why she was so afraid of needles.

Generally, if she didn't understand something, Matasha would search it out in a book in the library, or she would ask her parents. Her parents almost always gave a useful reply. But in this case Matasha was too afraid to ask what "treatment" might be; she didn't want to know the answer. Matasha thought of herself as someone who wanted to know everything about everything, so this was a humiliating development.

Matasha's class was at library now. Library was one of the best periods of the week, in a week filled with periods Matasha enjoyed. She enjoyed math, science, English, French, and history. She did not enjoy art. She could never get her shapes and colors to look like anything, whether the class was painting or doing pastels or cutting up construction paper for collage. She did not see the *point* in art class. She did not understand why Miss Fillmore, the art teacher, did not teach them useful and beautiful skills such as real drawing. Matasha's best friend, Jean, could draw marvelously, but Jean was never able to teach Matasha how to do what she did. Matasha would have given a great deal to be able to draw a flower that looked like a real flower and not a circle with flat teardrop shapes around it. She would have liked to draw real faces, and a house that looked like an actual house instead of a square topped by a triangle plus a rectangle with fake smoke coming out of it. (That was certainly not what Matasha's home looked like. She lived in an apartment, though it did have two floors.) What a talent that would be!

If Miss Fillmore would teach them such things—including how to make objects that were far away look far away and not close up—art would be interesting and worthwhile instead of boring and leaving Matasha always with a sense of failure.

Of course, Matasha knew that art was not always drawings and paintings of real-looking people and houses and landscapes. Her mother often took her to the Art Institute or to galleries where they looked at large canvases that were almost entirely black, except for an odd meandering thread of red, like a trickle of blood, in one corner; or pictures of people who seemed to have melted faces; or brightly painted constructions held together by wire; or even art you walked through wearing paper slippers. Matasha knew who Picasso was, and Van Gogh, and Matisse. She enjoyed going to the museum with her mother, who was good at explaining art: what to look for and why it mattered. (Once upon a time her mother had led tours at the museum; now she helped other people buy art for their homes and offices.)

None of this excused Miss Fillmore from teaching Matasha how to draw properly in art class, or justified her wasting Matasha's time with dopey collage. Once, in fourth grade, Matasha had asked Miss Fillmore when she was going to teach them how to draw things that looked real. An annoyed look had come over Miss Fillmore's face, and she'd said that the purpose of art instruction was not to impart narrow skills such as the reproduction of nature but to open children up to broader sensitivities such as symmetry, shape, color, and form.

The way adults talked exasperated Matasha. Sometimes, because she was earnest and bookish and could follow directions and sit still in her seat, they treated her like she was a little adult herself. They used all of their evasive and wordy grown-up language on her the way they used it on other adults, rather than giving her the straight answer she was looking for. When they didn't do that, they treated her like a baby, the way most grown-ups treated most children. It was almost always one thing or the other.

Except for her mother. Her mother, Matasha thought, treated her as the person she was—an eleven-year-old who was not an idiot—and was always honest with her. Sometimes a little too honest. Sometimes she wished her mother would tell her fewer things, and less clearly. Matasha was aware that people thought her mother was a little eccentric. She'd known this from the minute people had started asking her about her name, which was basically as soon as she knew it herself and could talk. "Matasha?" they asked. "Not *Natasha*?"

"Matasha," Matasha would say firmly, her toddler feet planted. For that was her name.

The grown-up would swivel to her mother with a questioning look. And Matasha's mother would explain that *War and Peace* was her favorite novel.

"But . . ." the other person would say, and Matasha learned at a very early age that one of the main characters in *War and Peace* was named Natasha with an *N*. So this did not solve the stranger's problem.

"I liked the sound of 'Matasha' better," her mother would say, and that would put an end to the conversation. As she got older, Matasha felt a sense of triumph when her mother got to this part. *Yeah!* she thought. *Who says it has to be exactly the same name!* She was proud of her mother for not caring to do what just anybody might do. Still, it always caused problems— whenever she registered for some activity outside of school, or on the first few days of summer camp, or when some nosy lady on the CTA bus struck up a conversation and asked what her name was.

The librarian, Miss Rostowski, was explaining the Dewey decimal system. She went over it nearly every week, but Matasha never got tired of listening. The Dewey decimal system might have been one of her very favorite things about school. They were on the two hundreds today.

"The two hundreds," said Miss Rostowski, "include all topics relating to religion. You can find books in the two hundreds on Christianity, Judaism, Islam, Hinduism, Confucianism, and other religions. You can find books on the building of churches and on hymns. What other topics might we find in the two hundreds?"

The class was silent. Jean was silent. She never volunteered in class; she said it was pushy. Matasha disagreed. She raised her hand. Jean emitted an audible grunt of disapproval.

"Yes? Matasha?"

"The Inquisition," said Matasha.

Miss Rostowski put her small plump hand to her mouth, a thing she did when she felt the conversation had gotten awkward.

"What's the Inquisition?" asked Elliot Gleason, a curly-headed boy who thought Matasha knew everything and wanted to know all the things that she knew.

Miss Rostowski removed her hand and tried a neutral look. "Matasha?"

"It was back in Spain in the 1400s when the Christians would arrest and torture Jewish people and try to make them become Christians."

"Oh," said Elliot. He looked down into his lap. He was wearing gray-green corduroys. Matasha liked the color and

13

thought they looked warm and comfortable.

"In fact," said Miss Rostowski, a bit miffed, "the leaders of the Inquisition also arrested and hurt many Christians as well. The leaders of the church at that time were worried about people not being Christians in a very particular way. They were worried about something called 'heresy,' which means . . ."

The class was growing bored. Matasha was irritated. She liked Miss Rostowski—Miss Rostowski wasn't afraid of knowledge, or of saying what was true, and she didn't act as if Matasha was an embarrassment because she read a lot and asked a lot of questions. It was surprising how many schoolteachers, people whose lives were supposed to be about getting kids to like learning, didn't approve of a girl who read so much. And Miss Rostowski was willing to explain things, even when not all the kids in the class cared about those explanations. But even Miss Rostowski slipped into that adult evasiveness sometimes. Why did she say the church leaders "hurt" people? They put them on racks, they pulled out their fingernails: they *tortured* people! It was not that Matasha didn't mind that word, "torture." She minded it very much. It made her head tingle in a nasty way. It made her feel she was going to throw up. Sometimes she had to skip ahead when reading about the horrendous things human beings did to other human beings. But she always marked the spots she skipped with a paper clip and made herself go back to them later. She'd force herself to read them, squinting so she would have to take in only a little at a time. She hated feeling that she'd been too cowardly to learn what was really what.

"What else might appear in the two hundreds?" asked

Miss Rostowski finally.

Gina Wilkins lifted her hand shyly. "The Bible?" she asked.

"Very good," said Miss Rostowski. Gina smiled, relieved.

The bell rang. It was an old-fashioned school bell, literally in a belfry on the roof. The custodian climbed up there at the start and end of each day and pulled on a thick rope to ring it. The kids were taken up there now and again to see him do it. The school, of stone and brick, had been built almost a hundred years ago, and it smelled pleasantly old and cool inside. There were black-and-white tile floors and big windows that were propped open in the spring with long poles. Matasha had seen other kinds of schools, newer schools on the West Side of the city and in the suburbs. They were long and low-slung and built of concrete. Matasha thought that if she went to one of those schools, it would feel like being in prison. She knew what their insides looked like from TV: long linoleum hallways, door after identical door, tall ugly lockers, too many kids passing back and forth. Mobs of kids, shoulders pushing, elbows knocking, mean and hurrying.

Matasha thought about the litany of religions: Christianity, Judaism, Islam, Hinduism, Confucianism, and whatever those other religions were. Her parents were Jewish; Jean's were Christian. None of them seemed really to believe in God. Matasha sometimes thought that was a shame; she was an orderly girl and the idea of a God in charge of everything, distinguishing between right and wrong, good and bad, appealed to her. So did the idea of having certain atmospheric rituals to follow, involving prayer books and incense and candles. But the only truly religious person Matasha knew was Sunset, who cleaned the Waxes' apartment and slept over during the week to look after her. Sunset was Polish and Catholic and used to be a nun, a fact that fascinated Matasha. She often tried to get Sunset to talk about it. She was keeping an open mind about the God question.

Jean interrupted her thoughts as they took the stairs to the floor with the sixth-grade lockers. "Why did you have to talk about the Inquisition?" she asked.

"What?"

Jean searched for the words she wanted. "It's like you . . . you always have to talk about bad things."

"No, I don't!" Matasha was taken aback. "I don't always talk about bad things!"

"You do!"

Matasha didn't know what to say. What was Jean talking about? Matasha talked about good things all the time, like small animals and ice cream and funny television programs such as *Happy Days—Happy Days*! She had a book called *The 1,001 Best Jokes Ever*!

Jean wasn't letting it go. "You're always bringing up stuff that's yucky. It's like your brain just goes to weird things."

Matasha was getting upset. "Miss Rostowski asked about the two hundreds," she argued. "The Inquisition is just something that would be in the two hundreds."

"There are a bazillion things in the two hundreds. Like, I don't know, priests and prayers and the difference between Catholics and Protestants. But you had to come up with something gross."

"It's part of real history," Matasha said limply. There were times when she felt that other kids had access to some sort of rule book that no one had shared with her. They seemed to know intuitively that there were certain things that were not nice to talk about, not nice to do. So that Matasha, who blithely assumed that anything was fair game for conversation, and that it was all right to do just about anything that didn't hurt someone else, would be brought up short and made to know that she had broken one of those rules yet again.

But why did *Jean* have to go on about it? What was wrong with Jean these days? Matasha wondered if it had to do with the fact that she, Matasha, had gone away for the summer, first to summer camp and then to Michigan, while Jean hadn't gotten to go anywhere. Her mother had had a new baby back in February, and there was too much to do. And now Jean had three younger sisters. She had complained mightily about how boring the summer was, how busy her mother had been with the baby, how messy the house was with all the baby stuff.

Whatever it was, Jean was being unfair. "You're just cranky," Matasha said, which was something her mother sometimes said to her, although Matasha frankly felt it more often applied to her mother than to herself.

Jean stopped dead and stared at her. Her face reddened and her look was so angry that Matasha felt afraid.

"I hate you," Jean said.

What? What had Jean just said? Matasha and Jean had had plenty of arguments over all the years that they had been best friends—five years and two months, to be exact—but Jean had never, ever used the word "hate" before. She looked a little stunned herself.

"I'm not coming over to your house," Jean said, more quietly. They'd had a plan, as they did on many days.

Matasha felt dizzy. Jean walked on ahead toward the lockers. Matasha ran to catch up.

"I'm sorry," she blurted. It was an all-purpose solution for fights with Jean. It didn't really matter whether you were at fault or she was, she seemed to need to hear an apology, and it calmed her down.

It worked again this time. Jean waited, let Matasha walk on with her. "Okay," she said, accepting the offer. "But I'm still not coming over today."

Matasha kept her mouth shut. She didn't have access to that rule book everyone else did, but she knew enough to accept what she'd gotten and not try for anything more. Jean would be herself again tomorrow. Probably. It usually panned out like that.

2.

Two years ago, Matasha had started to read the newspaper each morning before school. Before then she hadn't read it properly—only the comics and Dottie Summers's advice column, her favorite. One day she finished those and then turned to the front page and read it as well. So she knew about Patty Hearst, the multimillionaire's daughter who had been held hostage by a crazy political group; about Watergate, which had led to President Nixon resigning last year; and about the war in Vietnam, which was finally over. North Vietnam was Communist and South Vietnam wasn't, so the US had been helping the South Vietnamese fight against the North. But the South had lost. This past spring Matasha had watched on TV while a helicopter landed on the roof of the American embassy in Saigon, the South Vietnamese capital, and Americans had scrambled up into it to escape before the North Vietnamese marched in and captured them. She saw people dangling from the rope ladder to the helicopter and feared they'd fall off and die or be left behind. She'd read about the South Vietnamese families who were fleeing the country in boats and about the children who had lost their parents on the way. Her mother said she wanted to adopt one. A girl.

Matasha's father said, "We'll see." That was what he always said whenever he wanted to buy enough time to let his wife's latest enthusiasm fizzle out. In this way the family had emerged unscathed through Mrs. Wax's plans to buy a lakeside cottage in Quebec, spend six weeks living with a Palestinian family in the West Bank "to hear the other side," and start a business selling handblown glass. (Why handblown glass? Matasha never knew.) It wasn't that she never saw her projects through. But on the most expensive and expansive ones, Mr. Wax withheld his approval, and usually that was enough to deflate his wife's energies eventually.

This time, however, she'd continued to raise the topic: the orphans, their poverty, the United States' responsibility for their condition, the fact that they were in a position to help. They talked everything out right in front of Matasha, the way they always did.

"But a second child," said Mr. Wax. "It's not like a puppy, or like sponsoring one of your Soviet families." Mrs. Wax had adopted a family in Leningrad that she was trying to help emigrate to the US. The Soviet Union mistreated Jews yet wouldn't let them leave for other countries. There were groups trying to get the Soviet Union to change that. Matasha's mother had made a pledge to the Leningrad family—a mom and dad and three teenagers—to pay for their housing for one year, if they were successful in getting out. Mr. Wax had found that a bit extravagant.

Mrs. Wax looked at Matasha, who was sitting in one of the oversized living room chairs, reading *Studs Lonigan*. The living room was two stories high, and through its tall windows you could see the expanse of Lake Michigan. It was a Sunday, after dinner. Sunday was the one day the family always ate together. Matasha's father was enjoying a cigar. *Studs Lonigan* was old-fashioned and slow, but Matasha still liked it because it was all about Chicago. At the same time she had been half listening to her parents, and her antennae told her when their eyes suddenly settled on her.

"I wanted another," said Mrs. Wax.

"Who stopped you, Jenine?" asked Mr. Wax genially.

"I waited too long," admitted Mrs. Wax. "And I don't want a baby now."

"Are you sure you're thinking about this for the right reasons? This isn't just something to pick up like macramé—a distraction, an entertainment."

"Of course it's not about *entertainment*," said Mrs. Wax sharply. "I understand the responsibilities."

Matasha didn't think her mother did. Most likely Mrs. Wax would simply plant the girl in their apartment and then more or less leave her on her own. She'd hire an English tutor or something, but that was about it. Matasha's mother wasn't someone who got *involved*. Matasha knew the difference from school. The parents of her classmates came to school assemblies, helped with costumes for plays and on Halloween. They took their daughters to sell Girl Scout cookies. (Matasha's mother had dropped her off with her order sheet in an unfamiliar neighborhood and left to do an errand. Matasha, who was seven at the time, was too scared to do anything but sit on a stoop until her mother returned.) They took pictures of family events, helped with homework, cooked meals, insisted on piano practice, generally kept tabs on what their children were up to. Jean's parents did all these things, especially her mother, who cooked a lot. At Matasha's, Sunset made all the meals and did the laundry and the sewing, and she was the one who was there when Matasha got home from school. Matasha's mother took her on outings from time to time—to the museum or the ballet—but at other times seemed to forget about her altogether. She spent most of her evenings at "functions," which had to do with her volunteer work. Matasha's father went to the office on Saturdays, and on Saturday nights, he and her mother went out with other couples. Matasha was used to spending a lot of time on her own, but she didn't think this system would work very well for a stranger, much less a scared, skinny little Vietnamese girl who didn't speak any English.

"I have to say I don't understand," said Mr. Wax. He touched his mustache. He had a bushy tan-and-red mustache that put other fathers' scraggly mustaches to shame. "Even before getting to all the practicalities, like private school expenses, college expenses. These are not small items, Jenine. We have a happy family. We have a family that works. We have our beautiful Matasha. Why, as they say, mess with success?"

"Matasha is just not enough," Mrs. Wax replied.

Matasha clapped her book closed, loudly, and stood up. "Okay, okay, Mom. I'm right here. See? Me?"

Mrs. Wax uncrossed and recrossed her long legs the way she did when annoyed. Her pantyhose made a shushing sound. "It has nothing to do with *you*, Matasha. It's just I always saw having two."

"I'm with Dad," Matasha said petulantly. "If you'd wanted another, you should have done it before. You had eleven whole years." Her mother was so impractical at times. It was tiring.

"We'll see," said Matasha's father.

Matasha decided she didn't need to worry about her mother's plan going forward.

3.

Margaret E. Marvin was in the process of building a new combined middle school and high school building, and Matasha's class was going to be the first to use it, next year, the 1976–77 school year. The old middle-high school, close to the elementary school, was a four-story structure much like the one for the younger children. But it was to be sold off, and the new building would be larger and modern, with big panes of glass along the sides, a swimming pool, an up-to-date science lab, and a genuine library. In the elementary school gym, there were drawings and models of what everything would look like.

Right now it was just a hole in the ground.

The hole in the ground was on Matasha's route to school. She took the public bus, the CTA, to North Avenue and walked the rest of the way, ten minutes or so. Usually she passed by when the excavators and other big yellow machines were still parked on the grayish earth that lay under Chicago's sidewalks and roadways. By the end of the school day, though, there were men in the pit and vehicles that rumbled forward and backward and dropped and lifted their claws, apparently accomplishing something, although it was never clear what.

Matasha was sure that the boy's bones were buried there.

The boy was Martin Kimmel, a nine-year-old who had disappeared from Lincoln Park four months ago, just as school was letting out for the summer. He'd been there with his housekeeper, a twenty-seven-year-old woman whose name was Gloria James. The newspapers actually used the word "maid," not "housekeeper," to describe Gloria James, and Matasha had also heard both of her parents refer to Sunset as their "maid." But it was a term that made Matasha uneasy. A maid sounded like someone who had to curtsy and wear a frilly apron, someone you practically *owned*. Matasha had tried to get her parents to change their language, without success. "There's no use pretending we're the *proletariat*," said her mother, sending Matasha running to the dictionary.

The thing was, Martin Kimmel had vanished very close to Jean's house, about three blocks away, and that made the disappearance feel very real. Jean's parents no longer let her walk alone in the neighborhood; whoever had taken Martin still hadn't been caught. Matasha, horrified, thrilled, read every single news report there was to read about Martin Kimmel; she knew all the details. It had been four thirty in the afternoon. The sun was warm; it was seventy-two degrees out. Martin Kimmel was swinging on the swings. At some point he got off and walked away. Gloria James assumed he had gone over to the water fountain to get a drink. When she couldn't catch sight of him after a minute or two (Matasha got skeptical at this part of Gloria James's account; she suspected it had been more like seven or ten minutes; she saw how the housekeepers and babysitters behaved in the park), Gloria James became worried and began to search around for Martin. Then she alerted the other housekeepers and finally—this revealed true desperation—the mothers. Martin

Kimmel was not found that afternoon, and he still hadn't been found, though about once a week there was an article in the *Sun-Times* or *Tribune* about a possible lead, or the interview of a new witness, or some such.

It used to be that the Wax family took in only the *Sun-Times*, plus the *New York Times* on Sundays. When the Kimmel case began, Matasha, fascinated, talked her mother into subscribing to the daily *Tribune* as well. "It's a more serious paper," she told her, something she assumed because it had fewer photos and came folded in half like the *New York Times*. "I could learn a lot from it about current events."

Every morning she scanned the front pages of both papers and then turned to the city sections to see if Martin Kimmel had been found. In part, she was looking for answers for Jean. Though she was frightened herself about the somebody who might still be out there, scouting for other kids, it was worse for Jean, living where she did. So Matasha hoped to read of a sighting and an arrest. Maybe Martin had been located in a basement, or on a train in Ohio, or begging on a street in California. As time went on, though, she grew less confident there'd be good news. One day a detective was quoted as saying that children not found within a week after their disappearance were usually not found alive. That gave Matasha a chill. The detective's comment was followed by a statement from Martin's father that they were certain Martin was still alive and that they would never give up hope. But after that, whenever Matasha thought of poor lost Martin Kimmel, she thought about bones. She imagined Martin dead and his bones lying in a heap in Lincoln Park, bleached clean and dry as the dinosaur bones in the Field Museum. Then she realized this made no sense: a pile of bones out in the middle of the park. The bones must be under or inside something. She thought about this for some time, and gradually, without knowing exactly why, she ended up being convinced that the bones were in the pit where the new school was being built. The murderer, the sicko, had come one night and deposited them in the pit and covered them up with the displaced soil. Maybe he had used the earthmoving equipment. Maybe he was one of the men who operated the earthmoving equipment! The school, after all, was mere blocks from the park, although the area where Martin had disappeared was farther north. Maybe one day while the men were working, the bones would be tossed up by a big mechanical claw and the mystery would be solved. Or maybe the bones would be packed underneath the earth forever and, next year, three hundred seventh through twelfth graders would be walking back and forth on top of them. Opening their lockers, shooting baskets, putting on plays, and dissecting frogs right on top of them. The idea was very concerning.

She had yet to tell Jean about it, though. As Matasha had expected, the blowup they'd had after library last week—which Matasha now thought of as "*that* thing"—was quickly forgotten by Jean. Nevertheless, talking to her about Martin Kimmel was touchy. Jean was ready with her list of complaints. She couldn't walk to or from the CTA by herself anymore; morning and afternoon, her mother was at the stop, with Jean's baby sister and the twins, who were five, in tow. If Jean was going to Matasha's after school, she had to use the school pay phone to let her mother know, and none of the kids were allowed anymore to play in the yard behind Jean's house. Jean was incredibly lucky to live in a real house, not an apartment, and even have a real backyard; no one else Matasha knew at school did, and here Jean's mother wasn't even allowing the family to enjoy it. Jean hated and resented the whole fuss, and as a result got very irritable whenever the subject of Martin Kimmel came up. Matasha was at a loss to find the right time to talk about it.

But there was an urgency to the discussion. Martin was like a tickle at the back of Matasha's throat, a constant prickling that she needed relief from. If he could be found and put in a grave with a headstone like a proper dead person, she might be able to forget about him. His story would be over, and there would be some explanation, however horrible. If instead he got sealed under the concrete and brick of the new school, no one would ever know what had happened, which meant it could happen again. And what if the body haunted the school? Matasha did not officially believe in ghosts, but nevertheless she pictured angry rays shooting into the hallways and the lunchroom from beneath the unquiet foundation. It seemed reasonable that people who hadn't correctly been put to rest could harm you. Why *wouldn't* they be upset?

4.

Matasha woke at six thirty each school morning to her alarm clock, which had a wheel with oversized numbers that flipped with a satisfying click as each minute turned to the next. She dressed in front of the radiator in the bathroom, where it was warm. Then she went downstairs, retrieved the newspapers from outside the apartment's front door, and had a bowl of Froot Loops in the silent kitchen. Her father worked late into the evenings and didn't get up until around eight; her mother woke at no particular time. Matasha scanned the headlines for Martin Kimmel news, then read Dear Dottie and a couple of comic strips. She saved Dear Eleanor—the similar advice column in the *Tribune*—and any interesting news articles for later. She brushed her teeth, got her knapsack and her keys, took the elevator down to the garage, said hello to Jim, the garage man, and walked out into the early-morning light of the alley. The alley took her to Sheridan Road, where she caught the 153 bus, which made a few stops and then meandered into Lincoln Park and along the lake until it reached a tall building on the Outer Drive where Matasha got off for school.

This morning Tamar Pinsoff was on the bus. She got on two stops before Matasha. Tamar lived in a huge apartment, four stories tall. The place was so big that Tamar's parents had a second, separate kitchen and living room all for themselves.

Tamar and her brother lived on the first two floors and their parents lived on the top two. The Pinsoffs also had an entire enormous room that was just for art. Tamar had snuck Matasha up there once—the children weren't supposed to go on the parents' floors. There were blobby forms of brushed steel bolted to the ceiling and hanging down like silver ferns, and neon letters that blinked from the walls when you turned them on, and, most intriguingly, a large pile of loose nails on the floor that Tamar said was not part of a repair project but an art piece.

"Wow," said Matasha. She liked the room. She wondered if her mother had helped the Pinsoffs buy any of their artwork.

"We better get out of here," said Tamar. She flicked off the lights and they hurried downstairs to ask the housekeeper for egg salad sandwiches.

It was standing room only on the bus this morning.

"I'm going to try out for synchronized swim, are you?" asked Tamar. She was thin and freckled and wore her hair in two tight braids that made her whole body look taut.

"I don't know," said Matasha. She was always making up ballets and gymnastics routines in the club pool they went to near their summer rental in Michigan, and she thought she might like synchronized swim. You didn't get to do it until the second half of sixth grade. Next year, of course, they would be in the new building with its own pool instead of having to go to the Y, and they could have synchronized swim right in school. Right over Martin Kimmel's bones. Yikes.

There were two problems with the idea of synchronized swim. One was that Matasha was physically lazy. The thing she most liked to do after school was go home and sit in the kitchen and read while spooning peanut butter out of the jar. Or else lie on the carpet in her room listening to her Beatles records and working on the novel she was writing, which was about a family just before and after the Great Chicago Fire. Once a week she had a piano lesson in the Fine Arts Building downtown. She didn't love piano, but her mother said every child should learn an instrument, and whenever Mrs. Wax had errands to do, which was often enough, she would drive Matasha to her lesson, which meant Matasha got to spend an hour in the car with her mother. So she didn't protest about the lessons.

The second problem with synchronized swim was that Matasha was worried about her legs. Camille Janklow had said that Matasha had hairy legs. This was at the pool in South Haven, over the summer. The Janklow family went to Michigan for the summers too. Camille said straight out to Matasha, "You have hairy legs." Matasha looked down. For the first time she saw that she did have hair on her legs, a light brown that was visible against her pale skin. She got out of the pool and took a lounge chair by her mother, who was reading a book on Chinese porcelains. She covered her legs with a towel and peeked at her mother's, which were bronzing in the sun and hairless. How come Matasha had hair on her legs and her mother didn't? But it didn't entirely surprise her. Her mother was beautiful— everyone always said so. When her name was still Jenine Ostrander, she'd been named Miss Cook County 1955 and had gotten a scholarship to college, although later she'd dropped out to become a stewardess. She had large, beautiful gray eyes, thick, dark hair, and long, tapered fingers. Her fingernails were always polished a pretty pink. Matasha was immensely proud of having such a beautiful mother, one whom people stopped in the street to ask if she was the film actress Jacqueline Bisset. When Mr. and Mrs. Wax's friends asked Matasha if she planned to be as beautiful as her mother someday, she mumbled that she didn't know. The truth was she didn't think so. No one ever went out of their way to tell her she was pretty, so she probably wasn't. And the hairy legs, along with being inexplicably tiny, were tip-offs that beauty was not her destiny.

On balance, Matasha thought that she would not do synchronized swim.

Tamar yawned and looked sleepy. Sometimes in the mornings, if the two girls ended up on the bus together, they didn't talk much, which was just fine with Matasha. Tamar's conversation was not scintillating.

At Armitage, Camille Janklow got on. Matasha instinctively tensed and moved closer to the pole she was holding. She made herself ready. Fortunately Camille was often late to school and so didn't end up on Matasha's bus, but when she showed up it was terrible. You always had to be prepared for some sly remark that you would be thinking about for hours afterward, wondering if it was an insult, unless she did come right out and make an obvious insult. You had to worry about "friendly" invitations that turned out to be opportunities to humiliate you, conversations that took a sudden veering turn so that you crashed into an obstacle you hadn't foreseen.

Camille's father was a client of Matasha's father's. As a result, ever since Matasha was a baby, they were supposed to have been friends. When Matasha was younger, she had spent a certain amount of time at Camille's. She remembered those times mainly as a blur of shampoo, hair spray, shaving cream, and Dippity-Do. There was always something viscous and strong-smelling that Camille wanted them to put in their hair, smear over their bodies, or eat on top of toast. The rest of the time they would spend doing Camille's hair. She had thick, wavy hair that Matasha would have to put in rollers or twirl up into what Camille called a "chignon," or braid and pin around her head so that she looked like she was wearing some sort of cinnamon bun. At some point, Matasha had extricated herself from having to make any more of these visits. She didn't remember exactly how, but now no one expected her to go anymore. Least of all Camille.

Matasha and Tamar stood miserably holding on to the same pole, waiting for Camille to decide what their interaction was going to be like this morning. It was very unlucky that Jean didn't take the 153 to school—she lived on a different route. Matasha suspected that if Jean rode with her, Camille wouldn't get so bold.

"You got 100 on your history test," Camille said to Matasha.

"Uh-huh." Matasha didn't give Camille the satisfaction of asking how she knew this. It would just be the usual thing anyhow. Camille was famous for looking into teachers' desk drawers while they were out, opening other girls' knapsacks, intercepting passed messages, and using psychological torture techniques to get classmates to give her information she hadn't managed to get on her own.

"Why are you so smart?" asked Camille.

Camille really was ingenious. It was impossible to tell, from her inflection, whether she was asking a straightforward question or saying the opposite of what the words seemed to mean (*You aren't so smart, you just think you are*) or saying that Matasha *was* smart but suggesting that this was a matter for ridicule. No matter which version you responded to, Camille would make sure you knew she'd meant something else.

Matasha shrugged. Tamar, her guard down in the early morning, replied, "Her parents."

"Your dad's a lawyer."

"Mmnh," said Matasha.

"Isn't your mom going to school or something?"

"No, that was before." After marrying Matasha's father, Matasha's mother had gone back to finish college and then started graduate school in art history, but left when she'd decided being an art consultant was more to her liking. Camille was aware of this.

"Why isn't she going anymore?"

"She got bad grades," Matasha said. She looked at Camille very seriously. "She got Fs."

"Ha ha," said Camille. "You are *so* smart, Obnoxia." That was Camille's special name for Matasha. Supposedly it rhymed with her actual one.

Tamar said, "I'm going to do synchronized swim."

Camille turned and looked at her coldly. Tamar dropped her gaze to the floor.

Matasha noticed that their hands on the bus pole were like

this: Tamar's on the bottom, Matasha's in the middle, Camille's on the top. Camille was wearing a gold ring with a blue stone on her fourth finger.

Camille, noticing Matasha looking, said, "That's a real sapphire. It's my birthstone ring. My father got it for me for my birthday."

In spite of herself, Matasha was envious. The sapphire was cut in an oval shape, but more pointy on the ends, with many facets that caught the light now coming in through the large bus windows.

"I had a diamond ring too but I lost it," said Camille. Matasha tried to decide if this could be true. Maybe the sapphire wasn't even a real sapphire.

The bus took long shifting curves around the bends in the park, making the interior slosh from side to side. Matasha steadied her feet and held on. The last thing in the world she could bear was the thought of losing her balance and getting crushed against Camille. No one in school would hear the end of it for months—years!

"How tall are you?" asked Camille suddenly.

Matasha hesitated. Camille had asked her this question at school only a week ago. She knew how tall Matasha was.

"I don't know," she said.

"You know."

"I'm four eight," said Tamar. She was trying to help, in her way.

Matasha's face felt hot. "Four four and a half, four five, something like that."

"You're not four five."

"Four four and a half."

"Are you going to grow up to be a midget?"

"No."

"How do you know?"

Matasha didn't know.

"North Avenue!" called the bus driver. They trundled off and started walking toward the school. Though it was still early fall, the wind off the lake was gusty and tinged with a chill. Ahead, Matasha was glad to see Kay Bledsoe and Glenda Berrigan, Camille's two closest friends. Matasha thought of the three of them as the Evil Triplets. Kay was already into smoking cigarettes. She did it on these walks, then threw the butts in the grass. Glenda was tall and pudgy and had a loud, grating laugh. Both were nightmares, but seeing them gave Matasha the hope that Camille might want to catch up with them and leave her and Tamar alone. But Camille acted as if she hadn't noticed her friends. She adjusted her headband and pulled up her fur hood. Tamar bowed her head as if trying to get under the wind. Matasha didn't have a hood on her jacket and pulled a knit hat out of her pocket.

"You'll have hat hair when you get to school," said Camille.

Matasha kept her face completely calm and expressionless, but while they walked she thought about putting her hands around Camille's neck and squeezing really hard. She pictured Camille beginning to squawk like a loud bird, then a quieter one, and finally like a teeny little expiring parakeet. She smiled.

"What's so funny?" Camille asked. A misstep.

"Oh, I don't know," Matasha said, turning the full force of her smile on Camille.

"You don't know much for such a smart girl," retorted Camille. The comment fell lamely between them.

Matasha kept grinning.

"You're so weird," said Camille.

5.

Mrs. Wax told Matasha that an agency that placed Vietnamese children with American families had approved their initial paperwork and scheduled them for a home visit. Matasha was taken by surprise. This sounded serious—other people besides her mother were involved now, which suggested that the adoption might be for real. Mrs. Wax explained that a home visit was when someone from the agency came and saw your apartment, talked with you, and stayed for dinner. This was to make sure that you weren't alcoholics or crazy people, that you were a family that could take proper care of a child. The visit was going to be next week, on a Wednesday.

"Does that mean Daddy's coming home for dinner?" asked Matasha.

"It does. Mrs. O'Connor and Miss Lacey know that Daddy usually works in the evening, but he'll be here so they can meet him."

"Did you tell them that Daddy said 'We'll see'?"

Her mother said, "What they care about is that Daddy has a stable job and that we get the bills paid and that the child will be safe here and all her needs taken care of."

Matasha tried to imagine another child in the apartment. It didn't seem as strange as she might have expected. She was good at being alone, but she liked having someone around, and

Jean couldn't always be available. Jean came over less and less often lately, even not counting the day of *that* thing, and even though she regularly complained that her house was too noisy and chaotic. It used to be that at the end of the school day, Jean or Matasha could just say to the other, "Wanna?" and wouldn't even have to finish the sentence; there would be a nod and off they'd go to one of their homes. But since their return from summer break Jean often said she didn't feel well or that her mother had told her she had to do something or other.

A sister, on the other hand, would always be available, and Matasha began to come up with appealing scenarios. The new girl could sleep in a sleeping bag on the floor in her room and they could talk until way after lights out. The big stack of board games in her closet would get much more use. Well, board games might be hard for the new girl at first, but in the meantime, Matasha could teach her to read English and help her with her schoolwork and show her how things worked in America, like playgrounds and ice skating and swimming pools. And Matasha would be saving someone, doing good in the world, the way her mother did with her organizations and her Soviet family.

Apparently Mrs. Wax's comment about Mr. Wax being home for the agency visit was a bit of wishful thinking, because Matasha heard them fighting about it later. It was a Sunday evening again. She wasn't used to loud voices coming from their bedroom and was alarmed. Her parents rarely argued, and when they did, it was a brief spat, right in front of her and quickly over.

She'd come out of her room for a glass of water and heard the raised voices. Mostly it was her father. He was telling her mother, loudly, that he was not going to come home and meet two agency people about an adoption. There wasn't going to *be* an adoption. You could not unilaterally adopt a child into a family (Matasha knew what "unilaterally" meant). This was something two married people did together or not at all. The fact that she—Matasha's mother—could even think of sending off the application without consulting him . . .

"I consulted you, Robert," Mrs. Wax said. It was harder to hear her mother; Matasha had to sidle closer to the door. She didn't want to get too close, in case one of them suddenly came out. "I told you I wanted to look into this."

"'Look into it,' yes! There is a big leap between looking into it and *home visit*."

"It doesn't commit us to anything. It's just so they can clear us to proceed, if we want to."

"Well, 'we' don't want to. *You* want to. You think you're going to draw me, step by step, into this process, until somehow I'll change my mind. I can tell you right now that's not going to happen. I don't care how charming this Mrs. O'Connor is. I don't care how many photographs of handsome, sad, orphaned Vietnamese children she shows us. I don't want another child."

"We wouldn't have had the first child if it wasn't for me! You had to be coaxed into that too! You are the most . . ."

Matasha froze and didn't hear the rest. A wild static rose up in her head. Had her mother just . . . had her father not . . .

Had her father not wanted her?

She sat down on the top step of the stairs. She drew up her knees and held them. The static crackled again. She told herself: *It doesn't matter. I'm here now. My dad loves me, I know he does. I know he does.* She rocked back and forth, repeating this to herself.

"You're wasting the agency's time" was the next thing she heard. She got onto all fours and scuttled closer to the door. "You're wasting their time, you're wasting my time . . ."

"Yes, I know that's the real point. We're taking two or three hours out of your precious time at the office. If I could adopt this child without you having to take fifteen minutes out of your life to do it, I'm sure you wouldn't object."

"That's insulting. You're talking about a girl's life. You're talking about being responsible for someone for the next ten, fifteen years—and forever after that. I live in this house too, Jenine. It is not a question of the time for a home visit."

"Do you live in this house? *Do* you? I'm not at all sure about that."

Her father's voice dropped to a low menacing mumble, which scared Matasha more than anything he might shout. She couldn't make out the words. Her mother said something equally unintelligible. Matasha thought she had better go back to bed, pull the covers over her head, and try to forget she'd heard anything, but then her father's voice rose up again and she couldn't help listening. "It's a question of profoundly changing the way things are. You can't just bring someone into our family, someone you're going to be tied to for the rest of your life, our lives, without thinking it all through, Jenine! And without me being on board. Which would seem obvious to any grown-up who is not you."

"I think it would be good for Matasha," Mrs. Wax unexpectedly said. "She's too much alone. The only real friend she has is Jean. And lately they quarrel all the time. I sense something going on there, and it worries me."

"The way to fix Matasha's social problems is not to adopt a child! And don't make this about Matasha, anyway. This is about what *you* want. I don't know what's behind it exactly, it isn't rational . . ."

"Oh, *rational*. Everything in life has to be rational, doesn't it? *Feelings* are completely imaginary, they don't mean anything, who cares about *feelings* . . ."

Matasha's mother's voice was getting very high and she sounded, frankly, a bit unhinged. Matasha retreated to the steps again. She was a child who hadn't been wanted, whom her mom had had to talk her father into, maybe that was why he spent so much time at the office. And her parents thought she had "social problems." Did she? It was true that Jean was Matasha's only real friend; it had never before occurred to Matasha that this might be a bad thing. And she and Jean had always quarreled some. Jean had a temper; it was simply the way she was, and Matasha had learned to deal with her little eruptions of meanness via properly timed apologies and waiting her out. It probably *was* the new baby, although Matasha had trouble understanding it. She thought Charlotte was very cute.

Matasha stood up slowly and smoothed down her nightgown. The voices were lower again, hard to hear, back to a vicious muttering. She made her way downstairs. In the kitchen she filled a glass of water and sat with it at the counter, brooding. No matter how many friends Matasha ever made, she would never be popular the way her mother had been when she was in school. You could see Mrs. Wax had been popular from the photo albums she still had, pictures of herself and bunches of pals making human pyramids on beaches and playing softball in the park. Matasha couldn't picture herself becoming that laughing, free-spirited kind of person. Maybe her mother wanted to adopt another kid in the hope that the new one would come out different.

Matasha finished her water and went back upstairs to bed, past her parents' door. The talk seemed to have stopped. She wondered what they were doing in there. Was it hard to sleep next to a person when you were very angry at them? Would her mother make her father sleep on the floor, or vice versa? That was what Jean told her she'd done when she and one of the twins, Diane, had had to share a room for a couple of weeks last winter. The other twin, Kelly, was sick with the flu and Mr. and Mrs. White said she needed her own room until she was better. Jean said Diane kicked in the bed and so she'd made her sleep on the floor.

Matasha got into her own bed. It was a four-poster, with the mattress well off the floor, and the best thing about it was that it had curtains she could close around her. She did this now, sealing herself away. She thought of the story of how her parents had met, which she was able to get them to tell her every once in a while. She'd always thought it romantic. When her mother dropped out of college to become an airline stewardess for Pan Am, she'd had a little cap and a light blue suit and white gloves, and she'd served alcoholic drinks to passengers. Her mother said they'd had real meals on airplanes in those days, meat and vegetables you could enjoy rather than the nasty stuff they gave you today. When she wasn't working, she could fly first class to just about anywhere she wanted. She'd been to places many people would never go, like Ghana and Thailand and Japan. It was one of the few jobs for women that wasn't being a nurse or a secretary, neither of which appealed to her, and she had been able to afford to live on her own and meet all kinds of people, some of whom she stayed in touch with to this day although they lived far, far away. She'd met politicians and diplomats and TV announcers. She had Saul Bellow's autograph on an airline menu card—Saul Bellow was a very famous Chicago writer whom she said Matasha would read one day. Every so often she got a week off to take care of errands and doctor's appointments. During one of those breaks she was at the dentist. In the waiting room was a serious-looking man who looked a little older than she was (he was four years older, it turned out) and who had an open briefcase beside him. He was frowning intently over some papers. "Working, working, working," laughed Matasha's mother when she told this story. "Who, I wondered, was this man who was working so hard even at the dentist's office?" The man's name was called out by the receptionist—Robert Wax, which Matasha's mother also found a little comical—and he had to fuss to gather and arrange his papers. It took several long moments, and Matasha's mother thought he'd been silly to spread them all out like that given that he knew he was going to be called in soon. He stood up and some sheets dropped to the floor. Matasha thought this the most astounding part of the story. Her father was so orderly, so in control of his things. When he was around to be part of the recounting of the tale, he would chime in at this point: "Your mother was so beautiful that I was very flustered. I actually hadn't gotten any work done since she walked in. I kept looking at her." Her mother picked up the dropped sheets and handed them to her father. "Just like a movie," her father told Matasha. Then he went in to have his teeth cleaned.

Later that evening Matasha's mother received a phone call from Matasha's father. After his appointment, he'd asked for the name of the woman in the waiting room who'd been seen after him. Then he'd looked her up in the white pages and that was that.

Matasha thought this was a great story, though it also made her uneasy. What if her parents had not happened to go to the dentist on the same day? Then she would never have been born. It seemed like a near miss—Matasha could have been nothing, invisible, vapor. Matasha's mother said that if you really thought about it, everything in life was quite accidental. Matasha hoped this was not true, but it was hard to come up with an argument that contradicted it, unless you believed in God, which was yet another reason that religion was an appealing idea.

Her parents loved each other. Matasha really believed they did. She saw it sometimes in the way her father looked at her mother, as if dazzled that someone so elegant and lively had chosen him. He knew how to tease her and elicit one of her rare laughs, usually by doing something utterly at odds with his regular persona, like rolling his eyeballs back into his head while making a fish face. And her mother depended on her father, Matasha knew she did. She could be brusque and flighty, but she looked to him for his opinions and his explanations of the many things she didn't understand, like world politics and math and what to do when the car started making strange noises. Matasha thought about these things, but they didn't entirely dissolve her unhappiness. It sat on her chest and in her throat. Her belly was what she called "washy." It always got that way when she was upset. If her father was angry about the adoption, they definitely shouldn't do it. Matasha had been warming to the idea of a sister, even getting excited about it, but it wasn't worth it if her father didn't want it. Couldn't her mother see that? Matasha didn't want her parents to fight. They never used to fight. The change was scary.

6.

Some afternoons later Matasha finally talked to Jean about Martin Kimmel. They were at Matasha's, sitting on the four-poster bed. It was one of the days Jean had agreed to come over. She'd been fidgety, and she'd groused that Matasha didn't have any good snacks in the kitchen, but after a while she'd settled down, especially once she started drawing. Usually when they got together, Jean drew and Matasha worked on her Chicago Fire novel. The sixth graders were going to be studying the Chicago Fire soon—in history, the whole sixth-grade year was given over to the study of Chicago—but everyone already knew the basic story. Matasha had been working on her novel since the end of the summer. When her grandma Nan still lived in the city, before she'd moved to Ohio to be near Matasha's uncle Edward, she had once pointed out to Matasha a drugstore on Fullerton Avenue and told her that the Chicago Fire had stopped *right there*. The fire had burned right up to that building—a house then, not a pharmacy—after destroying tens of thousands of homes to the south and west, and just petered out. That gave Matasha the idea to write about a family that lived in that house, the terror of the fire's approach, what happened to the neighbors, and how everyone rebuilt afterward. One problem she'd run into so far was that she didn't want to describe people dying, and quite a lot of people had died in the Chicago Fire. She couldn't imagine dying by fire; the time she'd accidentally grabbed a saucepan heating on the stove had been terrible. She solved the dilemma by deciding that all the deaths in her novel would involve people running into Lake Michigan to avoid the flames, which had also happened and was much easier to imagine and describe. The victims could just go farther and farther into the water until they sank out of sight.

Today, though, Matasha had come up with something of equal interest to writing her novel: making a list of all the sixth-grade girls who were already wearing bras. There were three lists: Definitely, Maybe, and No. Matasha and Jean and Tamar Pinsoff and a number of others were Nos. Camille Janklow, Kay Bledsoe, Lisa Marcus, and Molly Jentel were Definitelys. Glenda Berrigan, Wendy Urquhart, Billie Taylor, Helen Lake, and Gina Wilkins were Maybes. Matasha went back and forth on the remaining classmates, moving some from Maybe to No and back again. From time to time she asked Jean for her input. The Definitely list had gotten longer and the No list shorter since the two of them—Jean much more enthusiastically then—had done the same lists last spring. Matasha figured she was likely to be the last one off the No list. She hoped it wouldn't take forever, but she would almost certainly have to be very patient. Was it a coincidence that the meanest kids in the class were in the Definitely category? Probably. Camille and Kay had been horrible even when they were little.

"Do you hope you'll get into the Definitelys soon?" Matasha asked Jean. Jean looked at her, appalled. "No!" she said. "Breasts are gross." Matasha differed on this but didn't feel like a debate. When she'd gotten as far as she could with the lists, Matasha asked Jean once again to try, just try, to give her some drawing lessons. She'd had another hateful day in art class. Jean agreed with Matasha about art class; she thought it was dumb. She didn't want to do collages or wax transfers or stuff with masking tape any more than Matasha did. She just wanted to draw. And she was very, very good at that. But Jean always replied to Matasha that she didn't know how to teach it, she just *did* it. And then she'd draw a face and say: "See, just do it like that," which wasn't very helpful.

Today, for once, Jean was more amenable. She got a faraway look in her eyes. "Like if I were going to draw your foot"—Matasha instantly unfolded from her cross-legged position, removed one sock, and stuck out her leg—"I would first look at the overall shape—it's sort of oval—and that shape kind of stays in my head while I draw the edges"—she took a pencil and drew two confident lines and connected them with a swoop Matasha took to be her heel—"and then I just *look*. Like, your toes are more little ovals"—*whoop* and *whoop* and *whoop* and the toes appeared at the top of the drawing—"and every foot is a little different so you have to kind of follow its shape with your pencil—see?" It all made perfect sense and Jean had drawn a beautiful foot, a foot that really looked like a foot, and yet there was a mysterious factor that Matasha couldn't quite grasp, a leap Jean seemed to make in her mind. Nevertheless she took up her pencil, asked Jean to take off her sock, and looked and looked until she saw that, yes, Jean's foot was a sort of oval, an oval broader than her own, with toes that were a little shorter and stouter, and she tried to make her pencil follow what her mind was seeing, and while her oval got a little smooshed in the execution, the picture that came out was not half bad. Matasha was thrilled, and convinced a new age was dawning for her as an artist. And then out of the blue, Jean started talking about her mother.

Her mother was a *nutball*, Jean said, bending over her drawing (she had grabbed a new page of loose-leaf paper and was sketching a big field with a horse sticking its head over a fence). She was embarrassed that her twin sisters had to come meet her at the bus stop every single day. "Like they can't be in the house for two seconds alone. So there's this whole *crowd* every time I get home from school. In the morning it's not so bad because my dad sometimes walks me. But even that is stupid."

"Your mom would feel better if they found the killer, don't you think?" asked Matasha leadingly. She'd had some thoughts recently—about something she and Jean might be able to do together to solve the crime. But it involved talking about the bones and the school construction site.

"God, I wish they would." Matasha wanted to ask Jean if *Jean* was worried about being stolen off the street and killed. She'd wanted to ask this forever, but she suspected Jean might get angry. If she were Jean, and lived three blocks away from where Martin Kimmel was taken, she'd be pretty scared. She'd probably ask her parents to move. But Jean made it sound like only her mother was bothered.

"Maybe they need more police to find the guy," Matasha

suggested.

"Maybe." Jean feathered some more grass into her field.

Something told Matasha to hold her tongue for now about the construction site. Instead, she said: "They need some clues. Just one good clue. If they can get that, they can find him."

"Yeah," Jean agreed. "That would be good." She sighed. "I gotta call my mom and see when I have to come home."

Matasha didn't want Jean to go. "Wait! Let's go see Mr. Bunny."

"Okay." Jean had three cats at home and liked all kinds of pets.

Mr. Bunny was a rabbit that Matasha had talked her parents into buying the summer before last when they'd been at a county fair in Michigan. He'd spent the summer in a cage in the yard of the South Haven rental. When September came and they moved back to the city, Mr. and Mrs. Wax said that Mr. Bunny couldn't stay in the apartment because of the smell. So the cage was put on the fire escape out back. The problem was that then Mr. Bunny was no longer under Matasha's eyes and she often forgot about him. Two or three days would go by and something would make her remember, and she would be pierced with guilt that he hadn't been fed or visited. She'd rush out and fill his bowl and pet him and swear she wouldn't forget anymore, but then it would happen again. And again. Winter came and Mr. Bunny's cage got covered in snow, and sometimes Matasha would come out and find his water bottle completely frozen. He'd made it through that winter, though, and in the summer they'd taken him back to South Haven, and now Matasha was determined to do better, to visit and feed him every day.

The two girls put on their coats and went out the back door of the apartment and across the cement hallway to where the fire escape door was. The fire escape always felt to Matasha like that part of a dream where you find another room in your house, one you'd somehow forgotten was there. It had a metal table and two chairs that were never used, and its floor was made up of narrow iron slats painted black. It was weird to walk on a floor with gaps. At times it brought an odd flash of Martin Kimmel, who had tumbled down through some sort of gap himself, into the pit for the new middle-high school.

"Mr. Bunny, Mr. Bunny," coaxed Matasha.

"Let's take out his hutch so he can't hide."

Matasha felt bad that Mr. Bunny always retreated into his hutch when she came out, as if he was afraid of and disappointed in her. They removed the hutch, and Matasha hoisted his surprisingly heavy body into her lap. She petted Mr. Bunny and crooned to him and told him she was sorry his food bowl was empty, as indeed it was. Jean took a turn holding him while Matasha went to the spot under the back-door overhang where the pellet bag was kept.

"I wish my mom and dad would let me keep him inside."

"Maybe you should get a cat," said Jean. Her family's cats were all boys; thank God, Jean said. Otherwise the place was overrun with girls.

"I wish I could," said Matasha. She took Mr. Bunny back. *Oh, Mr. Bunny*, she thought. *Why can't I remember better?* His fur felt reassuringly thick under her hand, and his muscles rippled emphatically. One thing that would be nice about having a cat was it would purr. Rabbits didn't make any noise, so you were never sure exactly how they felt.

They put Mr. Bunny back in the cage and replaced his hutch and closed the cage top. They went inside and Jean called her mother.

Back in the kitchen, Jean rummaged around again for cookies. "These are stale," she said, holding up a gingerbread round after taking a bite out of it.

"I'll get my mom to order some new ones," Matasha said placatingly.

Jean made a huffing noise. Matasha saw something more coming.

"Why does your mom order groceries over the phone?" Jean asked.

Matasha had never really thought about it. "I don't know. I guess it saves time."

"My mom goes to the *grocery store*," said Jean, as if this weren't the obvious alternative to calling in your order. "Even though she has to take the baby and sometimes even Kelly and Diane."

"So?" Matasha asked. She'd been having such a nice time with Jean. Jean had seemed like her old self, like she was coming out of whatever bad phase she'd been in for weeks and weeks.

Jean shrugged. "I'm just saying," she said.

Matasha bit her tongue. Whatever it was Jean wanted to

say or argue about, Matasha didn't feel like giving her the chance. They found some peanuts that Jean didn't have any objections to, and ate them together quietly. By the time Jean's mother arrived to get her, Matasha felt tired of her presence and ready to say goodbye, a feeling that was unfamiliar to her.

7.

The Waxes were going to have a visit from the adoption agency after all. Matasha couldn't imagine, after what she'd heard, how her father had come to agree. But apparently he had. It wasn't going to be a dinner anymore but tea on a Tuesday afternoon. And the Saturday night following, her parents were throwing a party, so it would be a busy week in the apartment.

There was an early snow that Tuesday. Mr. Wax arrived at 3:30 p.m., just after Matasha did, and his unaccustomed shape in the doorway, snowflakes sprinkling his hat and his dark wool coat, made her fly to him and throw her arms around him. He always smelled like Old Spice and Listerine. He laughed, patting her. His ungloved hands were strong and dry and cold. "Missy," he said. "Missy Matasha. What a pleasure to see you."

He stamped the snow off his shoes and put his briefcase down by the padded entryway bench. Matasha always wanted to know what was in her father's briefcase. It was a hard black case with her father's initials, RLW, inscribed in the brass lock. The inside lid had a silken pocket that held a slim sheaf of papers. It was very orderly inside, row after row of neatly filed sheets. Matasha occasionally asked to read them, but her father said he didn't want to get them shuffled.

Her father rubbed his hands together briskly, warming them. "I think it's time for a hot cup of tea," he said.

"I'll make it!" Matasha cried, and she ran ahead of him into the kitchen, filled the kettle, and turned it on. She knew what he wanted: English breakfast, even though it wasn't breakfast time. Her father didn't have English breakfast at breakfast time. He had coffee.

At ten of four, her mother came down in heels, a skirt with a cardigan sweater, and pearls.

"You look pretty, Mommy," said Matasha. Her mother's outfit signaled that the meeting, even if it was still afternoon, was going to be formal and serious. Matasha's stomach began to flop around excitedly and do its washy thing. If her father had changed his mind, maybe she really was getting a sister, and one from awfully far away.

Her mother smiled at the compliment and told her not to eat so many crackers. They would have cookies, she said, when Mrs. O'Connor and Miss Lacey got there. Matasha grumbled and put down the box of Triscuits.

The doorbell rang promptly at four. Mrs. Wax greeted the two agency women and made a comment about the weather. The women fluttered apologies for their wet shoes and coats, and Matasha's mother politely insisted they not be silly. Her father cleared his throat in his characteristic way and shook hands solemnly. Then Mrs. Wax introduced Matasha. Matasha stuck her hand out, remembering Mr. Evinrude's advice. Mr. Evinrude, her science and math teacher, had once explained to their class, for no particular reason, that you should never shake hands with a hand like a limp fish; it made a bad impression. Since then Matasha always made sure to shake with a very firm hand. Matasha squeezed Mrs. O'Connor's hand and Mrs. O'Connor gave a surprised little laugh—Matasha guessed she had been too forceful. She squeezed less hard with Miss Lacey, a slim woman in a dark floral blouse and dark pants, and seemed to get it right this time. Mrs. O'Connor was older, with gray hair, and plumper, with a skirt and sweater and heels like Matasha's mom, though with a butterfly pin on her sweater instead of pearls. She didn't have pierced ears, Matasha noticed. Matasha was attentive to pierced ears lately because many of the girls in her class now had them and she was starting to want them, too, except that getting them involved needles.

They sat in the living room. Sunset had put out a tray there, with the good china and the silver teapot and creamer that Matasha loved. "What a beautiful home you have," said Mrs. O'Connor, looking up and around at the marble fireplace, the crystal chandelier hanging from a chain anchored to a rosette in the high ceiling, the grand piano (passed on to Matasha's father by Grandma Nan; no one but Matasha played), the art.

"Thank you," said Matasha's mother, and she presented the cookie plates to Mrs. O'Connor and Miss Lacey. Mrs. O'Connor sighed and said she was on a diet—just one!—but Miss Lacey took a couple, so Matasha figured it was safe to do so as well.

"What made you decide that you were interested in a Vietnamese adoption?" asked Mrs. O'Connor, once they had all settled in with their tea and made some small talk.

Matasha's mother leaned forward earnestly. "I think about the *crime* that the war was for these children. It doesn't matter whether you were for or against the war," she added carefully, looking from one woman's face to the other in case a pro-war position might be evident there. "These children were victims either way, the victims of forces much greater than themselves. I feel that as Americans, we can try to address the suffering we've been part of."

Matasha was impressed. She recognized it as a talent her mother had, to get fervent about things and infect everyone with her fervency. It didn't matter if she might change her mind tomorrow. She believed what she was saying *right now.*

Mrs. O'Connor seemed impressed, too, and smiled warmly. "Do you share that feeling, Mr. Wax?"

"I agree it's been a humanitarian tragedy," he replied. "But for me, an adoption would have to be for more purely personal reasons. I'm not as positive that adoption is the right idea in our individual case, but I think it's an honorable thing to do."

Matasha's mother didn't look surprised or angry at this comment, so Matasha guessed they'd worked out an agreement: they could have the meeting with the adoption service so long as her father would be free to express his reservations.

"Fair enough," said Mrs. O'Connor, nodding. "Many families wrestle with the pros and cons, and this meeting is one of the ways we try to help you sort them out. So you, Mr. Wax, are a lawyer, and you, Mrs. Wax, are an art consultant, I see." She was checking a binder. "Matasha is your only child, age eleven—twelve in May. And your family is Jewish?"

"Yes," said Matasha's mother and father at once.

"Would you plan to raise an adoptee as Jewish?" Mrs.

O'Connor asked. "Many of our children have had a religious Christian upbringing." Miss Lacey reached for a third cookie, and so did Matasha.

Mr. and Mrs. Wax looked at each other as if they hadn't anticipated this question.

"We would be respectful of the child's upbringing and find a church to attend as well as a synagogue," said Matasha's mother. "We attend synagogue only on the High Holidays as it is. We have Sabbath dinners occasionally but they are really more of a family ritual and could be adapted . . . adapted . . ." She seemed to lose her train of thought.

"That's fine," said Mrs. O'Connor, ticking off something with her pencil. "Perhaps we should talk about any concerns you may have about bringing another child into the family. And age. On the application you put down that you prefer a girl, of any age through eleven."

"Yes. We think it might be difficult to handle a child already in her teen years. A younger child is going to be, well, more resilient and more able to adapt to a new home, isn't that generally the case? And with Matasha always having been an only child, it might be hard suddenly to have an older sibling."

"Understandable," Mrs. O'Connor said. "Though perhaps you'll think about this a bit more. The older the child, the harder he or she is to place, so it's a great blessing when we can place the big ones."

Mrs. O'Connor then began to speak about the challenge of integrating refugee children into American homes. "Some of them have been through very rough experiences. Miss Lacey can speak more to that, and to the resources we have to support our adoptive families."

Miss Lacey illuminated the many issues for Vietnamese children coming into American homes. They often had nightmares, and some feared going to sleep. It could be hard for them to trust their new parents. A few were aggressive, although depression and anxiety were more often the case. Some had continuing health problems due to infections and malnutrition during the war. In some instances their growth might be permanently stunted. They would be several years behind in school, of course, although the agency found that once their English became fluent—and this often happened quickly—the children were ready learners and made up the gap after a year or two, especially if the family enrolled them in supplementary schooling, which was strongly encouraged. If Mr. and Mrs. Wax were going to continue on the path to adoption, they would be required to attend six sessions on emotional, physical, and educational issues among the Vietnamese refugee children population. "The good news," said Miss Lacey, "is that we have a strong network of services we can refer you out to if these problems emerge. Both state and private."

Mrs. Wax assured Miss Lacey that the family had the finances to pay for any kind of services or therapy that might come up. Matasha's father cleared his throat. Matasha thought: *How interesting. Maybe we will have two growth-stunted kids in the family.*

At a certain point Matasha's attention began to wander, as the two women and her parents began to mix talk about the adoption with what Matasha thought of as time-wasting adult conversation about the early snow, last winter's snow activity, and how the two winters might compare. All at once she was aware that attention had been turned to her. Mrs. O'Connor was asking how *she* felt about the whole idea of a little sister: Was she excited? Worried?

Matasha was unprepared to be asked her opinion. Her parents, of course, would want to know what she thought, but usually adults didn't care what children had to say. Once in a while Jean told her that she had no idea what it was like to have siblings, and Matasha guessed this was true. She knew it was unusual to be an only child. The only other one Matasha knew of at Margaret E. Marvin was a fifth grader named Stacey Owens, whose father had died in a car accident when she was two. Matasha never had to share her things or fight over what to watch on TV. On the other hand, she never had anyone to play Mastermind or Battleship with. Sometimes, when she had a sleepover at Jean's, Diane and Kelly would sneak into the room after their lights-out, and Matasha and Jean would tell them ghost stories. Matasha enjoyed that immensely. If you had a sibling, you could do that. There were other things that Matasha had always wanted to do but that seemed to come only with having a TV-style family of at least two kids and a house in the suburbs. Such as: building a snowman. This was a challenge when the only thing that came close to a yard was a small square of grass opposite the front door, bounded by a low iron fence. How did you get the base so big and round? Where did you find stones for the eyes? If their family adopted a refugee girl, they still wouldn't have a house in the suburbs with a snowy lawn, but maybe they'd do a few more normal-family things like snowman building.

The two women and her parents were looking at her. It was quiet in the room, in the whole apartment. It was *always* quiet in the apartment, Matasha realized.

"I would like it," she said, discovering that she definitely would. A sister!

The agency women smiled. "Well," Mrs. O'Connor said, getting up. "It was lovely to meet all three of you, and we'll be glad to answer any questions you have, assuming you move forward. We hope that you will. You seem as if you would be able to provide a loving and stable home for one of these children who need so much."

Pleased, Matasha's mother put her warm, long hand on Matasha's shoulder, and Matasha shivered contentedly under the contact. She looked at her father, whose expression wasn't giving up much. It occurred to Matasha that she might have sealed the deal, at least as far as the two visitors were concerned. She wished she knew what her father was thinking. If he was unhappy, they didn't need to adopt the girl. They didn't! But then her mother might be the unhappy one. Matasha just wanted the option that would make both of her parents glad. Why was that so hard?

8.

The party her parents were throwing that Saturday night was a Russian party; everybody had to come dressed as Russians.

"Russians?" Matasha frowned when she heard this. Russians had the hydrogen bomb and might start a nuclear war with the US someday. Russians threw people in jail just for speaking their minds. "Not Soviet Russians," her mother explained. "Russians before things over there got all gray and ugly."

Matasha was surprised her mother hadn't come up with this idea before, given *War and Peace* and all. Matasha's mother dreamed up all kinds of parties. Last December, she'd thrown one where everyone had to come in bathing suits. It was hilarious seeing all the women moving through the living room in their one-pieces and little skirts, and the men bare-chested. (Some of them, more embarrassed, covered up with button-downs.) The women outdid themselves finding the most amusing bathing caps—one was printed all over with kings and queens of England, and one was a blinding Day-Glo green. Another party had an astronaut theme. Mrs. Wax had served those moon sticks, brown and chewy, in chocolate and peanut butter flavor, that Matasha adored, the ones the box said astronauts took with them on their flights.

Matasha's mother said she could stay among the guests until ten o'clock. Matasha usually was up reading in bed until eleven or so on Saturday nights, because neither of her parents stirred the next morning until late, and she argued to be allowed to remain longer. But Mrs. Wax wouldn't hear of it.

"Will anyone interesting be there?" asked Matasha. She meant anyone who would listen seriously after asking her what she wanted to be when she grew up. She meant anyone who knew good jokes or some Beatles trivia (she didn't expect anyone to know as much as she did).

"Well, I've been meaning to tell you," said her mother. "Dottie Summers will be there."

"Dottie Summers?" yelped Matasha.

"That's right," said her mother.

"I *love* Dottie Summers," said Matasha, as if her mother didn't already know. She started to run around the room. She did a hop, a skip, and a jump. Then she pretended to be jumping rope, very fast. Matasha preferred Dottie Summers's advice column in the *Sun-Times* to Dear Eleanor in the *Tribune*, and not just because she'd been reading it for much longer. Dear Eleanor got way more letters from women complaining about their husbands' sloppy habits, or asking what was the best way to sweep under beds or launder hand towels. It seemed half advice and half housekeeping. Dottie Summers occasionally had those kinds of letters, but mostly she replied about more exciting things such as divorces and affairs and scheming friends. Matasha would read each letter and put her hand over Dottie's answer. First she would decide what she, Matasha, would say to the letter writer if she were writing the column. Then she would guess what Dottie Summers would say. These two responses could be different because Dottie was often harsher than Matasha would have been. Dottie was likely to call the letter writer something somewhat rude and sarcastic, like "bub" or "honey," and tell them right to their faces that they were stupid or selfish. Well, not their faces, of course, but right there in print. Matasha thought that the letter writers probably felt pretty bad when they got those kinds of answers.

Sometimes she disagreed with Dottie. One woman wrote in to say that her husband had lent his brother some money. Some of *her* money, which she'd brought into the marriage and always kept in a separate account. She'd agreed to let her husband make the loan, but now it was looking as if the brother-in-law was never going to pay it back. He had used it to start a business that had quickly collapsed. The thing was that he never, ever mentioned the money he'd borrowed, and five years had gone by. The letter writer, "Burned in Boise," had urged her husband to ask the brother for the money, but her husband kept putting it off. She wanted to know if she should take matters into her own hands and write to the brother herself. Dottie told Burned in Boise that she'd been dumb to lend the money. "When you lend to family," she said, "you'd better be prepared to look at it as a gift, not a loan." Insisting on payment might cause tensions between Burned in Boise's husband and his brother. In the end, family harmony was more important than the money. Matasha thought this was wrong. If you borrowed money, you should pay it back.

Matasha stopped jumping around. She was panting. "You know *Dottie Summers*?" she asked.

"We've always known Dottie Summers," her mother said. "She's Daddy's law school roommate's aunt."

"Why didn't you *tell* me?"

"I'm sure I have told you."

"No, you did not," said Matasha. "You think you tell me things and you don't."

"I'm sorry, honey. Well, we'll have to make sure you get to talk to Dottie."

"I'd like to ask her how many letters she gets a day. And how she decides which ones to answer. And does she write back to some people but just not put it in the paper. And which was the weirdest question she ever got."

"I'm sure she'll answer all your questions," said Mrs. Wax.

The day of the party not only Sunset but Sunset's grandniece came over to get things ready. Matasha's mother had ordered special food from a Russian restaurant in the South Loop. At 6:30 p.m., the bartender arrived. He was serving only vodka. He lined the bottles up, clear and glittering, on a snow-white tablecloth. Mr. Wax crouched in front of the fireplace, building a tepee of logs and kindling. Matasha played with the chain-link fireplace curtains while she watched, scrunching them up and letting them fall. Her palms got greasy with fireplace dirt. She twirled the brass-tipped poker until her father told her to set it down. Then she walked around the room, visiting all the familiar art. There was the grainy-looking woman holding a huge cement ball in front of her stomach, as if she were pregnant on the outside. There was a four-by-six-foot picture of a bright red car that looked like a shiny photograph but that her mother insisted had actually been painted. Occasionally Matasha got on a stepladder to investigate, and even way up close it still looked like a photograph, with the perfect lettering on the license plate and the gleam on the car's windows. She could not see brushstrokes of any kind. There was a painting of a girl that for some reason had feathers and buttons glued all over it. And there was a drawing that always made Matasha uneasy. It was a sketch of a man's face—just one hooked line for a nose, a couple of lines for the eyes, and a small line for the mouth—with a big X over it, the lines of the X thicker than the lines of the face. Matasha could never quite get over it: a big cross-out over a face. It seemed violent. When she'd asked her mother about it—for of course it was her mother's purchase; her father didn't care much about art—her mother said that Matasha's reaction was exactly the point: the artist wanted to show us that we reacted to art as if it were real, that we could feel about the drawing of a person as if it were really a person. And it made us very uncomfortable to put an X over a person. But the artist hadn't put an X over a person, just over lines on paper. This seemed unnecessarily complicated to Matasha. Since Xs over a drawing of a person made people uncomfortable, the artist just shouldn't have done it.

Mrs. Wax already had out the records that would be playing tonight: classical ones that Matasha assumed had something to do with Russia. The LPs were kept in a long low cabinet against one living room wall, underneath a turntable that slid smoothly out on rollers and had a heavy arm for the needle, unlike the flimsy arm on Matasha's phonograph, which leapt out of her hands and bounced onto her records and scratched them. Most of her parents' LPs were classical, but they also had Bob Dylan, Jefferson Airplane, Joan Baez, Judy Collins, and Simon and Garfunkel. Matasha had already appropriated all the records by the Beatles.

Matasha went upstairs to watch her mother getting ready. Watching her mother get ready was almost as good as being at the party. Her mother sat in her bra and slip at her dressing alcove, which was bounded on three sides by mirrors. A zillion Mrs. Waxes and Matashas looked right and left and up and down as Mrs. Wax applied her mascara and a pale crayon that she said took away the circles under her eyes. Once upon a time Mrs. Wax had put on false eyelashes for parties; Matasha could remember it. Many times she had begged her mother to do it again—her mother looked so glamorous when they were on. But her mother said that these days false eyelashes were a little vulgar. Mrs. Wax dabbed Chanel No. 19 on her wrists and at her collarbone, and let Matasha put some on too. Then she unlocked her jewelry drawer with a tiny key and laid out all the things she would wear when she was fully dressed: pearl-drop earrings that looked like mini replicas of the living room chandelier, a bracelet of square gold links, and, best, a long rope of pearls that, though doubled, still reached nearly to her waist.

"What are you going to wear?" asked Matasha. Her mother indicated the floor-length, deep blue dress in the walk-in closet. It had voluminous skirt pleats, a narrow bodice, and loose, lacy sleeves. Awed, Matasha wanted to know if it was a real Russian dress.

"I had Mrs. Szalai make it up," her mother told her. Mrs. Szalai was the dressmaker her mother went to on Briar. "It's Russian-*y*." Matasha reached under the dressmaker's plastic; the skirting was filmy and very silky to the touch. She breathed in the slightly chemical new-fabric smell. Sometimes, when her parents weren't home, Matasha cleared a space in the closet amid her mother's pointy shoes and sat behind all the dry-cleaning bags, just enjoying being near her mother's fancy things and her father's sober ones—handsome, dark, polished shoes, dark suits—on the other side.

Maybe she was wrong and she would look and be something like her mother one day. She *was* her daughter, after all. Last week, trying to make up her mind about synchronized swim (in the end she'd definitively decided no), she'd asked her mother why she had hairy legs, and her mother said all girls got them eventually, and that if Matasha wanted to get rid of the hair she could shave. Mrs. Wax bought a razor and shaving cream for Matasha the next time she was out and explained to her how to do it. So that had cleared up one problem. Maybe Matasha would also begin to grow and become prettier. You never knew—it could happen.

Matasha went into her room to get ready herself. That was easy—she had one party dress. It had a white underlayer with a top of white net embroidered with little strawberries. She and her mother had picked it out at Marshall Field's. Every August her mother took her to Marshall Field's for school clothes for the year and one new dressy outfit. In May they went back for summer clothes. It was a routine that was partly pleasant and partly not. Her mother pulled things off the rack quickly, hurriedly, and once they found something that fit, she would insist on buying two or three of them, just in different colors. The only thing she let Matasha take her time on was the dressy outfit, so Matasha always tried on a lot of things and indulged in a lot of second-guessing before making up her mind. By that time her mother would be wild for a cup of coffee, so they would head to the ice cream parlor in Field's and Matasha would get to order a sundae.

In two minutes Matasha had on her dress and her white socks and white Mary Janes, and in another two she had her hair brushed out and in braids. All done: how disappointing. There really should be more to it. At least she smelled like Chanel No. 19.

The party had been called for 7:30 p.m., and at 7:15 Matasha stationed herself by the front door, waiting to let people in. She also wanted to see Dottie Summers right when she arrived. Her mother had said no one would come early, but Matasha didn't want to take any chances. Her mother was right, though, and 7:30 came and went. Her father appeared in a tuxedo with a red sash across it. He really did look like he might be a Russian officer of some kind, with that sash and his thick mustache. Matasha inspected his boxy silver cuff links. She was delighted when her father wore cuff links.

Matasha was nearly dying of boredom by the time the downstairs buzzer rang and she could finally press the button to unlock the door to the building. Then she flung open their own. The Pinsoffs were the first to show up.

"Why, hello, Matasha," said Alexandra Pinsoff. She was

a strange-looking woman, extremely thin and with white hair even though she was probably about thirty-five, the same as Matasha's mother. The Russian aspect of her outfit seemed to be that she was wearing a flattish, wide-brimmed straw hat; Mr. Pinsoff for his part had on a kind of naval cap with an insignia on the front. What made someone's hair go white so early? Maybe Mrs. Pinsoff had seen something terrible as a young girl. She also had a very high, little-girl voice. Mr. Pinsoff was shorter than his wife and round and so boring that you never remembered what he said right after he'd said it. Mr. Pinsoff was clearly where Tamar had gotten her boringness from. When Matasha saw the Pinsoffs, she could never forget that they had built an entire kitchen for themselves that they didn't let their children use.

"How's school?" asked Mrs. Pinsoff, which everyone knew was a ridiculous question. If Mrs. Pinsoff wanted to know about math class, Matasha would be happy to tell her (they were doing intersecting sets, something Matasha liked). If Mrs. Pinsoff wanted to know what they were reading in English, fine. But there was no way to answer a question like, "How's school?"

Mrs. Pinsoff didn't wait for an answer anyway. "Tamar tells me you're going to be doing synchronized swim," she said.

Matasha was taken off guard. "I don't think so, actually," she said.

"Oh." Mrs. Pinsoff had run out of conversation topics. She began waving energetically at Matasha's mother, who emerged from the kitchen, where she'd presumably been conferring with Sunset and Sunset's grandniece and the caterer. She'd put up her hair in a glamorous, glossy swirl that made the chandelier earrings stand out. Mrs. Pinsoff gave her mother a forceful kiss on the cheek, which Matasha knew her mother disliked. Her mother was not kissy. If you had to kiss her, you had better keep it just a little brush against her skin, and *never* wet.

All at once, the buzzer started buzzing repeatedly. People, nearly all of them couples, came up the elevator and through the front door, one couple after the other. Some of the women had on old-fashioned long dresses. Some had tiaras. A lot of the men had had the same sash idea as Matasha's father. Someone Matasha didn't recognize turned up in a very authentic-looking jacket with epaulets and gold braid. Some of the guests wore ordinary party clothes and had just added a jokey touch, like Carol Shapiro, one of her mother's oldest and closest friends, and Carol's husband, Arthur, who wore matching signs that read "NICHOLAS" and "ALEXANDRA," the names of the last emperor and empress of Russia, the ones who got killed by revolutionaries. Carol was a gentle, friendly middle school teacher who always had time to talk to Matasha and was up on all the subjects Matasha was studying in school. Jean's parents never came to the Waxes' parties; even though Matasha and Jean were best friends, their parents didn't spend time together. Camille's parents, the Janklows, came. You would never know from the Janklows that their daughter was such a beast. There didn't seem to be anything wrong with them as there was with, for instance, the Pinsoffs. Mrs. Janklow didn't pretend to be interested in Matasha, which was just fine. She let Matasha take her coat, a silvery black mink, delicious to the touch. Matasha was nervous about somehow spoiling it until she got it hung up in the coat closet.

Matasha eventually tired of greeting people and waiting for Dottie Summers to arrive, and went into the living room to join the party. She hoped Dottie Summers wasn't going to be a no-show. Many of the women smiled down at her as she wove through the milling bodies, and she tried to ignore it. She knew that smile. It was the one that told her she was an oddity—so tiny!—and not to be taken seriously.

Matasha went over to the food buffet, which was set up on a white cloth draped over the LP cabinet. Everything looked suspect. She stayed away from the main dishes entirely, knowing she wouldn't like them, whatever they were, but even the appetizer spread had little that was safe, other than the thin slices of smoked salmon on triangles of dark bread. She put six of these on her plate. Sunset had given her dinner at five o'clock, but Matasha could make room for smoked salmon anytime. Other serving dishes held bits of hard-boiled egg, which Matasha didn't like, tiny green balls of something, asparagus (ugh), and sliced beets (ugh ugh). She left all of these alone.

Some fast Russian-y music with strings was playing on the stereo. Matasha was talking to Carol Shapiro about her Chicago Fire novel when she thought she heard her name. She turned and, over by the glass coffee table, saw a woman she was pretty sure was married to a client of her father's.

". . . should take her to a good specialist," the woman was saying to Matasha's mother. "You wouldn't want to wait until . . ."

Matasha tuned out the music and listened hard. *Was* the

woman talking about her? She couldn't make out the conversation, but she heard her name again for certain. And then her mother said coolly, in a louder voice, "Well, thank you, Maxine. I'll file that away. Now I need to go check up on the kitchen."

Matasha followed her mother so she could ask what she and that woman had been talking about, but as soon as they were out of the room, her mother stopped and gave a little exclamation. "Dottie!" she said, and bent down to give Dottie Summers, who had just arrived, a kiss. A kiss! She must really like Dottie Summers, thought Matasha. Dottie was sitting on the entryway bench struggling to remove her galoshes. She had a high blonde helmet of hair and looked about the age of Grandma Nan. A man nearby walked over and gallantly got down on one knee to pull off Dottie's overshoes. Matasha wondered why Dottie Summers didn't have a husband to help with her galoshes. Was he dead? Or maybe he just hadn't come to the party.

"Dottie," said Mrs. Wax, "this is my daughter, Matasha. She reads your column every single day. When we go away, we have to get someone to clip the columns and save them for her."

"Hi, Mrs. Summers," said Matasha politely, holding out her hand and offering her firm handshake. Dottie Summers had a firm handshake too. She opened a large embroidered velvet bag and pulled out a pair of gold lamé pumps. Her helper had disappeared, and so had Matasha's mother. Dottie was wearing a skirt suit in a color the exact match of the shoes. Matasha wasn't sure if there was anything Russian about her outfit, but she guessed not. Dottie was probably so famous that she didn't have to follow the rules when it came to parties.

"I like your shoes," said Matasha, who very much did.

"Well, thank you," said Dottie. "So you read my column?" She patted the bench next to her, directing Matasha to sit down. She seemed prepared to talk for a few minutes.

"Every day!"

"How old are you?"

"Eleven."

"Wonderful." Dottie did not do the double take so many adults did when Matasha told them her age. "Which topics do you most like to read about?"

Matasha knew right off the top of her head. "I like to read about people's problems with their kids. And what's polite or not. And pets. I don't like reading about money and wills."

Dottie smiled. "Those things become more important when you get older. Money and health. But you've got a long time until you'll feel that way."

"I have so many things to ask!" burbled Matasha. She felt starstruck and a little out of control. "How many letters do you get? Are some of the people who write you ever crazy? What do you do with the letters you don't answer?" Matasha was aware that it wasn't completely polite to barrage a grown-up with questions without even asking if that was okay first.

Dottie didn't seem to mind. "Oh, you would be amazed," she said. "I get about three thousand letters a week, from all over the country—even the world. That's one hundred and fifty thousand letters a year. I have three assistants who read all the letters and then pass on to me the ones they think I'll be interested in. I make the final choices. We answer some of the letters that don't go in the paper, but we can't answer everyone." She tapped Matasha gently on the knee. "Are you wanting to write me a letter?"

Matasha blinked. Oddly, she had never thought of this, but now that she'd been asked, yes—yes, she did want to write Dottie a letter. But what about? There were so many things she'd been wondering about lately. The Vietnamese adoption: Was it a good idea? Was there a way to get her parents to stop fighting about it? Was it okay to have just one friend, and what if she was too often kind of mean to you, and how did you know if you had "social problems"? If Martin Kimmel got buried under the new school, how could she stop thinking he might haunt it? And, most of all, what would happen if she never grew taller than four foot four?

But—"I don't know," Matasha mumbled, and felt ashamed. She prided herself on being straightforward when asked a question, and this answer was not just evasive but childish. But she couldn't seem to assemble the right words just now.

"Well, if you ever decide you want to," said Dottie Summers, "you don't need to sign your real name, you know. And here's a little secret. At the bottom of your letter, just make a small circle and draw the capital letter *D*—for Dottie—inside it. That's a special code that means it will come directly to me. Then watch the newspaper."

"And you'll answer?" Matasha couldn't believe her good fortune.

"I'll answer," said Dottie. "Watch the newspaper."

●

The chandelier had been dimmed, and most of the light came from dozens of candles set all around the room: on the buffet, the drinks table, the windowsills, the fireplace mantel. It was past eleven, and Matasha was upstairs on the balcony looking down. She was supposed to be in her room, but she kept back to one side and would be out of sight if someone bothered to gaze up. The candlelight was warm and wavery and everyone looked a little blurred. Even the talk seemed muted. Things were still lively but not loud. Sometime during the evening Dottie Summers and a few other of the guests had left; the rest floated from sofa to drinks table to easy chairs, talking, laughing softly, leafing through coffee table books, refilling their plates or glasses. Her mother glowed blue as a dusky jewel. Her father looked neat and trim in his dark jacket, his olive skin picking up the flickering light. He was sometimes stiff and abrupt in company—he was actually very shy—but tonight he seemed at ease, enjoying himself, making jokes. He put his arm around Matasha's mother and she leaned into him, going off-balance in her high heels. Her pumps were silver, with heels like long spikes. A salty smell rose to the second floor. The fireplace was roaring. Suddenly her mother disentangled herself from her father, walked to the fireplace, cried, "*Nostrovia!*" and aimed her glass inside. There was the sound of shattering and then the glass ignited, sending up a blue flame. A burst of surprised, anxious laughter. Matasha's father stepped up to the grate. "*Nostrovia!*" he cried, and hurled his glass in. Again, the blue explosion. Now the guests pushed forward to the fireplace, tossing their glasses, sometimes two people at a time, and a few times fire bellowed out from the grate so quickly that people had to jump back. "No, no!" cried Carol Shapiro. She was trying to keep her husband from wresting her glass from her hand. But he did it anyway, and her glass was fed to the fire. There were broken shards on the carpet near the fireplace. The fire roared up one last time, then subsided, and everyone watched it, mesmerized. Over a minute, two minutes, it banked down dim and gray. The room looked dim now too. All the excited noise had stopped. People sat down silently; women tucked strands of hair behind their ears.

Matasha's mother stood up and strode to the buffet, placed a few small items on her plate, and returned to sit down on the sofa. She picked up a triangle of bread and took a bite. She ate quietly. Others got up now and returned to the buffet and put food on their plates. People began to talk again. Some coughed; the room was smoky. The bartender handed people fresh glasses of vodka. The leftover smoke had begun to reach up to the balcony and sting Matasha's nose. She put her hand over her mouth until she got safely to her bedroom and then coughed and coughed until the coughing turned to giddy laughter. She wiped away the tears from the laughter and the coughing and went to the bathroom and spat several times and washed her face. Then she got under her cold sheets and hardly had time to think about everything that had happened before she fell asleep.

9.

One Friday Mrs. Wax picked Matasha up from her piano lesson downtown and stopped with her at an office where she needed to get some documents relating to the Vietnamese adoption. They waited a long time in a room with molded plastic chairs in cotton candy colors, and eventually they were called up to a window. The window man was skinny and old and wore suspenders and a small cap cocked to one side. He looked like a railroad engineer in an old-fashioned photograph.

The man spoke impatiently to her mother, and then they had to sit and wait again. Matasha kicked the base of her chair with her heels until Mrs. Wax told her to stop.

"So Daddy decided to say yes?" Matasha asked.

"He didn't," said her mother. "I just decided to go ahead."

"He didn't?" Matasha's eyes widened. "He doesn't know that I'm getting a sister?"

"He does. I told him. I told him I was going to do this whether he was okay with it or not. I told him it was important. There's a crisis out there, and people have to do something. We can't always be curled up in a little ball, pretending we don't see. And I always wanted you to have a brother or sister, Matasha."

"You did?"

"I did, but I waited too long. Oh, who can explain all these things? Somehow the years went by. I really don't much like the baby stage. Maybe that was it. If I could have had a six-year-old right away, I wouldn't have kept putting it off." She looked off into a corner where a large woman was waiting with a girl and a boy who might have been twins, maybe seven or eight years old. All three were dozing. "Every child should have a sibling."

"But you don't even get along with your sister." Aunt Sondra and Uncle Howard never came to Thanksgiving or any other holiday. Matasha's mother hadn't spoken to Aunt Sondra in years.

"That's true. But still."

You couldn't argue with Matasha's mother. She was never trying that hard for logic, so there was no point bringing logic to bear against her. You just had to accept what she told you, knowing that there was some sort of truth in it for her.

"But how can the girl come if Daddy doesn't want her to?"

"He doesn't exactly not want her to. But he's anxious about it. It's a big responsibility, having another child."

"I could do a lot of the work," offered Matasha. She had spent time lately mulling over scenarios that involved her getting to be a kind of combination teacher, boss, and mom for the new girl. These were gratifying fantasies. Matasha had been cautiously hoping that her father would come around, and her comments now were aimed at convincing his absent presence.

"I'll look after her at school," she continued. "I'll even learn some Vietnamese so we can talk to her better."

"That's lovely," said her mother. She was trying to fill out some sheets that the railroad man had given her. "I'm so glad you want to do all that. You'll be a huge help."

Seeing how pleased her mother was, Matasha figured she'd pile it on a bit. "I'd *so love* a sister," she said theatrically, and loudly enough that maybe the woman with the twins would hear and be impressed. The word "sister" did have a kind of magical potency. It was a warm, sparkling one, one that seemed to promise nighttime secrets, silly games, limbs entangled on a bed.

Wait. Whose bed? She'd never asked about where the new girl would sleep. In her mother's office? It was the only extra room in the apartment besides Sunset's, which was of course occupied by Sunset herself. Matasha asked about this now.

"We'd get a bunk bed for your room, sweetheart. Bunk beds are fun. That's a ways off, though."

A *bunk bed*? Matasha had to sleep in a bunk bed at summer camp. It was one of the few things she outright disliked about camp. She was scared of the top bunks—what if she rolled out in the night?—and always worried on the first day that she'd get stuck with one. What if the girl, being the newest member of the household and more needy, got to have the bottom? Also, what about Matasha's beloved four-poster bed with the blue-and-green floral curtains?

"What will happen to my four-poster bed?"

"We'll give it away, Matasha. There isn't enough space in your room for two beds. It's not even happening yet. I need to focus on these forms."

Matasha was trying to be grown up about all this. "Couldn't we at least keep it in storage?" In the basement of their building, in a large, damp room, there were lockers for families to put their extra belongings.

"We'll see. Your questions are making me tired, Matasha. It's too much right now." Mrs. Wax turned back to the papers in her lap.

Matasha kept quiet for a time, but there was a question she couldn't wrap her mind around. Softly, she said: "I still don't get how she can come if Daddy doesn't want her to."

Her mother put down her pencil. "Well, first of all, I told him she will be entirely my responsibility. I will be the one to make sure she adjusts to school and learns English and has lessons in whatever. I will handle any problems that come up."

"Yes, but . . ."

"Daddy will come around, Matasha. He doesn't like change. He never has. If it had been up to him, we never would have gotten married."

"You wouldn't have gotten *married*? Mommy! What do you mean?" Her father hadn't wanted a child, and now it turned out he hadn't even wanted to get married? What about the story of meeting in the dentist's office?

"I don't mean that he didn't love me or anything. Just that he can never make any big decisions, unless they're work decisions. He hates taking a plunge. So finally, after a year went by and he still hadn't asked me to marry him, I said, 'Look, is this going to happen or isn't it? Teddy Garmin wants to marry me, and I think I'm going to tell him yes.'"

"Teddy Garmin?" Matasha was confused.

"Yes, well, Teddy Garmin hadn't actually asked me. But it lit a fire under your father. And we got married six months later."

"Who is Teddy Garmin?" Matasha asked. And her mother

had *lied*? She'd never been aware of her mother telling a lie before. She held on to the sides of her curved seat. It wasn't very steadying.

"He was the son of the undertaker," her mother explained unhelpfully.

"So you could have married Teddy Garmin?"

"No, no. He was sweet on me but he was scared to ask. He was right, since I never would have married him. He wasn't intelligent like your father."

Matasha was beginning to lose the thread of what all this had to do with the adoption.

"So the thing about your father: if he doesn't say no, you can take it as a yes. If he doesn't have the energy to say no, then he doesn't deserve a no, does he?"

"I guess," said Matasha. She reached under her chair and brought out her current novel, *The Once and Future King*. The complications in it were easier to understand than her mother's.

"Listen, Matasha." Her mother didn't seem to notice that Matasha already had her nose in the book. "Something's not right about you and me and your father just sitting around in our big apartment, and all the quiet and sameness. Our world is too small. We are shutting too much out. And I just felt . . ."

Matasha looked up. Her mother's voice sounded odd, and her face was screwed up as if she had bitten her tongue.

"What, Mom?"

"Everything needs to be shaken up," her mother said fiercely, and it struck Matasha with awful clarity that her mother didn't know exactly what she was doing, that she was gambling:

with Matasha, with her father, and of course with the girl who was going to be coming to live with them. Matasha wanted to get up and take her mother's hand and lead her right out of that office, away from the man with the suspenders and the forms. But then she thought of returning to their apartment and understood what her mother was talking about. Their house was lonely. There was no way around it. They had a lonely house. A house was supposed to have some noise and commotion in it, like Jean's house had. It was supposed to have more laughter and more conversation and more food. Something was missing, and maybe it was another person who was meant to be there.

"Jenine Wax!" called the man in suspenders. Her mother went to the window and handed over her forms. She stood there awhile, responding to the man's questions. Then finally she was done. "I need some coffee," she said, returning to Matasha's seat.

They left the building and walked until they found a coffee shop. "Oof," said her mother, placing her purse on the booth seat and signaling aggressively for a waitress. "A cup of coffee, black," she told the waitress. Matasha had noted that her mother never said "please" to waitresses.

"Can I have rice pudding?" Matasha asked.

"And a rice pudding."

The coffee came and her mother had a large swallow. Instantly she seemed less furrowed, more relaxed. "And now I have a surprise for you," she said. She took a letter-sized envelope out of her purse. "The agency sent a photograph of a possible match."

"Oh, Mom!" Matasha was almost wild with anticipation.

"She's ten and her name is Qui." Her mother pronounced it like "key." "She's been living in a temporary foster placement in Idaho."

"Show me, show me!"

Her mother opened the envelope and removed a folded sheet with a passport-sized black-and-white photograph inside. She passed the photo to Matasha.

Matasha was startled. The face in the picture did not match the image that she had carried around ever since her mother had brought up the adoption idea, of a perfectly oval face and long, shiny black hair, big almond eyes, and a shy smile. The pictures of refugee girls she'd seen in the newspapers almost always looked like that. This girl's—Qui's—face was wide and a bit swollen, and her hair was short in ragged bangs. Her eyes were squinty and she was not smiling. She stared grimly into the camera, like someone who did not expect any good to come of this.

"What do you think, sweetheart?" Her mother's voice was tender, concerned.

"She's not as pretty as I thought she'd be."

Now it was her mother's turn to be surprised. She drank her coffee. Then she said, "I think she has a strong, stoic face."

It took Matasha a moment to remember what "stoic" meant.

"She looks like she might be mean." Matasha put the photograph down and pushed her rice pudding away. She had a sinking feeling.

"Mean? Maybe she's just someone who's been through a lot."

Mean, thought Matasha. *I can see it in her face. I don't want that one.* "Is it too late to get someone else?" The girl did not look like someone who would be nice to play with, or patient while Matasha taught her about ice-skating and jacks. She looked the way Jean looked when Jean got into one of her moods and refused to be pleased about anything. This was not a girl who was going to be fun. Matasha could just tell.

Her mother cocked her head. "Why don't we talk about this later?"

"Okay," said Matasha. She remembered Mrs. O'Connor and Miss Lacey talking about how some of the adoptees were aggressive—Matasha had taken that to mean that they had loud tantrums and got into physical fights. That they might try to hurt people. Could you tell from someone's face that they would be like that? Matasha began to think so. She wanted a sister but not a *problem* sister. She wanted her mother to get the right kind of orphan. But she could sense her mother was speeding along toward her idea just as she sped through the racks of blouses when she and Matasha did their May shopping. Her mother didn't want anything to slow her down. Matasha crumpled up her napkin as her mother slid the neglected glass of rice pudding over to her own side.

"This is really good," her mother said, spooning up the pebbled cream.

10.

They came home to the dining room table set for Sabbath dinner. The Waxes had Sabbath dinner four or five times a year. All the other Fridays, Matasha's father was at the office, or he and Mrs. Wax had theater tickets or a dinner party. But every few months Sunset got out the china and the crystal wineglasses and an embroidered cover for the loaf of challah Mrs. Wax had picked up. Mrs. Wax put lace over her head and lit two candles, making small circling motions with her hands, her pink nails catching the candlelight. She sang the blessing in her off-key voice, and Mr. Wax did the prayer over the wine (grape juice for Matasha) in his low, true one. Matasha did the prayer over the bread. Then Mr. Wax said "Good job" to Matasha and sliced the bread with the big silver bread knife. They chewed on the bread while they zipped through some prayers Mrs. Wax had typed up and stapled together into a booklet. There was one about a woman's price being far above rubies that Matasha's father always said to Matasha's mother, and this was Matasha's favorite part of the service. Then something else, with a beautiful rhythm, about binding these words upon one's hands and upon one's forehead and upon the gateposts, which aroused some strange images.

Finally they ate the meal. Sunset brought in and cleared plates and refilled water glasses when necessary. Sunset lived in a house on the West Side with her sister, but Monday afternoon through Saturday morning she spent at the Waxes'. Her big Polish family consisted of four brothers, three sisters, and gaggles of nieces and nephews. She had never married. Matasha's questions about her years as a nun had started with the clothing: Had Sunset worn the big white head thing? the black dress? a big cross? Sunset said the head thing was called a "coif," and yes and yes and yes. Sunset looked like someone who had once been a nun. She was tall and straight and had a long gray braid down her back. She told Matasha that a lot of the women in her family became nuns, but it wasn't as popular a calling as it once had been. Only one of her nieces had gone into the church, and none of her grandnieces.

The meal was very quiet. When Matasha and her mother had gotten home, Matasha had been able to put thoughts of Qui aside by plunging into *The Once and Future King*, and now she was daydreaming about King Arthur and his wife, Guenever, and his best friend, Lancelot, and how Guenever and Lancelot were having an affair, and how they both loved Arthur and felt so guilty about deceiving him, and yet they didn't stop. Somehow T. H. White had written the book so that you didn't think Guenever and Lancelot were terrible even though you knew they were doing something very wrong. And you didn't necessarily think that Guenever should go back to Arthur even though he was the most virtuous character in the book and should have had the best things happen to him. It didn't seem like it was going to be that kind of book, where the best character got the best ending.

So Matasha had been dreaming, and feeling rather in love with either Lancelot or King Arthur, she wasn't sure which, and twisting her cloth napkin with a kind of delicious tension that, looking down, she suddenly thought might be a sign of lovesickness—a condition she'd read about but had never been certain she understood. Was it whatever she was feeling now? No one had spoken for practically the entire meal. Her father had been attentively cutting up his roast beef into small pieces—he was one of the slowest eaters she'd ever known, slower even than Grandma Nan, who was very slow—and her mother kept reaching for her wine and taking a swallow. Sunset moved in and out of the room like a steady, silent breeze. Matasha had even forgotten to chatter on about her week at school, what they were studying in history, what Mrs. L'Enfant had said about *Tom Sawyer*.

"Matasha," said Mrs. Wax, jarring her alert. "I've made an appointment for you to see Dr. Andrews, to check your height."

Matasha froze. Of course she'd known that her half birthday was coming up, but she'd been hoping her mother would forget. Her mother was often scattered enough that it seemed just possible she would. In the meantime, Matasha had done her best to forget about it herself.

"I don't want to go," she said, her voice wavery.

"I know you don't. But it's better to catch this now than to wait until you're older."

"Catch what?" said Matasha. The tears were sitting in her eyes, ready to spill over. She did not want to cry at the table.

"Well, if there's some problem, then we should know about it, sweetheart. So we can do whatever we need to."

Matasha slid from her seat and rushed out of the room. All the thoughts she'd been avoiding in recent weeks came hurrying in. There was something wrong with her, or at least the grown-ups thought there was, which was what mattered in the end. Why couldn't they just leave her alone? She was fine! The doctor was going to examine her and *look* at her and then do some *treatment*. Why would her parents allow this?

It was Mr. Wax who came and found her on the living room sofa, curled up small and shuddering in one corner. He didn't mind when she cried, whereas her mother did. Crying irritated her mother, made her speak angrily. Her father stroked her back silently. Then he said, "Matasha?" She looked up with her face red and bunched up with misery.

"You're just going to get measured," her father said. "Let's take this one step at a time."

Matasha didn't like this talk of "steps." One step led to another. "I don't want them to do *anything* to me!"

"There's no reason to assume you're going to need to do anything at all," her father told her. "This is just a checkup. And, look, if you do need something, it won't be so bad. There are hormones in our bodies that make us grow. You may not have as much of those hormones as most children. That's no big deal. It's just a physical thing. The doctors can give you that hormone and you will start to catch up with the other kids."

"But do they give it with a *needle*?"

Her father paused, realizing his mistake. "I don't know. I believe so."

Matasha began to wail. "No!" she cried. "I won't do it! I don't care if I'm not like other kids. I like being the way I am!"

"But you might not like it when you get to be a teenager and the differences get even bigger."

"I won't care. Why do I have to do it if I don't care if I'm small? I DON'T CARE! Isn't this my choice?"

Mr. Wax didn't have an answer to that.

"It's just a consultation," he said at last. "You're just going to talk to the doctor." He fished a handkerchief out of his pocket. It was clotted at one end with something her father had already blown into it. Matasha gingerly took the clean end and wiped her nose and eyes with it.

"How do you know? Do you promise?"

"I promise. No shots, no nothing on this visit. Just talking. And then we'll see."

Matasha finished drying herself. "You promise?"

"I promise."

They walked back into the dining room, holding hands. Mrs. Wax sat in her seat looking as if she wasn't sure what to do with herself. Matasha, to her horror, felt coming on the compulsive hiccups that she used to get when she cried very hard as a young child. The kind where after you were done actually crying, you still gasped convulsively every few minutes, so deeply it hurt your chest. It was a baby's way of crying. She wanted to run out of the room again but she stayed put, pretending to be unaware of each gasp and willing her parents to be unaware of it too. If she willed hard enough, it would somehow not be happening even as, in fact, it was.

They all poked some more at their food, and then her mother said, "Matasha and I saw a picture today of a child the agency says is available for adoption. Her name is Qui."

Now it was her father's turn to look uncomfortable. He

cleared his throat.

"She's not very pretty," said Matasha.

"Well, that doesn't matter," said her mother. Although Matasha knew that things like that did matter to her mother. It was complicated. Mrs. Wax thought about beauty all the time, and when she pointed out a child she thought had beauty, she seemed as happy as when she pointed out to Matasha certain statues and paintings in the Art Institute. She talked about beauty as if it were some magical thing that added to the goodness of the world and which you couldn't try to have, you either did or you didn't. There was a girl in Matasha's class, Jackie Fellows, whom her mother had described as "beautiful." Matasha tried to figure out what it was about Jackie that was so special. She couldn't see anything herself. Jackie had long straight hair and an ordinary face, eyes, and nose. Mrs. Wax said Jackie was "ethereal." Matasha looked the word up. "Celestial," "heavenly," "immaterial," the dictionary said. What did these have to do with Jackie Fellows, who walked around with cakes of soap in her pocket and then sniffing her fingers?

Yet Mrs. Wax didn't seem all that interested in the way Matasha looked, or whether she was ethereal or not. Maybe, Matasha thought, it had to do with the fact that her mother said she'd inherited her father's brains. If you were brainy and a little odd, like Matasha (and like her father), pretty didn't come into it. You weren't, and you didn't need to be. On the other hand, Matasha was discouraged that her mother had seemingly given up on her from the beauty point of view. She thought there was still a chance she'd turn out nice-looking. She didn't care that much about her looks, either, but it would be better to be pretty than not pretty, and she hoped her mother hadn't written her off too soon.

Matasha was surprised it didn't matter to her mother whether Qui was pretty. But maybe Qui wouldn't be smart, either, or at least she might not seem smart, after months on a boat and in a refugee camp, not even going to school.

If Qui was neither pretty *nor* smart, what would Matasha's mother find in her to like?

"And how did you happen to see this photograph?" her father was asking.

"The agency mailed me some information."

"Some information that you requested?"

"She looked a little mean," Matasha broke in.

Her father turned to her. "Mean?"

"Like she might not be friendly. Or might . . ." Matasha searched for what it was she needed to put into words, what the impression was that she'd gotten. "Like she might cause trouble in school. Not listen to the teacher. Not do her homework. Get in fights." There weren't too many kids like that at Margaret E. Marvin. There might be one or two a year, and then they disappeared; their parents took them out and they had to go somewhere else.

That wasn't completely it. There was something in the girl's expression that frightened her.

Mr. Wax looked alarmed. "You have a vibe about this girl?" he asked.

"Yes," Matasha said. "I think she's bad news."

Mr. Wax began to laugh. Matasha, realizing that her

phrasing had been comical, began to laugh too.

"Come on, now," said Mrs. Wax. "That's ridiculous. There's no reason to think . . ."

"She's bad news!" giggled Mr. Wax. Matasha laughed harder, egging her father on. "Bad news. She's bad news!" they gasped. When Mr. Wax got going laughing, it was difficult for him to stop. He got positively hysterical. The sound of his high-pitched laugh, so unlike his usual formal demeanor, was in itself so funny that it made Matasha get hysterical too, and then it would be a long time until either of them could calm down. Months later, if one of them referred to whatever it was they'd found so amusing, it would set them right off again.

"Very funny, you two," said Mrs. Wax. "You two jokers. Very funny."

"Oh-oh-oh!" Eventually Mr. Wax pulled himself together enough to get a fresh napkin to replace the moist one he'd balled up in his fist, and to apply himself once again to eating his potato. Matasha kept giggling softly.

"But seriously—hee hee—you don't have a good impression from the picture, Matasha?"

"Oh, Robert, how can you go on about it? It's like a mug shot. They line these children up and photograph them straight on and the kids are scared half out of their wits."

"Show me the picture," said Mr. Wax.

"We're eating dinner, Robert!"

"Let's take a look now."

Mrs. Wax rose resentfully and left the room. She returned with the envelope containing the photo. Mr. Wax shook the photo out and held it up, squinting at it, then put it down near his plate and removed his glasses, bending close to see it better.

"Matasha's right," he said. "I don't like the look of her."

"Robert," said Mrs. Wax, exasperated. "To be using Matasha's . . . I mean, to . . ." She looked helplessly at her husband and then at Matasha, then at Mr. Wax again. Matasha could see that she was extremely angry. "This is something we should be talking about at another time," she said finally. Matasha never heard her parents say that to each other—that they should talk about something at another time. And after all, her mother was the one who had brought the whole subject up.

"You mean without me!" Matasha trilled. She still felt hysterical, as if she had risen above her seat and was staying aloft by flapping her arms wildly. Her voice sounded loud to her.

Mrs. Wax stared at her husband.

"Why do you want to talk about this without me?" shrieked Matasha. "She's going to be MY sister. MY sister! MY sister! MY sister!"

"THAT'S ENOUGH!" shouted Mrs. Wax.

Matasha closed her mouth abruptly. Her mother almost never shouted, so it scared Matasha when she did.

"Well, she is," murmured Matasha very quietly. "Mean-looking." She was on the edge of something dangerous, about to topple off.

"Matasha feels uncomfortable about something," said her father. "We have to take account of that."

"You are just saying that because you do not want to do this thing at all!"

"I've never said that," replied Mr. Wax calmly. That was always his trump card—even Matasha was old enough to know it. Whenever the going got really rough, Mr. Wax would calm way down and say something noncommittal and completely inarguable. He would refuse to take sides, have any definite opinion. It drove everyone crazy.

"I need . . . I need . . . I need . . ." stuttered Mrs. Wax. She didn't say what it was she needed. Matasha was beginning to feel sorry for her, and a little regretful. All of a sudden she wished this would stop. Her mother was looking flushed, confused, and still very angry. Matasha wished her parents had in fact talked privately before dinner, or waited until after. She wished she hadn't gotten all silly with her father and provoked her mother.

But she couldn't help saying what she'd said about the picture. She didn't want that girl inside their house. She wanted a sister, but she didn't want *that* one.

Her parents rose from the table. They didn't seem to notice that they were both only halfway through their meals. Sunset hadn't been in since the giggling incident. She knew when to stay out. Mr. and Mrs. Wax walked upstairs together, Mr. Wax ahead, Mrs. Wax behind. They both looked rigid, tired, and miserable. The moment they were out of sight, Sunset reappeared. She cleared away the plates and the water glasses, and Matasha helped her. She liked clearing the table, and it gave her a way to stay near Sunset.

"You all were laughing like the circus had come to town," said Sunset. Matasha began to giggle again and had to make a conscious effort to stop herself.

"I'd better not get into it," she told Sunset.

Matasha put the dirty things next to the sink. Sunset would rinse everything and run the dishwasher and unload it again tomorrow.

"Looks like just you for dessert," Sunset said. She put out a boxed apple pie from the supermarket.

"Do you want some?" asked Matasha. It embarrassed her that Sunset had to be invited to partake of the food she served. Once it was leftovers, Sunset was free to have whatever she wanted. But even then she never ate until after the family did.

"Well, all right, dear one. I think I will."

They sat down on the kitchen bar stools, side by side, and ate the pie. Matasha asked if Sunset knew who was going to be on Johnny Carson tonight. Sunset usually checked *TV Guide* to find out.

"George Gobel, Cloris Leachman, and Truman Capote." Sunset pronounced the last name "Ca-POTE." Matasha had only heard of Cloris Leachman.

"Can I come watch with you?" Matasha asked, even though Sunset always said yes.

"You can. Get in your nightgown first and wash up and then you come down." She made a groaning sound when she stood up to clear their dishes. She often made this sound when she got up. When Matasha was younger, she had asked why, and Sunset said it was because her legs got swollen from standing too much and that she had arthritis in her hips. In any case it always took a little time for Sunset to stand up all the way and start moving.

Matasha went upstairs, past her parents' bedroom, where she could hear her father's slightly raised voice and her mother's now quieter one. She put a 45 on the turntable: "Be-Bop-a-Lula," by Gene Vincent and the Blue Caps; it always cheered her up, especially the scream toward the end. She listened to that a few times and then to the Beatles' *Rubber Soul*. She read *The Once and Future King*. At ten she changed into her nightgown, hung up the clothes she'd worn that day, brushed her teeth, and went down to Sunset's room. It wasn't quite time yet for the show, but if she showed up early, there might be a few minutes for Sunset to tell her more about being a nun.

Sunset's bed had a quilt on it with enormous sunflowers that she'd embroidered herself. Matasha wondered if Sunset liked sunflowers because they had the word "sun" in them, like her name. On the other hand, Sunset wasn't big on the sun itself. Her face was very pale, very soft and rather saggy, and she said she never went to the beach, didn't care for it. Matasha loved going to the beach when the weather got warm. You could walk there from the apartment in under ten minutes. It was just on the other side of the park. Sunset said you couldn't pay her to sit in the sand under the hot sun. Sand got in everything, and it made her itch for days. And the sun put spots all over your face.

"It does not!" Matasha insisted. "I get freckles, but I don't get *spots*."

"It puts them there when you're older, believe me."

On the wall above her bed Sunset had hung a picture of Jesus haloed in golden light, and on her dresser there was one of the Virgin Mary. There was also a picture of Saint Sebastian, who had several arrows in the sides of his body with blood dripping down. Matasha didn't know why anyone would want such a picture, but she didn't ask. It might turn out to be rude. There were a lot of people to keep track of in the Catholic religion— Sunset had once run through an explanation of seven or eight of the saints for her, and added that there were dozens more.

Over time Matasha had been able to put together the story of why Sunset had stopped being a nun. It was a long time ago now. It had to do with a younger sister she loved very much, who had also become a nun. They were in the same convent. It was a strict convent that allowed you to see your family only once a year. When her sister contracted polio and died, Sunset had been allowed to go home to her parents for a few weeks, and found that when the time was up, she could not go back.

"I just couldn't go to the place where my sister had died. It had been all right when I had been able to watch over her and be company for her, but now that she was gone, I just couldn't." Sunset had prayed and prayed for her faith to be stronger than her grief. She thought about asking to be sent to a different convent, but by this time her sisters and brothers had a lot of children they needed help taking care of, and so she decided to do that. She'd always liked children.

"I'm so lucky you left," Matasha always told her fervently. Sunset had come to work for the Waxes when Matasha was eight. She'd recently stopped working for another couple who'd moved to San Francisco. Matasha never asked about that couple's children, though she knew there had been a boy and a girl. She didn't want to feel that Sunset might have loved them more than she loved Matasha.

Sunset was watching the news that came on before Johnny Carson. The news rarely mentioned Martin Kimmel anymore. But as usual something else terrible had happened. This time, a man had been shot at a gas station on the West Side, and a reporter was interviewing a woman who'd witnessed the incident.

"Do you live near there?" asked Matasha, worried. Sunset said she didn't.

"When you were a nun," blurted out Matasha, "did God ever actually talk to you?"

Sunset got up and lowered the sound on the TV. She turned to Matasha very seriously. "Once, I thought so," she said.

"What was it like?" This was intensely exciting.

"It wasn't a voice. It was like a . . . an atmosphere. Like the air filled up with softness and light and I felt a presence breathing through me. Talking to me without talking."

"What did it *say*?"

"It said that everything was going to be all right. It was not long after my sister died. I had prayed that she was in a better place and not suffering. I prayed about whether I should go back to the convent. I heard him say that she was well, that she wasn't suffering anymore, and that everything was all right. And I knew that whatever I decided would be all right too."

Matasha was awed into silence; any further questions would be noisy and frivolous.

"I don't know if I should be telling you these things. You have your own religion. I don't want your mother and father to think I am trying to meddle in any way."

"It's not meddling. You're just telling me. Anyway, I get to decide what religion I want to be when I grow up."

"Is that right?"

"Of course! I guess it will be easiest to be Jewish, but if I want I can pick something else. I like that Catholics have all the saints and things."

"It keeps things lively," Sunset agreed. She pointed out that Johnny Carson was coming on.

Ed McMahon did his introduction of Johnny Carson and Johnny did his monologue, making some jokes about President Ford, and then a man in a sparkly jumpsuit sang a song with too many melodramatic flourishes. The cameras caught the sweat on his forehead and upper lip. The next guest was this Truman Capote, pronounced, apparently, "Kuh-PO-tee." He had a large puffy face and dark glasses and a high voice. Matasha couldn't believe he was an author. *This* person was an author? Johnny Carson was talking to Truman Capote about a short story he'd written that had upset a lot of people.

"It's fiction," Capote insisted. "Do I need to remind these people what the definition of a fiction is?" He emphasized the word "fiction" strenuously, and swayed and waved his hands, one of which held a cigarette.

"That man is drunk, or he is on drugs," said Sunset.

Well, there was certainly *something* strange about him. And yet Matasha almost immediately began to imagine what it would be like to be him, sitting on Johnny Carson's couch and talking about her books and her stories. She would say, "Well, it started when I was seven years old. My first story was about a rooster who gets stuck on the roof of an apartment building and can't come down . . ." And she would talk about her most recent book, which was a best seller.

As if Sunset could read her thoughts, she said: "That will be you in fifteen years, Miss Matasha. You better wave to me from that couch."

Matasha laughed and felt very hot. She would love to be on TV, under all those lights, millions of people watching her in their houses. She did not want to be famous, exactly. When you were famous, bad things happened to you. You got kidnapped, like Patty Hearst or that billionaire's grandson who got his ear cut off. Or you got shot at, like President Ford. But it would be nice to be on TV, talking to people like Johnny Carson and having people read your stories.

Sunset let Matasha watch until 11:15 and then told her she should go to bed. The next day, there was a special report in the *Sun-Times* about Vietnamese refugees who had made their way to Europe and the United States. The report described the boats some had escaped from Vietnam on, small and rickety, and the pirates who intercepted the boats. The refugees swallowed any small valuables they'd been able to take with them—coins, rings—to keep them from the pirates. People were crammed sixty or eighty to a thirty-foot boat and some had only half a cup of water to drink a day, and no food. Matasha got a measuring cup from the kitchen and filled it with half a cup of tap water to see how much that was.

Sunday was the morning her father always made matzoh

brei for breakfast. When Matasha woke up, she claimed to have a stomachache and skipped both breakfast and lunch, and she measured out another half cup of water and sipped at it for the rest of the day, making it last as long as possible. She made it until dinnertime, when Mr. Wax went to pick up Chinese food. The smell of the roast pork was intoxicating, and Matasha lost her will to explain to her parents about her experiment. She ate a heap of spareribs, her father praising her appetite, along with two very large glasses of orange juice, and finished up with some matzoh and a big bowl of ice cream. After, sated, she ran up to her room to be away from her parents, ashamed that she'd had bad thoughts about a refugee like Qui. She still didn't want Qui to come. But she felt in the wrong.

11.

At school on Monday Matasha told Jean about the pirates, and about the photograph of Qui. They were sitting on the counter-top next to the sinks in the fourth-floor bathroom. The fourth-floor bathroom was where they went to have serious and private conversations. It was smaller than the other bathrooms in the school and shared the floor only with the big art room, so it didn't get a lot of use. You could count on having a little bit of time before another kid came in.

"So do you think you'll get somebody else?" asked Jean.

"Probably," said Matasha. "I won't let Qui come."

Jean frowned. "Yeah, you can probably just say that to your parents and they'll listen. They do whatever you want."

"That's not true."

"It is true. You're kind of spoiled, actually."

"I'm not spoiled!" Matasha was hurt.

"Yes, you are. Like I go over to your house, and you can never have just one thing of Magic Markers in your closet. You have like four packages of them. And you never even use them! You're always keeping them 'nice'! And you have a stack of drawing paper this high. You have about three hundred board games. Your parents get you anything you want."

"No, they don't," said Matasha, although she couldn't think of anything she had asked for that she hadn't gotten, sooner or later. She didn't *feel* spoiled. She didn't badger her parents for things she saw on TV or make a big fuss when she had to do things she didn't want to. She wasn't a *brat*. Jean was just mad because Diane and Kelly came into her room and took her drawing things and then lost or broke them, and her mother didn't do anything about it. Jean asked for replacements, but her mother was distracted with the baby and took a long time about getting them. Then Jean would be angry because she had to use her allowance and didn't have enough left over to buy record albums.

"I'll give you some of my markers. I don't care."

"No, you won't. You say you will but you won't." Matasha had to admit this was true. She hated giving away her things, and usually "forgot" whatever she had promised.

"Your mom cooks," Matasha said, which she saw as a great advantage.

"That's not *spoiling*. That's just eating."

Matasha wanted to say something about what it was like to eat Sunset's limited repertoire day after day—tough hamburgers, spaghetti and meatballs, or tacos from the box—but just then a little kid came in to use the bathroom, and anyway, she didn't think she would be able to make Jean understand. Jean was the one person who could undermine Matasha's usual confidence that she knew what she was talking about. Matasha couldn't figure it out. If Jean insisted to her that two plus two equaled five, and Matasha said, no, it's four, Jean would somehow end up making her believe that five was the right answer. Jean had always been stubborn, even more stubborn than Matasha, and seemed to care less about keeping a good feeling between them. In contrast, Matasha cared quite a bit about that, and it put her at a distinct disadvantage.

The little kid washed her hands and left.

"My family has four kids and yours has just one," Jean said primly. She flicked a crumb of something off her velour top. "So we can't have just everything we want."

Matasha closed her eyes, shutting out Jean's nastiness. "Well, I'll be getting a sister soon."

Jean slid back against the mirror. "So maybe you'll have to learn how to share."

Matasha had given that some thought, ever since the discussion about the bunk bed. What *would* she have to share? Well, dessert might be an issue. She wouldn't be able to count on being the only one to like mint chocolate chip ice cream. Her mother bought that flavor because Matasha liked it, and no one else ate it; it was always there when she wanted it. Likewise no one raided the Ho Hos, the Sno Balls, or the egg matzoh. They were all hers. But in all honesty she thought she could handle this. Other than that, what was there? Clothes? Her mother and father wouldn't expect her to share those. Books? She didn't mind sharing books; she swapped with Jean all the time.

"It will be okay," said Matasha.

Jean let out a big, slow breath, and Matasha knew that whatever had been bugging her was dissipating. Matasha kept reminding herself of that—Jean let go of things, and afterward her brain seemed to be swept clear of all memory of it. The problem was that Matasha didn't forget, couldn't seem to clear her head in the same way. For the rest of the year she'd probably be worrying that she was spoiled. She would notice how much blank paper and how many pencils she had, and wonder if it was too much. She would feel bad if her parents took her to a restaurant; Jean's parents never took their kids out. She always remembered all the cutting little things Jean had ever said to her, the explosions, the accusations, the days of snubbing. Jean was rarely genuinely cruel, but her snubs were lonely times for Matasha.

"I can't believe you're really getting a sister. A sister from Vietnam."

"It's going to be so interesting."

Jean rolled her eyes and Matasha saw her temper flare again. "If you had brothers and sisters you wouldn't think they were so *interesting*. They're mostly a big pain."

"Okay, okay. Give me a chance to find out."

"I swear, Matasha, you talk like a book sometimes. Like a little pointy-head. 'Interesting.'" She put on a fake English accent: "They're going to be so terribly interesting."

Matasha lost patience.

"Where else do you want me to get my information? If I don't know something, what's so bad about finding it out in a book? I can't just KNOW everything AUTOMATICALLY like you. I guess you were just BORN knowing everything, you never have to LOOK for it."

"Oh, stop it," said Jean, but Matasha could tell she was in retreat, and after they moved on to another subject, Jean asked if Matasha wanted to come over after school.

Matasha did. At day's end they caught the bus together. Mrs. White was at the stop, of course, with the baby and the twins. Jean stared straight ahead, ignoring all of them as she marched the blocks to their house. Matasha was left answering Mrs. White's questions about what they had done at school that day. After lunch there had been an assembly with a hypnotist. It was fascinating. The hypnotist had asked for volunteers, and Gina Wilkins had gone up, on a dare from Jonathan Villaneuva and Victor Stein. The hypnotist had told Gina she was six years old again. He'd then asked her to write her first name on a big chalkboard on wheels. When she did, it was exactly as a six-year-old would have done it: tilting, uneven capital letters, some of them backward. Matasha was astonished. She would love to hypnotize Jean from time to time and get her to confess what she was thinking. Sometimes, at a look on Jean's face, Matasha would say, "What?" and Jean would say, "Nothing." Once, in fourth grade, Matasha had kept asking and insisting that Jean had to be thinking *something*, until Jean told her to shut up or she'd sock her in the mouth. She looked like she might actually mean it, so Matasha backed off, puzzled. What could be such a big deal that Jean couldn't just say it? She'd mentioned the incident to her mother. "Maybe Jean doesn't even know what she's thinking," her mother said. Matasha wondered if that could possibly be the case.

Mrs. White was less impressed by the afternoon's activity. "I pay too much to that school for them to be giving assemblies on hypnosis," she said. "Someone who could tell you a little something about history or world affairs would be more in my line."

Jean spoke up at last. "That's all we do in classes, Mom. Assembly's a chance to hear about something that's different."

"That's different, all right," said Mrs. White. To the baby: "Charlotte, ouch, stop pulling at my hair."

The Whites' house smelled of chocolate chip cookies. Mrs. White had baked a huge batch during the afternoon, along with an applesauce cake. Jean was immediately in a better mood. Mrs. White put out paper plates, and all four kids tucked into the cookies. The cake was for after dinner.

"What are we going to have, Ma?" Jean asked.

"I'm thinking a ravioli with red pepper sauce." Mrs. White was peering at a cookbook with a cover showing a bright array of eggs, tomatoes, and shiny cooking pans.

"Yum," said Jean. She was an adventurous eater. Matasha rarely stayed for dinner because she had a feeling she wouldn't like the food. She wished Sunset would cook something different once in a while, but the food at the Whites' was a little *too* different.

The two girls took a last cookie each and ran up to Jean's room, which had a curtain of purple and black beads for a door. They made a lush sound as you pushed through. Jean's bed was a mattress right on the floor, covered with a purplish, exotic-looking quilt. Jean finished her cookie and then grabbed a roll of flesh at her belly and said she was fat.

"No, you're not," said Matasha. That was something else new this year: Jean claiming she was fat, a porker, which Matasha could not understand at all. Jean was round and soft, unlike Matasha, who was scrawny, but she wasn't fat. Molly Jentel was fat, and the other girls at school never let her forget it. They drew ugly cartoons of fat people and taped them to her locker. They called her Blubber Molly. Matasha cringed when she saw and heard these things, but she never objected or spoke to Molly about them. She never even thought of it. She didn't want to be friends with Molly, and if she talked to her and acted sorry about things, she'd have to become her friend. That was just the way it was.

Matasha lay on Jean's bed doing cat's cradle with a red cord while Jean put on Lou Reed's "Walk on the Wild Side" and then sat cross-legged on the floor, drawing the *Transformer* album cover in her sketchbook.

"I'm playing this real low. My mom caught Diane and Kelly listening to it and she got so upset!"

Matasha laughed, but she didn't know why "Walk on the Wild Side" wasn't something five-year-olds should be listening to. It was just a strange but appealing melody to her.

They listened to the song four times. They didn't like the other songs on the *Transformer* album, so after that they put on the Beatles' *Revolver* and listened to that straight through. Jean seemed relaxed and content, so Matasha decided to take a chance and talk to her about her developing plan to solve the Martin Kimmel case. It was a plan that would allow her and Jean to do something genuinely important and that might also bring them closer again. They'd used to have more adventures together, secret things they did that had set them up as a team against the world. Once, they'd stolen Mars bars from the Osco near Jean's house. That wasn't nice, but it was exciting, and they'd only done it once. Another time, they'd written an anonymous note to Mr. Herbert, a history teacher who'd since left the school, suggesting that he brush his teeth more often; he'd had truly horrible breath. They slipped the note into the drawer of his desk one day after the dismissal bell, terrified of being caught in the act, and they still talked about how dangerous but necessary it had been. They never knew for sure if Mr. Herbert had discovered the note, but they still believed that he had left the school out of shame when he'd learned the truth about himself.

"What if the police found where Martin Kimmel is buried?" Matasha asked. The question felt more out of the blue than she'd thought it would. But now that it was spoken, she had to persist. "I mean, if they found him, then they could look at the bones"—she couldn't believe she'd said that word out loud—"and that would be a big clue. They could get evidence and then they could find out who did it."

"I wish." Jean rolled her pencil between her thumb and forefinger. "But nobody *can* find him."

"Well, I have an idea . . ."

Jean looked up suspiciously. Those small crimes Matasha and Jean had executed together hadn't been ideas so much as spontaneous capers; later they couldn't have said who initiated them and who followed. But Matasha's ideas were in a different category. They were ambitious, they were all hers, and sometimes they didn't work out very well. For instance, there was the time she found out about a huge record warehouse on the West Side that had tons of LPs you couldn't find anywhere else, like bootlegs of the Beatles' early days playing in Hamburg and odd Swedish versions of their albums. She'd seen ads for the warehouse in the *Sun-Times*. It would be like walking into a room in a fairy tale heaped with emeralds and rubies. She'd gotten Jean excited about it, and Mrs. White agreed to drop them there. That was in the old days of course, last year, when Mrs. White was easygoing about Jean and Matasha's plans. But it had been a mistake. The warehouse, which Matasha had pictured as a big open place like an airport hangar, was actually a warren of dusty and dim rooms with low ceilings, the layout was confusing, and the manager was an obese man who followed them from room to room as if suspicious that they meant to stuff things into their knapsacks and run. Once they were left alone, the other people they came into contact with were even worse: a skeletal, odorous man in a limp, filthy T-shirt; a middle-aged guy who grinned at Matasha with no teeth. There wasn't a single woman in the place. At some point the two girls got accidentally separated and Matasha frantically searched for Jean, getting more and more disoriented as she kept reentering rooms she thought she'd been moving away from, until she sat down on the floor and began to heave with fear, tears trickling from her eyes. Moments later, Jean, furious, found her, demanding to know why she'd walked away. Bucking up their courage, they asked one disturbing-looking patron after another how to get to the exit before finally making their way out. They sat on the sidewalk in front of the warehouse, in an unfamiliar neighborhood of mysterious and shabby storefronts, and waited until it was time for Mrs. White to pick them up. Two different men stopped and asked, leering, what two little girls were doing sitting alone on the street, and a stout older woman told them sternly that they should not be hanging about on their own. Matasha meekly replied that her friend's mom was picking them up any minute. In the back seat of Mrs. White's car, Jean gave her the silent treatment. Matasha could feel the contempt radiating from her: another one of Matasha's stupid ideas.

So Matasha almost backed off then and there. Her new idea was far worse than the one about the record warehouse, or the time she decided they should make ChapStick from scratch and Jean burned one of her hands in the boiling water. But this was one of those occasions when electricity seemed to crackle in Matasha's brain and make her positively reckless, convinced that Jean, if not right away then a little down the line, would see the beauty and wisdom of her plan, which *just had to be done.* And so she said: "I think I know where Martin Kimmel is buried."

"Shut up," said Jean slowly, low-pitched, warningly.

"Well, I do," said Matasha, hearing herself dig in, commit. And then she saw it in Jean's eyes: despite herself, Jean wanted to hear.

So she did something rare for her: she played hard to get. She lay back on the bed, making a Jacob's ladder with her cord, and waited Jean out.

"So where, smarty?"

"If you call me that," Matasha said without turning her gaze, surprised at her steeliness, "I won't tell you."

"Sorry."

Matasha sat up.

"Where do you think he is?" Jean asked.

Matasha told her. At first Jean's face closed down; she looked almost offended. But Matasha kept going, explaining. When she got to the point of describing how the new middle-high school building would soon be on top of Martin Kimmel's bones, sealing him in, Jean began holding her knees and rocking back and forth. "That's so . . . horrible . . ." she breathed.

"So what we should do is go down there and look!" finished Matasha triumphantly.

"No!" cried Jean. "No way! That is so weird, Matasha. I can't believe you even thought of it."

Matasha hated when Jean said she shouldn't have thought of something. It put her in a very strange position. She'd *already* thought of it, so what was she supposed to do?

"But see!" insisted Matasha. "If we do it, if we really do it, we'd help the police solve the mystery!"

Jean buried her face in her knees. Matasha pressed her advantage. "Everybody could stop worrying. Your mom could stop worrying. The murderer would be in jail! We could play in your yard again."

Jean turned her cheek to one side. "I don't know," she said.

"Everything could be normal. And we would probably be in the newspapers for helping!" Oops—wrong move. Jean looked alarmed. "Well, probably not. We're just kids. But also, we would keep everyone in the school from *walking on Martin Kimmel's body forever.*"

Jean nodded. She seemed transfixed.

"Well," Matasha said cannily, after a pause. "I don't know.

Maybe we shouldn't." She lay back with her cord and started working on a bird's nest. She could feel Jean's mind turning over the conversation. She had a feeling Jean would come her way. It might take a while, but it would happen.

When it was time for Matasha to take the bus home, Mrs. White insisted on walking her to the stop, so the whole crew had to go out again, and they had to wait for the baby to be put in some sort of heavy one-piece sweater with feet and the twins to tie their shoes and zipper up their coats. Jean was exasperated, and Matasha could understand one of the reasons she so often avoided after-school visits: unless her father was available, pickups and drop-offs did involve an entourage. But Jean's complaints today had less fire in them than usual, and Matasha believed she was busy thinking about Martin Kimmel. Matasha's belly was anxious-washy but also happy-washy. If Jean agreed, the two of them might be heroes. She'd always believed that someday they would do something wonderful and important together, something that would make people link their names forever, the way you never said Laurel unless you said Hardy, or Romeo unless you said Juliet, or Simon unless you said Garfunkel.

Diane and Kelly and Charlotte and Mrs. White and Jean and Matasha: they all waited at the stop until the bus came, and Mrs. White gave Matasha a compliment. She said Matasha had very good posture. Matasha was surprised, as Mrs. White rarely handed out praise, and she was pleased, but she also suspected this was not likely to put her in Jean's good graces, or to encourage her receptiveness to the Martin Kimmel plan.

"I have good posture too, Ma!" Jean protested.

"I never said you didn't," Mrs. White said mildly. "Bye, Matasha. See you soon."

"See you tomorrow," Jean said, waving. So she wasn't too miffed, apparently.

12.

Dr. Andrews told Matasha to stand on the scale. He nudged the chunky metal marker down and down until the moving pointer balanced. "Sixty pounds," he announced. Then he asked her to straighten up and he brought the measuring bar down on her head. Matasha thought he was mashing it too hard and making her lose an inch or two. "Okay," he said. He had her step back, then forward again. He brought the bar back down on her head. Finally he told her she could return to the examining table. "Four foot four," he informed Matasha's mother.

Matasha was outraged. Two weeks ago, she'd asked Sunset to measure her against the back door. Sunset had marked the door with a pencil just at her head. Then Matasha had measured with Sunset's tape measure and she had come out four feet five inches, just what she needed to make Dr. Andrews stop being concerned. She was sure Dr. Andrews had shaved off some height.

"That's not even second percentile on height and weight, I'm afraid," said the doctor. "But what concerns me more is that she's grown only a quarter inch since her last visit. If she were growing at least two inches a year, I would be less concerned. She would just be destined to be a very short young lady."

Matasha sat quietly, wanting to tear the horrible paper gown from her body, listening to the grown-ups talk.

"Mother, I'm going to recommend that she have an X-ray to determine her bone age. We take an X-ray of her wrist and compare it to an X-ray of a child of average size and development for her age. The results will give us an indication of where we are in terms of Matasha's growth potential. For now we'll just do some blood work, to see what's going on. I may want to send you to the specialist I mentioned, Dr. Karnow."

"Blood work? What's that?" Matasha snapped to attention.

"We draw some blood from you. It's very simple."

"Is that with a needle?" Her eyes were enormous.

"Yes, of course. It won't hurt. Just a pinch."

Liar, thought Matasha. And not just him—her father too. Her father had said "just a conversation"! He had said "no needles, no shots, nothing." She couldn't stop the tears, hot and huge, that sprang up. While she was trying to maintain control of herself, the rest of Dr. Andrews's comment sank in. What did he mean, the specialist he'd *mentioned*? He hadn't mentioned anyone.

"Who is the other doctor?" she asked.

She saw Dr. Andrews and her mother exchange a glance over her head.

"He's someone who does research into children with growth problems," said Dr. Andrews, in an unnaturally slow and patient voice, the kind of voice you used with someone you suspected couldn't understand. In that moment, Matasha realized that he and her mother had already talked about this. That was what he had let slip with "mentioned." Her father had maybe even been in on this too. That was how he'd known about "the hormones."

"Will he give me *hormones*?" Matasha asked angrily.

"Well, that is one possibility," said Dr. Andrews. "Yes, one possibility is growth hormone injections."

Matasha felt sick to her stomach. Injections! Injections! That monstrous, dreadful word! She pictured the horrible piercing of her skin, and then something yellowish and thick going into her veins, spreading throughout her whole body. It would be like a poison. It would probably give her cancer. She read about that all the time in the papers: how people took some kind of medicine for years and then it turned out it gave you cancer. Matasha didn't want injections, and she certainly didn't want to take something that was going to give her cancer. As she got back into her street clothes, she felt a new wave of tears, tears of mourning for her early death: at thirteen or fifteen, or maybe she would last until nineteen.

She saw that Dr. Andrews had left the room and there was a nurse there now, arranging needles on a bright tray.

Matasha jumped up from her chair and ran to the door. She moved so quickly no one had time to react before she was in the corridor. Then the waiting room. Now where could she go?

Out, that was where. Just out. She didn't want to chance waiting for the elevator, so she started down the stairs. Dr. Andrews's office was on the twenty-seventh floor, and she wondered if she could make it all the way to the lobby. After ten or twelve flights at top speed she knew she couldn't. She exited onto a floor, her breath scraping her throat, her skin covered with cold sweat. She banged on the elevator button, willing it to come. She waited to hear steps behind her, the stair door opening, but nothing happened. There were no noises at all. No one was coming to get her. *My father lied to me*, she thought.

The elevator came and she pressed herself into a corner, even though no one else was inside. The doors opened at the lobby, and when she walked out her mother and a nurse were standing there. The nurse grabbed her arm so hard it hurt. Matasha's mother looked tense and annoyed.

"Let's not be silly, now," said the nurse, and Matasha thought that if she were braver, she would haul off with her free arm and punch her.

Matasha was brought back into the doctor's office, a prisoner. He was sitting at his desk now, scribbling on some papers. He put his pen down when she came in. His look said that he had only so much time for this nonsense.

"Mother," he said to Mrs. Wax, "please keep your daughter still. This is just a little blood work and then we'll be done."

The nurse made Matasha sit back up on the examining table and put a cardboard box under her arm for it to rest on. "Hold her around the waist so she doesn't jump up," the nurse told Mrs. Wax.

"Oh, really," said Mrs. Wax.

"I don't want this needle to go astray," threatened the nurse.

Mrs. Wax held Matasha around the waist. Her painted nails clicked together in front. Matasha was afraid that she would not be able to stop herself when the needle approached, that she would jump off the table. Maybe she would get the needle in her eye. The nurse turned to her with the gleaming tip in her hand, and Matasha slid forward.

"I said *hold her*," the nurse said loudly. Dr. Andrews had already left the room. Mrs. Wax grabbed Matasha convulsively around the waist, squeezing her tight. The breath went out of Matasha again and for a moment she didn't know where she was. Her arm was held in a strong grip and something stuck her and went deep. It was *wrong wrong wrong so wrong!* She couldn't even cry out to protest. The nurse pressed her fingers against the injection site. "It's not coming very fast," she complained. The finger pressing made Matasha nauseated. The nausea and the pain alternated until finally the nurse withdrew the needle. Matasha thought she might throw up onto the floor. She was shaking. The nurse was stretching a Band-Aid over the injection place. It was over. *My father lied to me!* she thought again, but was too spent to be outraged anymore.

"She's going to need to get over this someday," said the nurse.

"We don't need your opinion," replied Matasha's mother.

Matasha's arm, near the elbow, felt stiff and bruised. She moved it carefully, then stopped moving it. She watched the nurse's large hands as she briskly labeled the three vials of her blood with "Wax, M" in blue marker. Somehow the blood didn't bother Matasha once it was out of her body. Even the idea of it coming out didn't bother her. It was just how they had to stick her that was awful.

Once she and her mother were outside, the cold lake wind oddly enough soothed Matasha's shivering. Still, she huddled inside her coat as they walked down Michigan Avenue. Her scrambled mind drifted to Martin Kimmel. How would she ever be brave enough to look for him—*dig* for him—if she couldn't even sit still for a doctor's needle? She hated herself right now.

"Would you like to get some hot chocolate?" her mother asked.

That sounded good.

They stopped in the nearest coffee shop, a grimy little place with a cigarette machine at the front, and Mrs. Wax ordered two hot chocolates with whipped cream. Matasha didn't like whipped cream, but this way she could scoop hers off and her mother would get double. There were photographs on the wall of famous Chicago people Matasha knew about or had seen on TV: Jack Brickhouse, Harry Caray, Gene Siskel and Roger Ebert, Irv Kupcinet. And Dottie Summers, whom she'd now met for real. All of them were signed with greetings and appreciation for "Paulie," the owner.

Matasha spooned her whipped cream onto her saucer before it could ruin her hot chocolate, and pushed the saucer to her mother. She blew on the liquid and took a sip. It tasted wonderful.

"I hate when they call me 'Mother,'" said Mrs. Wax.

"Well, I hate Dr. Andrews," said Matasha.

They smiled at each other.

"Do I have to have the X-ray?" asked Matasha.

"Yes," her mother said gently. "Yes, you have to have the X-ray. There are no needles with an X-ray."

"All right," said Matasha. She didn't ask for any promises.

13.

In her head, Matasha wrote:

> *Dear Dottie:*
> *I'm scared I'm going to have to get treatment*
> *for being very short. It might involve injections. I'm*
> *really really REALLY scared of needles. And the pain.*
> *What should I do?*

It wasn't a good letter. The shots were not something Dottie could be that helpful about. She couldn't make them not happen, for starters. It wasn't like when someone asked her how to talk to a rude coworker, or what to do when your mother was upset that you were marrying a Catholic instead of a Protestant. What could Dottie really say about it? "Be brave"? Matasha *hoped* Dottie would not say anything like that. That was something Matasha absolutely did not want to hear.

> *Dear Dottie:*
> *I would really like a sister. I'm an only child.*
> *My mother is thinking of adopting one but my father*
> *doesn't want to.*

Matasha stopped mentally composing. She'd been thinking

Dottie might give her advice on how to talk her father into the adoption, but this probably wasn't the case. Dottie would say what any grown-up would say—what her father actually had said when she'd overheard him that night—that both parents had to want an adoption. Dottie might even scold Matasha, saying that an adoption was serious business, that you didn't talk someone into getting a child the way you might talk them into buying a sweater or going somewhere in particular for vacation. Matasha didn't want to get on Dottie's bad side.

All these years that she'd been reading Dear Dottie she'd assumed it was simple to write Dottie a letter. You just put down what your problem was and sent it. But now that she wanted to do it herself, she saw it wasn't so easy. First you had to decide exactly what your problem *was*. Then it had to be the right *kind* of problem. It was distressing to discover that there were certain kinds of problems Dottie wasn't that suited for.

Matasha put aside the idea of a letter for now. She was convinced that she had something to write, and that there would be a way for Dottie to help, but it might have to wait. In the meantime, she went for her X-ray. It wasn't scary. A nurse draped a heavy bib over Matasha's chest and flipped a switch while she sat on a table. It didn't hurt. It didn't feel like anything at all. The X-ray showed that Matasha had the bone development typical of an eight-year-old, which was more evidence, Dr. Andrews said, that she was low in growth hormone. The blood tests hadn't shown anything interesting, and Dr. Karnow, the specialist Dr. Andrews was sending them to, would likely do some more.

Matasha's mother told her the news one afternoon when

Matasha returned from school. She was sitting in the kitchen over a cup of instant coffee and nibbling at some biscuits. Matasha loved the smell of coffee and was happily anticipating one day turning fifteen, which was the age when her mother said she could start drinking it.

Matasha tried to speak calmly and maturely to her mother. "I don't mind if I'm very, very short," she said. "I don't see why I should have to be as tall as everyone else."

"It's not just height," said her mother. "You also need to go through puberty. You need to get breasts and start to menstruate."

Matasha thought about this. She had convinced herself she wouldn't mind always being short, but it might, in fact, feel weird to be twenty-five years old and have no breasts and look like a child. As bad as it was now to be mistaken for an eight-year-old, think what it would be like when she was twenty-five.

"There are other things too," her mother went on. "Your bones may not grow as strong as they should if you don't get proper levels of the hormone."

Matasha began to tremble. "Mommy, what are they going to *do*?"

Her mother did something unexpected then. She put out her arms and pulled Matasha close to her. She lifted her and Matasha went limp as she settled into her mother's lap. Her mother was often all edges, bony, but just now Matasha found her lap soft and enveloping, comfortable, a huge relief. She pushed back against her mother's chest and fought off the tickle in her throat. Her eyes grew wet against her will, but she somehow knew it would be all right, that her mother wouldn't scold.

Her mother bent down and kissed Matasha's hair. "We need to see Dr. Karnow to know for sure. I don't know exactly what he's going to do. But I have a guess. I think you do too."

Matasha nodded, miserable.

"If it's injections, you'll be able to do it, Matasha. It will seem hard at first, and then you won't mind so much."

Matasha couldn't speak and her eyes got dim—maybe she was going blind too. She was going to be mute and blind and they were going to be sticking needles into her. There was no way this was really going to happen.

Matasha's mother held on to her a little longer. Then she sighed and let Matasha slide off. Matasha thought about letting her legs collapse under her and sinking to the ground in a heap, but she knew the dramatics wouldn't be appreciated. She straightened up weakly. It was impossible to picture getting stuck with needles all the time. How often *would* it be? Once a month? Once a week? *Every day?* And what about those breasts, anyway? Were they really so important? She did want to look like a grown-up one day, and she wanted, she guessed, to get married. She hadn't thought much about it, but it would be nicer to live in a house or apartment with another person, to have someone to talk to, rather than be alone all day. Much nicer.

Her mother had taken her coffee and wandered upstairs. Matasha went to the cookie drawer to get some cookies. Her mother's big tin of Maxwell House instant was sitting in its usual place on the counter. Matasha turned on the flame under the water kettle. She'd seen her mother prepare coffee hundreds of times; you just used the scoop inside the tin to measure out the grounds. She did that now: put the grounds in the cup, and when the water was boiling, she added it. She stirred and bent her head. Mmmmmmm . . . the most heavenly smell. She poured in half-and-half, the same amount her mother did, and waited, patiently, for the brew to cool. Let her mother come down now and tell her she was too young to drink this! Everybody wanted her to grow up? Here she was, drinking coffee, being a grown-up! Let her mother come down and tell her to pour it down the sink! But the trouble was, Matasha's mother wouldn't come down. She was upstairs, absorbed in documents related to her art consulting or maybe a novel. She couldn't smell the coffee from there. And even if she could, Matasha suspected that her mother wouldn't come and stop her. It was almost impossible to be bad in this family. It was so aggravating. To make anyone really object she'd have to do something spectacularly wrong, and that did not appeal to her. Being genuinely bad took a lot of energy; it sounded exhausting.

She drank about a quarter of the cup—it tasted okay, not as good as she'd expected—and went to her room to work on her Chicago Fire novel. She hadn't yet decided on a title. Maybe *The Great Fire*—although what if someone else had already used that? Or what about *Rachel and Sam*? In her story, the family in the house where the fire stopped was Jewish and followed many of the traditional observances; this was 1871, after all. Their name was Levy. In the part she was now writing, the neighbors who have lost their homes accuse the Levys of some kind of Jewish sorcery that caused their house alone to be saved. The Levys are a mother and father and a daughter and a son—in stories it was good to have both a girl and a boy—and, thinking of Jean, Matasha had thrown in a baby as well. Babies made things more fun. Matasha of course had never had a brother, but she felt she knew exactly what it would be like. He'd be a cross between Elliot Gleason—earnest and dreamy and looking up to Matasha—and Tim Pierce, who was always good-naturedly roughhousing in the hallways and breaking a wrist or a toe. Maybe, thought Matasha, surfacing momentarily from her writing reverie, it would make sense for the Waxes to adopt a boy instead of a girl. Boys tended to be stupider and more immature, but they were also more malleable and often sweet when you got down to it. She should bring this up with her mother.

Rachel, the girl in her fire story, was twelve, and Rachel's little brother, Sam, was ten. Matasha's plan was to have the neighbors turn into a mob threatening to hurt the family, but eventually coming around as they see how the Levys throw themselves heroically into the rebuilding of the neighborhood just like everyone else. The Levys would have two other families over for Passover seder, and these other families and their friends would begin to understand what Judaism really was and lose their false ideas about it.

Matasha had a feeling that this second half of the book was not going to be as exciting as the first half, that she would need to come up with some things to keep it interesting. Maybe not all of it would have to do with the rebuilding of the city, which felt rather technical, frankly. There could be scenes just about family life after the disaster. Maybe something with Rachel at school. Matasha decided that because the regular school has burned down, classes have to be held in a temporary lean-to, with kids of all ages crowded together. Rachel's best friend, Christine, could get damaged lungs from breathing in too much smoke during the fire and be mostly absent from school. The new kids coming in from other neighborhoods would be tough and mean. There would be no insulation; everyone would be cold as winter approached. Rachel's old teacher could have gotten killed by the fire; the new teacher would be cruel and like to beat students with a ruler for the slightest infraction. Because of all the rumors about Rachel's family and the fire, he would have it out for her in particular, and in a scene Matasha now imagined, he would use the ruler on her and then force her to stand on a box in front of the class all day. Matasha realized she had lifted this scene straight from what happened to Amy in *Little Women*, but since she was writing about 1870s Chicago and not 1860s Massachusetts, she thought it would be okay.

14.

Matasha's appointment with the specialist was coming up, but she had plenty right now to distract her from thinking about it. Matasha and Jean talked every day—sometimes in the fourth-floor bathroom, hurriedly and in code; sometimes at one of their homes—about the plan to investigate the construction pit. Jean was eager to listen to Matasha's suggestions and to brainstorm. They were real partners! There were several challenges they had to address. Challenge number one: How would they get down inside the pit? Challenge number two: What tools would they need? Challenge number three: How could they avoid being seen? Challenge number four: *When* could they do all this without their parents knowing?

Matasha scrutinized the site each time she walked to and from school, and saw how the workers accessed the pit. There was a set of metal stairs from the ground level to the pit level, but the stairs were on wheels and sometimes they were absent. The workers almost always left one long ladder to the surface. That would be scarier than stairs, but Matasha thought they could handle it. As for when to do their exploring, a school day was out. There were never workers at the site when Matasha passed by around 7:45 in the morning, but if she and Jean—well, Jean, anyway—tried to leave early for school, it would raise questions. The workers probably knocked off around five, but at this time of year it was already dark then, and Jean said there was no way she was going into the pit in the dark. Matasha agreed. They weren't sure whether there was construction work on Saturdays, so a Sunday was the best bet. Sundays were family days for both Jean and Matasha, but they would figure out a reason to give their parents for their needing to get together.

That still left the question of other people noticing them down in the pit. Matasha was convinced it would be all right. They could approach the pit from the quieter cross street on the opposite side; there were just a few town houses there and not a lot of foot traffic. They would be super quiet. Besides, Matasha said, grown-ups rarely looked up or down or to the sides, they just went straight ahead in front of them.

The tools would have to come from Jean's house. The garden Jean's mother kept meant there were trowels, a shovel, and a rake in a toolshed out in the backyard. All Matasha had been able to find at home was a plastic shovel from a pail set she used to take to the beach when she was little. That obviously wasn't any good. A real shovel was too bulky to carry around with them, so they settled on two trowels. Jean was nervous about taking them, but the garden was fallow now, and her mother wouldn't be paying close attention to what was or wasn't in the toolshed. Matasha said they would return everything the very same day, not to worry.

"So what are we actually going to *do*?" Jean wanted to know, one afternoon at Matasha's house.

"We've talked about this! We're going to dig!"

"How can we dig everywhere with just a couple of trowels? It could take years."

As the designated Sunday grew closer, Jean's enthusiasm had begun to waver. She asked the same questions over and over, even though Matasha had given her perfectly good explanations. Matasha tried again.

"The dirt at the bottom of the pit is hard and smooth. They haven't filled anything in yet, so the bones can't be underneath. They have to be in one of the big piles at the side, the two near Spruce Street or the one near Belieu Street. Those would be the only places the murderer could hide something."

"So we're just going to dig in the piles?"

"Yes! We're going to dig in the piles."

"That's still a lot of dirt."

"It's doable," said Matasha, a phrase Mrs. L'Enfant, her English and history teacher, liked to use. She reminded Jean that they might have to go more than once.

Jean chewed anxiously on the end of her pencil.

"This is our chance," said Matasha. "Pretty soon we'll have a big snow and then we won't even be able to do it." Waiting was risky. Besides the chance of snow, the builders could start pouring a floor any day now. And Martin Kimmel would be sealed in forever.

"Won't the construction people find the bones once they move all that dirt around?" Another question Jean had already asked.

"They won't notice. They're in those vehicles, high up. And it's just going to be *shove, shove*, and so much dirt falling in all at once. The bones would have to be sticking *right out*, and even then the driver might not see." Matasha really had no idea about the logistics of all this, but it sounded right.

Jean clutched her knees and sighed. "I can't wait until this is over," she said.

"But then it will be so good," replied Matasha. "Your mom will stop worrying." *And I'll be able to stop worrying too,* she thought. She'd had dreams about Martin, a wispy boy disappearing around a corner, leading her down a corridor where it was too dark to see. She ran her hands along the walls— they felt like cave walls, damp and rippled—looking for a light switch. She'd woken up relieved none of it was real.

As if Jean knew her thoughts, she asked: "What will we do when we find—you know?"

Matasha had rehearsed this part in her head. There was a pay phone a block from the construction site. She would make sure to have a couple of dimes with her. They would call the police and tell them everything, and then Matasha—in a painful concession to Jean—would add that they didn't want their names publicized as the finders. They just wanted to do an anonymous good deed, no need for thanks.

While all this planning was going on, Matasha had her visit with Dr. Karnow. He measured Matasha all over and then took more blood, and Matasha tried not to fuss but ended up helplessly squirming and twisting and had to be held by two nurses. After the visit, she put aside those humiliating memories while she and Jean finished their preparations. They told their parents that they wanted to go ice-skating Sunday afternoon at the Saddle & Cycle Club. It was easy to get there on the CTA, and kids often went on the weekends. You had to belong, but they said they'd been invited by Wendy Urquhart, whose family did belong. Jean and Matasha did every once in a while do things with Wendy, so their parents didn't question them. The supposed plan was that after ice-skating they'd go back to Matasha's, and Mr. White would pick up Jean later. Jean's mother would be walking her to the bus stop, of course. The Saddle & Cycle was in the opposite direction from the pit, so Jean would have to get off after a few stops and then wait for a bus running the other way.

"She won't have to keep taking you to the stop anymore," Matasha told Jean. "After."

They chose school as their rendezvous point, which meant Matasha walked by the site on her way to meet Jean. It was very quiet. And they were in luck: the movable stairs had been left out. Nevertheless, an atmosphere of unreality settled around Matasha, muting her hearing and making her head buzz. She couldn't quite believe they were going to do what they were going to do. But you never believed in things before they happened. Matasha still remembered learning to swim when she was six. She kept sinking and flailing in the pool up in South Haven, and her father kept putting his hands under her back and insisting she could float if she stopped fighting. Finally she decided to believe him. And she'd floated! Maybe this would be like that—one minute it was impossible, and the next minute you were just doing it.

Jean had arrived at the school before she did. They nodded to each other, like spies in a movie, and turned back the way Matasha had come. Jean held herself stiffly and was absolutely silent. When the pit came into view, they detoured onto a side street and approached from the other side. The only figures out were a woman and a little boy; in an instant they had disappeared into a town house. Then: nothing, nobody out, the street holding its breath. Jean and Matasha walked up to the orange plastic netting slung along the dig site and stared down. There were the familiar vehicles: one with a front scoop, another with something that looked like a big saw attached. It seemed as if not much had changed since the start of the school year. What in the world were the men doing day after day? There were three large piles of dirt as always and, along two sides of the pit, stacks of brick and stone.

They looked at each other. "I don't want to," said Jean in a small voice.

"It's going to be okay," said Matasha softly. She wanted to leave, too, but if she backed out now, it would be admitting that maybe this had been a bad idea. If she could just get Jean engaged in the plan again, her own confidence would rise.
She checked once more that nobody was out, nobody watching, and then climbed down the steps. Jean hesitated only slightly before following. They reached the bottom and deposited their knapsacks along a wall. Matasha looked up. It was strange to see the town houses far above them, and the sky farther away than usual . It was cool and smelled of damp clay. The sounds of the city, sounds she was so used to she normally hardly heard them—cars rumbling, the wind creaking—floated above them, muffled but reassuring. It was peaceful, as if they were in a huge private room of their own. She was sure that any grown-up passing by would never think to gaze down. It was like being in a fairy tale:

the normal rules might not apply. They were under a spell of invisibility and would remain so until they climbed back into the world.

Jean seemed to have recovered some of her self-possession. She looked up at the machine with the sawlike appendage. "Wow," she said. "I wish I could ride in there."

Then it was time to approach the dirt piles. It seemed logical to start with the two that stood closest together. But first Matasha, encouraging Jean to follow, made a slow circuit of the entire site, just to see if there was anything else they should look into. They found only a metal box, unlocked, containing a pair of heavy work gloves, a discarded 7 Up bottle, and a couple of Snickers wrappers. The two girls inspected the brick and stone piles, but they seemed innocent enough. Besides, they didn't have the time or, likely, the strength, to lift and move everything to see what was underneath. This might amount to a lack of thoroughness in the plan, but Matasha couldn't worry about that right now.

"I wish I could ride in there," repeated Jean, studying the saw vehicle.

"Me too," said Matasha, but she didn't mean it.

Neither of the girls wanted to approach the dirt piles, but the pause was growing problematic. Soon they might chicken out. Matasha's heart thumped in her throat and she knew that the only way to go forward was to force it, just *go*. She marched forward clutching the base of her trowel to her chest, with the tip pointed out, as if she planned to fall on a pile and impale it. Their tools seemed meager now. The piles were taller than

Matasha was, taller even than Jean. She made the first thrust with her trowel and then let go of the handle as if it were red-hot. She looked at the handle stuck into the dirt and started laughing. Hysterical, high-pitched laughter.

"Stop it!" Jean hissed. She joined Matasha facing the pile. "This is really stupid," she whispered.

Matasha suddenly agreed. She strangled the noise she was making—but at the back of her throat she still laughed and laughed.

"There is NO WAY we can dig through all that dirt."

Matasha pulled herself together. "No, we can." She seized her trowel and began moving scoops of dirt from the pile onto the ground. The dirt was wet and dense. She worked quickly, blindly, making a small pile next to the big one. It reminded her of making sand castles. The dirt was just dirt, so far. She kept going.

Jean followed, more slowly building her own pile. For fifteen minutes they worked like this. Then Matasha's trowel struck something hard and she froze, electrified. She probed around carefully with the trowel to pull whatever it was toward the surface, far too frightened to reach in with her hands. Some sort of pale, narrow protrusion appeared and Matasha went faint with terror: *Bone! Bone!* Jean was occupied with her own digging and Matasha couldn't speak to get her attention. She pushed away the dirt around the object, whose outline seemed to swell. The vibration of her trowel against its surface reminded her of something, and as she moved it clearer of the dirt (Jean was watching now), she saw that it was a glass Coke bottle.

"Oh my God," said Jean. "I thought . . ."

"We're in the right place," breathed Matasha. "It's *the murderer's Coke bottle.*"

"What?" said Jean.

"He must have been drinking this when he kidnapped Martin! The bones are probably right there, deeper in!"

But Jean scrunched up her brow. "It's probably just one of the workers' Cokes," she said. "We saw those other bottles over there."

"Yeah, *their* bottles are over there. This is different."

Something in Jean shifted. "My jeans are totally dirty," she said. She sat back on the ground and inspected herself. "Look at my knees. My mom is going to ask what we were doing."

"No, she won't."

"Yes she will! You have a maid, but my mom is going to notice!"

"Can't you put them in the washing machine before she sees them?"

"I don't know how to use the washing machine!"

Matasha was losing control of the conversation. "You can figure it out. It won't be that hard," she said, although she had no idea how to use a washing machine.

"I'm going to get killed," said Jean.

Matasha looked around her. The site opened up again, enormous. She and Jean had made tiny hillocks next to their five-foot dirt mountains, and there was another dirt mountain across the way. Although it was still midafternoon, the sun was already quite low in the sky. It was darker down here than Matasha had anticipated, the pit getting cold sunlight only in fragmented shafts. And now Jean was starting to cry. "I just realized something. It isn't going to be *bones*. Killed people don't turn right into bones. It will be a BODY. The bones only happen later. First it's a body and it de-com . . . de-com . . ." Jean couldn't bring herself to say the word.

Matasha, horrified, realized Jean was right. God, how could she not have thought of it? Jean was heaving silently now, her eyes wide. Matasha had pictured a pile of bleached-clean bones, stacked in a neat pyramid like a Cub Scout camping fire; how could she not have realized that it would actually be a body, the way Jean said, something with legs and arms and a face but worse because de-com . . . de-com . . .

"Please, please let's get out of here," Jean sobbed.

"Okay, okay, okay," Matasha babbled, panicky.

They threw the trowels into their knapsacks, slung the packs over their backs, and scrambled up the steps. They broke into a run until they couldn't see any evidence of the construction site, not the tops of the vehicles standing in it, nothing. They stopped on a corner, panting. Matasha's eyes were watering from the effort and from some grit that had gotten into them. Jean brought her arm up under her nose and wiped. Matasha stole a look at Jean's pants, which were indeed filthy. Hers, the same.

They sat down on a stone ledge outside a town house, both of them crying. It was a brief storm, and then it was over. Jean stood up and then Matasha did. Jean started walking toward the bus stop on the Outer Drive, and Matasha trailed after. As they passed a doorman, Matasha, suddenly brought back to the day, asked what time it was.

It was 2:40. Matasha could tell Jean didn't want to come home with her, but if she returned so early, her parents would wonder. "We'll wash your pants," Matasha promised. "They'll look totally normal." Jean didn't respond, acting theatrically remote, and although they sat next to each other on the bus, Jean scootched up to the window to put as much separation between them as possible. Matasha knew that nothing she said or did was going to make things better.

When they got to Matasha's, her mother said her father was at work.

"But it's Sunday!"

"Well, you weren't home." Her mother didn't notice the dirty pants. Matasha realized she couldn't very well ask her how to work the washing machine. She wasn't even sure her mother knew how to work the washing machine. "You're back very fast. Was it any fun?"

"It was okay," said Matasha.

Jean asked to use the phone, and as soon as she reached her mother, she began to cry. "I have a bad stomachache," she said. "I had to leave skating. It's really bad, Mom. Please tell Dad to come pick me up."

Then there was nothing more to do but wait: twenty minutes, thirty, while Mr. White came. Jean curled up in a ball on the floor of Matasha's room and pretended to sleep. Matasha climbed onto her bed and watched Jean, stared into her own lap, and then watched again. Maybe Jean would open her eyes, maybe she'd say something. Even if it was to yell at her.

After a long time, the buzzer rang. Jean leapt up and ran out of the room and downstairs without saying goodbye.

15.

Nor did Jean speak to her the next morning, when they were at their lockers. Matasha, who had had a difficult afternoon and evening, unable to read or watch TV, soothed only by a short visit to Mr. Bunny, told herself to be patient. Jean would punish her awhile for her bad—okay, truly terrible—idea and then gradually forgive her.

The day was lonely, and the next few were worse; not only did Jean keep up the cold shoulder, but Matasha's follow-up with Dr. Karnow was due. She woke the morning of the appointment frightened, with such severe butterflies all through school that she barely focused on the strain between her and Jean. At lunchtime, not wanting to find out whether Jean would sit with her (she hadn't so far; Matasha had edged her way for now into a table with Gina Wilkins and Wendy Urquhart), she claimed she was going to throw up and spent the period in the nurse's office. Her mother picked her up at the bell. She'd promised her ice cream after the visit, and Matasha had said okay, even though the phrase "ice cream" might have been "sandpaper" for all the anticipation it brought. Twice in the waiting room Matasha thought she had to pee and dashed into the little toilet closet, but nothing came out.

When they saw the doctor, he gave them the good news that the tests had ruled out all sorts of exotic and unpleasant conditions that Matasha hadn't even realized were possibilities, but added that indeed Matasha suffered from a significant deficiency of growth hormone. She luckily just met the criteria for being eligible to receive treatment. She could be part of his research study—the results would help doctors know how best to treat other kids who had the same condition Matasha had. Matasha looked at her mother and knew this was a done deal. Her mother had already decided that if this was the doctor's recommendation, they were going to do it. Her father had been part of the decision, too, she was pretty sure. And the truth was, even Matasha now accepted that this needed to happen. She couldn't—didn't want to—look like an eight-year-old forever.

Dr. Karnow explained things. The shots—so, yes, that was what "treatment" did mean after all—were to be given every day (Matasha sank in her seat). The hormone came in a little transparent pouch and had to be refrigerated, so if Matasha ever went anywhere overnight, she'd have to travel with a cooler. Dr. Karnow showed them how you took out a pouch and drew liquid up into a syringe that had a needle at the end. Matasha went hot, then cold, then hot again. The best place to do the injection was in your bottom. *What?* Here was a new outrage, a new humiliation. If you were injecting yourself, it was hard to get to the meatiest part of your tush, so you could do more of the side part, near your hip. You could also do the side of your thigh or belly or your upper arm, but it was important to rotate through several places to avoid bruising and give each a rest. The doctor preceded all of this with a longish talk about how growth hormone in your amela Erens

body normally worked, and Matasha grudgingly appreciated it. She had come to respect Dr. Karnow. He was one of the rare doctors who didn't talk to you like you were a moron or a kindergartner.

"Will it give me cancer?" asked Matasha.

"There haven't been long-term studies of patients who have received these treatments, but the risk is considered quite low," said Dr. Karnow.

"So that means there's a chance?" said Matasha, alarmed.

"There's a chance of problems with everything," said the doctor. "There's a chance the carpeting in your home could give you cancer, or the water from the tap. But if the chance is very low, the benefits way outweigh the risk."

"The *carpet* in our home could give us cancer?!"

"The carpet in our home is fine," said Mrs. Wax impatiently. "Matasha, the doctor is simply saying what any doctor has to say. He's saying you don't need to worry about it."

Matasha looked at Dr. Karnow for confirmation. "You don't need to worry about it," he said.

Matasha closed her eyes, shut out both of the adults in the room. She spoke to herself quickly, urgently. *I know what they're saying*, she thought. *They're saying they don't really know for sure if the shots cause cancer, but they don't think they do, they hope they don't, and I'm supposed to think about this like a grown-up, which means I'm supposed to forget there's any chance at all. And that's what I better do, or else I won't be able to do this.*

The doctor was asking whether they planned to have Matasha's mom do the injections, or Matasha herself.

144

"My mom," said Matasha.

"Matasha," said her mom at the same time.

The doctor smiled. "Well, I guess you'll have to get that sorted out. But Matasha, you'll need to learn how to do it in any case. There could be times when your mom isn't available. And gradually you'll want to take it over as you get older." He'd already explained that she would have to do the injections for years; it was likely that she'd go on until she finished growing, which could be as late as seventeen.

Matasha asked how tall she was going to end up being.

"You won't be a giant. We're going to try to get you to five feet, all right? Four eleven, five at the very most." He said the bone X-rays showed that was the margin they were dealing with.

"That sounds fine," Matasha reassured him. She'd certainly never expected to make it to five seven like her mother.

That night, she and her mother sat on the bed looking at the syringe and the pouch they'd taken out of the fridge. Matasha had already realized it was unrealistic to expect her mother to do the injections; she was too often gone in the evenings. Then she realized she didn't even want her to: she was getting too old to have her mother see her bottom. Yuck. But this first night she definitely needed help.

"You have to do it the first time, Mommy."

"I think you should hold it, too, though, sweetie. You put your hand on top of mine. So you can feel how it should go."

"Okay."

Matasha waited for her mother to pick up the syringe. When she didn't, Matasha took it and handed it to her. Then, warm with shame, she lifted up her nightgown and tugged down her underpants to bare the part where the doctor said the needle could go in. She squeezed her eyes shut. She felt the tip of the needle against her skin, just a tiny touch of cold.

"Matasha, I don't want to hurt you!" her mother cried. Matasha opened her eyes and turned. Her mother looked genuinely stricken.

"It's okay, Mommy," she said. "We have to." She closed her eyes again and reached back to feel for her mother's hand. She covered it, and together they pressed the needle in. There was that queasy, this-is-impossible feeling of something sliding under her skin, although Matasha was surprised to discover it didn't hurt quite as much as having blood drawn did. She remembered the doctor saying something about that—that because the needle went into fatty tissue and not a vein, there was less sensation—but she hadn't believed him given that doctors always lied about pain. Matasha clenched at the hurt, but she didn't scream or jump up or run away. Together she and her mother pushed in the plunger of the syringe, and Matasha felt a burning that turned cold deep under her skin. Matasha dropped her hand, and her mother drew the needle out. They'd done it.

"How was that?" asked her mother.

Only now did the tears start.

"You were very brave," her mother said. She hugged her, and Matasha let herself shudder and sink into her. "You did great."

"Okay." Matasha felt incredible relief that it was over.

"I can help you again tomorrow," her mother said. "I'll be home."

"That's okay," said Matasha. She didn't want her mother to see her like this again. She would figure it out for herself. She had to.

She lay awake for a long time that night. She drifted off once and was in a car with Martin Kimmel, the kidnapper's car as it turned out, being taken who knows where. She snapped awake and then was afraid to sleep and return to the dream. She turned on the light and looked at some pictures of Yosemite National Park in her View-Master, a handheld viewer that showed photographs. Her mother's mother, Grandma Esther, had given her the View-Master ages ago, when she was very little. Grandma Esther had died three years ago. The Yosemite photos were static and dull—Matasha didn't find landscapes inspiring—but they were a way of getting other pictures into her brain. There was a second set of photographs, of the Everglades, and Matasha looked at those too. When she was finally unable to resist sleep any longer, she had no dreams at all. At least, she didn't remember any.

16.

Jean started hanging out with Tamar Pinsoff. Matasha couldn't understand it, even with what had happened between them. Tamar! Tamar had no interests, listened to no music. Everything that came out of her mouth made you want to go to sleep. She smiled and smiled but it never seemed to be about anything. Matasha kept thinking that Jean was just trying to make her jealous, but the days went by and the friendship began to seem serious. When Tamar got on the same bus as Matasha in the morning, she spoke to Matasha as if nothing had changed; Matasha had to give her that. She didn't act mean or exclusionary. But Jean did. Jean passed her in the halls with her eyes narrowed and a look that said, *Don't even try me.*

One afternoon in math class Matasha saw Jean pass Tamar a note. When they were dismissed for the next period, the note was still on Tamar's desk. Matasha grabbed it and took it with her into a bathroom stall.

M is a sicko. She has sicko thoughts and does sicko things. She loves everything to be about blood and guts and bad things.

Matasha felt ill. Jean wouldn't have told Tamar about the pit, would she have? She didn't think so. But what *had* she told

Tamar? Matasha needed to get to science class; if she was late, Mr. Evinrude would say something and she might start crying. She looked at the note again and saw that something was drawn on the back.

It was a small cartoon of a girl sitting in the posture of *The Thinker*—they'd looked at a picture of that statue in art class. Of course, because it was Jean's drawing, it really looked like the statue, except that *The Thinker* had bangs and was very, very *small*. Underneath it said, "Tiny Matasha thinks she has a big brain."

Matasha shoved the note in her pants pocket and ran. Mrs. Andretti, the music teacher, who happened to be at the sink, called after her: "Wash your hands!"

Matasha slid into one of the seats in science just as Mr. Evinrude was shutting the door. Jean was in this class with her, although Tamar wasn't. All year, like every year, Jean and Matasha had been partners in science. Together they wrestled with the Bunsen burners that flared up alarmingly when you lit them and the microscopes through which you could never see anything. Now Jean sat on a different side of the room and paired up with Allison Rodgers, and Matasha more than once had had to be with Jack Teague, a kid who liked to whisper dirty words to girls under his breath, knowing they'd be too embarrassed to tell the teacher. Matasha tried to talk to Jack as little as possible and not even look at him. But while they were making drawings of paramecia (why did they even need a partner to do drawings?), he asked her if she knew what living creature was smaller than a paramecium, and when she didn't reply, he said the answer was a

Matasha. "I could step on you and squish you," Jack Teague said.

Matasha pretended she hadn't heard him. "Squish squish squish," Jack repeated as they worked on their drawings. "*Squish*." School felt dangerous without Jean as her friend. Kids were freer to say anything to her, to dump their meannesses on her.

When their drawings had been turned in, the class went over some homework, and Matasha scooted her stool as far away from Jack's as possible. She looked out of the classroom windows, which faced in the direction of the school construction pit and the park. Matasha wondered if the police were still continuing to check the park for clues, or if they had completely given up on Martin Kimmel. Pretty soon there were going to be regular and heavy snows, and they would probably have to call everything off until spring.

When she got home that day, Matasha put Jean's note in her Messy Drawer, which was where she put everything she didn't want to think about just now but also couldn't bring herself to totally forget. The only good thing she had to focus on was the hope that her mother was working on a replacement for Qui. Surely the agency would send the right kid next time. Her mother hadn't said anything in weeks. But maybe if Matasha got a sister, she wouldn't mind so much being all by herself at school.

17.

"YES," said Mrs. Wax loudly. "YES, WE ARE HOPING YOUR VISAS WILL COME THROUGH SOMETIME IN MARCH. *MARCH*. WE ARE WORKING ON IT."

There was a long silence.

"HAPPY HANUKKAH." A pause. "OH."

Another long silence.

"I WISH THE BEST TO ALL YOUR FAMILY. WE WILL SPEAK NEXT MONTH."

Mrs. Wax hung up the phone. She looked bewildered. "They don't celebrate Hanukkah. Even *we* celebrate Hanukkah."

Matasha's mother had been making a call to the Leningrad family whose housing she'd agreed to pay for if they got to the States. She called once a month to keep up the family's morale. The phone calls were patched through Paris and were very expensive, about three dollars a minute, Matasha's mother told her. When the family knew that a call was scheduled, they would arrange for a neighbor who spoke decent English to be present to take the call and to translate during it. Mrs. Wax found these conversations, in which she had to yell to be heard on the faint, staticky lines, very taxing. Matasha found them fascinating. Once or twice she had quietly picked up an extension in another room and listened to the almost incomprehensible guttural English of the man on the line. She realized that half the time her mother wasn't able to understand what the man was saying and just went ahead and made conversation anyway.

"Are they going to get to come to America?" asked Matasha.

"Who knows?" said Mrs. Wax. "For eight months I've been calling this family and there's been absolutely no information. Every month I tell them it's going to be okay, that they're going to get out eventually."

"What if they never get out?" asked Matasha.

"What if nobody ever gets out?" asked Mrs. Wax nonsensically. She threw down the dish towel she was holding. She seemed in a very bad mood.

Somehow this seemed like an opportunity for Matasha to ask about the adoption. Mrs. Wax said she was still waiting for the agency to send another potential match. She didn't know what was taking so long. She sounded frustrated and tired. But maybe Matasha's question worked some strange magic, because when her mother went to get the mail an hour later, there was a packet from the agency. Her mother was smiling in surprise, and Matasha felt she'd done something extraordinary. The two of them went upstairs to take a look sitting in the twin oversized chairs in Mr. and Mrs. Wax's bedroom.

Mrs. Wax opened the envelope and shook out the papers in it. She detached a small photo paper-clipped to the pages, studied it, and handed it wordlessly to Matasha. The new girl looked younger than Qui. She had a rounded face, and her expression was soft and sad. Her hair was parted in the center and neatly cropped above her shoulders. She looked guardedly hopeful. Like she was sad but willing herself to make an effort in this sad, bad world.

"She looks nice," said Matasha.

Her mother consulted the papers. The girl's name was An. She was actually the same age as Qui, ten years old. She was living in a refugee camp in the Philippines.

"How tall is she?" asked Matasha.

Mrs. Wax ran her finger down the first page. "Four foot two," she answered. Matasha smiled.

"How did she lose her mom and dad? Does it say?"

Mrs. Wax looked through the pages again. "It says that her father was in the army, a corporal, and has not been heard from since 1972. No one ever told the family anything, but eventually they heard enough here and there to be pretty sure he died at . . . I'm not sure how to pronounce this." She showed Matasha the name on the sheet: Quang Tri. "Um . . . An's younger sister was sent to stay with an aunt out in the country right before Saigon fell. An and her mother made it onto a boat." Her mother read on silently and then put the page facedown, looking at its blank side.

"What happened to her mother?" Matasha asked finally.

"The boat was intercepted by a gang. They took the mother off the boat, along with some of the other women. Oh, Matasha."

"Mommy, what do you think happened to her?"

"Nothing good, sweetheart."

"Do you think maybe she's still alive?"

"No. They caught some of the pirates. The pirates claimed that after a few days they threw the women overboard."

"*Why?* Why would they do that?"

Mrs. Wax rubbed her eyes. "These men spend all of their time at sea and they take women to have as girlfriends. Then they . . . get rid of them."

Matasha could think of nothing to say. She tried to picture the mother's life on the boat with the pirates. She imagined the pirates playing board games with the mothers. Playing a radio, making the mothers dance with them. Kissing them even though they didn't want to be kissed. Sitting by them and telling them jokes. Maybe the mothers even laughed at times. The pirates shared their food with them, fed them cake. Read them poetry. Kissed them again. Then they got bored, or spotted another ship, and threw them overboard. Matasha tried to imagine this throwing. She saw them scooping up each woman and heaving her like a sack of potatoes into the sea.

"Does An know about her mother?"

"Of course she knows."

Matasha tried to imagine An living in her house, her room, this girl whose mother had been tossed overboard from a boat. She worked to conjure up the old pictures she'd gone over and cherished in her bed at night: of teaching her new sister English, building a snowman with her, showing her how to ice-skate. But the images seemed stilted now, unreal. She couldn't clearly see anymore the playing, instructing, having fun. She'd known that the girl who came would have been through some bad things. But now this struck her more nearly. Maybe it wasn't good to let so much bad history into your house. Maybe bad things were infecting. Matasha knew she shouldn't think this way. You were supposed to feel bad for people to whom bad things had happened. You should want to help them. But maybe Matasha didn't want to spend time near someone whose mother had been tossed overboard into the sea. Maybe other things had happened to the girl, too, things so terrible Matasha would never want to hear them. All these things would fill their home and maybe make bad things more likely to happen to Matasha and her mother and father.

Matasha looked at her mother for reassurance. She didn't find it there. Her mother looked spooked herself. And something else, too, something that frightened Matasha even more than the thought of An's bad things in their home. Matasha couldn't name it; maybe it had no name; that was what made it worse than anything. "Mommy!" she cried out, to shatter the moment. Her mother turned. She seemed very, very far away. "Mommy," said Matasha more quietly. And then, unable to bear the unnameable look on her mother's face, she ran to her room and crawled under her four-poster bed, the way she'd done when she was younger and wanted to pretend she was a small animal who lived under their house and whom nobody could ever find.

18.

For the rest of the school session before Christmas break, Matasha drifted from class to class not really attached to anybody anymore. She had kids to sit with in the lunchroom—Gina Wilkins and Wendy Urquhart in particular remained welcoming—but there was nobody who felt special, nobody she could rely on. Jean had been prickly sometimes, changeable, hard to read. But there had always been some deeper understanding that she and Matasha fit, belonged together, that they just made sense. It wasn't something you could explain. They'd become friends on the very first day of first grade. Matasha had been playing in the sandbox and Mrs. Delaney, their teacher, had called her over; it was her turn to make a handprint. They were making handprints in plaster of paris so that at the end of the year they could see how much bigger their hands had become. As Matasha walked to the table where Mrs. Delaney was sitting, Jean came up to her. She was new; she hadn't been at Margaret E. Marvin for kindergarten. "I'm looking for a friend," she said. "Do you want to be my friend?"

"Okay," said Matasha. "After I make my handprint." As it turned out, Jean's turn was right after hers—White after Wax—and Matasha watched, admiring a little bracelet of beads strung on a ribbon that Jean wore. Afterward, they ran together to the swings and Matasha swung higher than she'd ever swung before—she was generally scared of going high on the swings. But she felt exuberant with her new friend and wanted to look bold and carefree.

And that was that. Afterward, they'd rarely been apart. They spent countless hours talking about imaginary places they'd invented, like a world where people had wings and were only four inches tall. They buried trinkets in the playground dirt and tried to find them again later. They taught themselves magic tricks out of a book, and pretended to be twins named Phil and John. (This was during a period when Jean complained repeatedly about having twin sisters rather than twin brothers. She thought that brothers would be much more fun.) They described what things would be like when Matasha was a famous author and Jean was a famous artist, although Matasha wondered how Jean would become famous if she always hid her drawings away and got angry when people praised them. They didn't always get along. Jean sometimes found Matasha exasperating—show-offy and eccentric—but she forgave all that just as Matasha forgave Jean's contradictions and sour moods. And now Jean had reneged on the bargain. She had decided that Matasha was *just too awful* to forgive. It was like a death sentence, something you couldn't make better in any way. All she could do was hope that somehow, eventually, Jean would turn around and become the old Jean again. But with every passing week that seemed less likely.

So Matasha went on, walking to class alone and eating her lunch with other kids to save face. Nobody invited her over after school, and she didn't invite anyone else. What would they do together if they came? Nobody but she and Jean listened to the Beatles and Bob Dylan and Lou Reed. Other kids were into disco: KC and the Sunshine Band; Earth, Wind & Fire. Nobody else but Jean could draw pictures that Matasha wanted to jump into and live in: all those horses in fields of blowing grasses, old men fishing in rivers, characters from *The Wolves of Willoughby Chase*. Nobody but Jean understood Matasha's ideas and plans, even if she often poked holes in them.

The hardest part of the day was when Matasha got off the CTA and had to pass the construction pit and remember what had happened there. She no longer knew if she believed Martin Kimmel was inside. She pretty much thought not. Her idea about the pit was like a dream she had woken up from, that had evaporated almost completely. At one point it had all seemed obvious to her and now it didn't. Maybe—probably—those tall piles of dirt were really just dirt, and Coke bottles, and stuff that dropped out of workers' pockets. Maybe Martin's body was far away, somewhere she would never be able to help find him. Like Texas, or at the bottom of the ocean, with An's mom.

Still, the open hole bothered her. She wished it would get filled in, and soon. She wanted to see floors put down, doors and windows installed. She wanted the nothing that was there to turn into a real place. There were going to be long carpeted hallways in the new school with picture windows at each end, and a big auditorium. She'd studied more closely the model in the corner of the current gym. The workers should hurry up and build those things and the new science lab and the big new library. A new building would be a good thing, she'd decided. Being in it might make next year better than this one had turned out to be. Her best friend was ignoring her, she wasn't sure whether she wanted a new sister, and every night she had to have a shot.

The shots. Often during the day she remembered what was coming at bedtime and felt sick to her stomach: the washy feeling squared. Her mother had said she'd get used to the shots, and Matasha thought that meant they would stop hurting after the first few times. But it always felt the same. Matasha tried praying to God, willing herself to believe in him. She knew that Sunset prayed on her knees by her bed—she'd never seen this, but she'd asked Sunset how she did it and Sunset had explained. But given the height of Matasha's four-poster, when she knelt by her mattress, she was actually underneath it, and this felt ridiculous. Jews didn't seem to have to pray in any particular position—when she and her parents went to High Holiday services, they stood and sat and stood and sat repeatedly, according to the rabbi's instructions—so Matasha began to pray lying in bed, staring at the ceiling, beaming her words toward a God beyond it somewhere. She asked God to make her stop minding the shots and stop thinking about them during the day. That seemed like something he might be willing to do for her, as opposed to taking away the shots altogether. And she prayed to God to make her less lonely.

It wasn't working. The second-hardest part of the day was when Matasha got to school and Jean ignored her at their side-by-side lockers: "Wax," "White." The third-hardest was the end of the day when the same thing happened. At home, Matasha found herself thinking of Jean whenever she played the Beatles, so she turned more and more to other music, music she learned about when she bought herself a couple of issues of *Rolling Stone* magazine. There was Bruce Springsteen's *Born to Run* and Paul Simon's *Still Crazy after All These Years* and Bob Marley and the Wailers' *Live!* She bought these one by one at Fat Sammy's over on Clark Street and listened over and over to their unfamiliar, entrancing sounds. After dinner, she reread Dottie Summers's column and thought again about writing her a letter. What had happened with Jean seemed like something Dottie could give advice about, but Matasha got tangled up when she tried to figure out how to put it in words. Did she want to be friends with Jean again, or should she just try to make new friends? How did you do that if you weren't excited about it? Did she need to explain all about what happened in the pit, or would that take up too much room in Dottie's column? If she brought up the shots and the adoption, that would make the letter *really* long, but they were important too; how could she leave them out?

Toward the middle of December, despite the cold and some snow, work at the construction pit seemed to leap forward. One Monday, large pipes appeared in trenches around the perimeter, and later that week a concrete floor was poured. Whatever was under the earth was imprisoned there for good. It was probably nothing but clay and stone. The following week, large grids were planted upright along the perimeter. The building was going up.

19.

Jean invited her to a party.

Matasha was thrilled at first, then suspicious. It was January, after the Christmas break. Matasha and her parents had gone to Mexico last Christmas, but this year nobody had said anything about any plans and they had stayed home. Both her mother and father were busy during the break—it seemed clients of all kinds wanted more things just before the end of the year. They were often out at night, but in different places. Matasha spent a lot of time watching TV with Sunset or reading or working on her novel. Occasionally she remembered Mr. Bunny. Twice during Christmas week there were heavy snowfalls. After the first one she went out and brushed several inches off Mr. Bunny's cage and then proudly told Sunset what she'd done. But Sunset said that the snow would actually insulate Mr. Bunny from the cold. Matasha was alarmed and went out and mounded snow back on, but it was drippy by that time and probably she was just making things worse. When the second snowfall came, she let things be.

Jean and Tamar stopped Matasha in the hallway the very first day back. They said they were having a party at Tamar's, and did she want to come. It was going to be a cooking party; they were going to make chocolate chip cookies and a pound cake and set up streamers and play some games.

"Who else is coming?" asked Matasha.

Tamar looked at Jean.

"Just you and, um, Helen," said Jean.

"Is Helen really coming?" Helen Lake was a pleasant girl, someone who moved easily between groups at school. She'd come to Margaret E. Marvin only last year, when her parents moved from Saint Louis. She was friendly with the mean kids without being mean, and with the athletic kids without being athletic. She read books all the time, but nobody seemed to mind it as they did with Matasha. She had big gold-rimmed glasses and a goofy smile, and everyone helplessly liked her.

"Uh, yeah. We haven't asked her yet, but I'm sure she can come," said Tamar.

"No, thanks," said Matasha. Her radar told her some humiliation was in order, though she didn't know quite what. Probably there would be no cookies and no streamers and they would simply ignore her, move from room to room playing games without her, waiting to see if she would cry. Maybe they would even lock her in a closet. That had happened to Jean once when she'd been stupid enough to go over to Camille Janklow's back in third grade.

Why are they bothering? thought Matasha. *They've already made it clear they hate me.*

The party invitation was dropped, but about a week later, after dismissal, Jean turned from her locker and spoke to Matasha. "Do you want to come over tomorrow?" she asked.

Matasha was so surprised she didn't have time to stop a big smile from spreading onto her face. Instantly she wished she hadn't shown such ready pleasure. She wanted to keep her cool. She wanted to shrug and say, "I guess so."

Too late for that.

"Well, do you?" Jean already sounded less friendly. Actually she hadn't sounded friendly to begin with, just neutral, like she didn't particularly care if Matasha came. Maybe Mrs. White had told her to patch things up, and she'd felt forced to say something.

Matasha couldn't help it, though; she wanted to come. She wanted to see the big house and the coat tree by the front door, a wooden throne with a deep seat, tall mirror, and hooks from which always hung lots of scarves and hats. She wanted to noodle on the piano and go into the kitchen where Mrs. White probably had waiting a plate of homemade biscuits. She wanted to run her hands in the violet beads at Jean's doorway and hear them rustle and spit, then lie on Jean's bed and watch as Jean picked out whatever album they were going to listen to.

"Yes," Matasha said. Her throat had already filled up with worry, and she could feel her face crumpling. Her mother had once told her that she signaled the fact that she was going to cry from a mile away. It wasn't very nice, but it was true. Another thing she regretted and couldn't do anything about.

"Bye," said Matasha quickly, and instead of heading out of the building, she stopped in the bathroom. She sat on a toilet quietly shaking and letting the tears slide out. She tried not to make any sound, but every minute or so she had to take a big shuddering gasp. She heard children come in and out—she'd only had time to get to the second-floor bathroom, the busiest one—and waited until there was a pause. Then she dried her face and rubbed it in the mirror until she convinced herself that she looked all right. She walked with her head held high down the hallway toward her locker, confident that Jean would already have left for home.

Mr. Evinrude was heading out of the science room.

"You're still here?" he asked genially.

"I forgot my book," said Matasha. She walked fast.

"Do you have a minute?" Mr. Evinrude caught up as she opened her locker. "I want to ask you a question."

Matasha finished putting her things into her knapsack and hoped she looked calm.

"I'm setting up a social-service project for the school," said Mr. Evinrude. "You're a girl who pays attention to the world, so I thought you might be interested."

Matasha didn't know what a social-service project was, so she just nodded.

"Well, good! We're going to be partnering with an organization that does home visits to elderly people in the neighborhoods around here. The Little Sisters, that's the organization's name. I want to put together a group of students who will sign up for visits and also make a plan to raise some money for the organization."

"Um," said Matasha.

"This school needs more of a service conscience," continued Mr. Evinrude enthusiastically. "You kids have so much privilege and good fortune, and so little of it is spread around. You're one of the students I'd really like to have join in. You're mature and bright and organized, and I'm sure you'd have some good ideas. What do you think?"

What Matasha thought was that she didn't want to help anybody, for any reason. The whole idea of helping poor and needy and helpless people drained and depressed her and made her want to cry again.

"I'll think about it," she mumbled.

Mr. Evinrude was startled. "Oh," he said. "Well. Do that. Get back to me. But if you could get back soon . . . I'm trying to get this organized . . ."

Matasha nodded. She lowered her head and ran like a strange animal down the hallway and to the stairs and then out into the street.

20.

The next day Matasha took the risk of sitting next to Jean in math class and talking to her about their homework. Jean answered her in monosyllables, shrugging that infuriating shrug, the one that said, *I don't care about anything, and if you do, you're ridiculous.* The one that made Matasha feel—was meant to make her feel—that her excitements, enthusiasms, fears, angers, *anythings,* were despicable. Tamar sat on the other side of Jean, and the two of them leaned in toward each other and chatted about . . . *nothing*, Matasha thought. Whereas she, Matasha, had plenty of interesting things to tell—ideas, information, even jokes!

At dismissal, Matasha finished up at her locker before Jean—another miscalculation. She had to wait while Jean took her time getting her things, never acknowledging her in the meantime. Matasha shifted her heavy pack from shoulder to shoulder and at last put it down at her feet. When Jean was finally ready, she walked away without even speaking to Matasha. Had she forgotten the get-together? Had she changed her mind? Matasha had reached her limit: she wouldn't trot along begging to come. Down the hallway, Jean met up with Tamar, and the two of them continued on together. Matasha headed for the exit at her own pace; if Jean wanted her, she could say something. And if she didn't, Matasha would stop at the candy shop on the corner and waste some time so she and Tamar wouldn't end up on the same bus.

Outside the building Tamar and Jean turned in the direction of Jean's stop. So the two of them were going to Jean's together, and leaving Matasha out. Fine. Matasha continued on her way.

"Matasha," called Jean harshly. "Where are you going?"

Matasha stayed put. "I'm going home," she yelled back.

"Aren't you coming with us?"

And then Matasha's feet turned, of their own accord, and she was walking toward Jean. She couldn't help it. She didn't want to be around Tamar, and she didn't want to go to Jean's. She detected something bad in the air. But the house—it was almost as if the house, not Jean, pulled her, and she could not resist. The house with Jean's harassed, blunt mother, clothes and toys scattered everywhere, the coat tree, the twins making noise, the big, sloppy, easy feel of the place. She wanted to be there. She wanted to see Mrs. White, who scared her a little and yet made her feel comfortable, if that made any sense at all.

On the bus, as Matasha had already guessed would happen, the two girls acted as if she weren't there. They talked about synchronized swim. Jean said she felt like a whale in the water.

Tamar giggled. "Mrs. Porter"—that was the gym teacher who taught synchronized swim—"is going to be there on Thursday."

Holy moly, thought Matasha. Mrs. Porter was there *every* Thursday. She was the coach; it was her job to be there! Once again Matasha was grateful that she hadn't signed up for synchronized swim, where she would have had to spend two extra hours a week with both Jean and Tamar, not to mention Camille Janklow and Glenda.

"I'm already bored of sink-or-swim," said Jean, using the kids' nickname for synchronized swim. "It's more babyish than I thought it would be."

"Synchronized swim is twelve weeks long," said Tamar.

"I might start doing gymnastics twice a week," announced Jean.

That pricked Matasha's attention. Jean was good at gymnastics. She could do the uneven bars and jumps on the balance beam. She went once a week to Sunnyside Gymnastics, and if she went twice, she'd start being able to do even more stuff. For a while Matasha had joined her for lessons, but the old Hungarian guy there had yelled at her and shamed her for having trouble getting over the horse, and she'd quit. The only thing she missed about it was getting to see Jean do the things she could do.

"That's so great," Matasha told Jean. "Are you getting really good?"

Jean shrugged.

"I bet you are. Can you do a cartwheel on the balance beam yet?"

"Yeah. Sort of."

"I have history homework today," said Tamar.

Matasha thought she caught a flicker of irritation on Jean's face. Surely Jean was thinking the same thing as Matasha, that Tamar's comment was ... well, very Tamar. But Matasha wasn't sure.

They got off the bus, and Jean's father was waiting for

them. Every so often he worked at home instead of going into the office, and Matasha was always happy to see him. She thought he was very handsome. He had a head of thick, curly hair and laughed easily, and he sometimes put his hand affectionately on Matasha's head and called her "sis" for no reason. The streets were banked with snow laced black from car exhaust and from dogs and people splashing up slush as they walked. It was too bad that what was so pretty for a short while always turned so nasty. It had been so many weeks since Matasha had been in Jean's neighborhood that the streets gave her a funny feeling; they felt only half-familiar.

When they got to the house, Mr. White said that Mrs. White had taken the twins and the baby to a birthday party. "Help yourself in the kitchen, girls," he told them, already halfway up the stairs to the room he used as an office. "Your mom left some spiced cider you can reheat on the stove."

"Yippee!" said Jean. As usual, food was the only thing she was willing to get openly excited about.

"Your kitchen is red and blue," said Tamar.

They heated up the cider and spent a long time blowing on it before finally drinking it up and going to Jean's room. The house was very quiet without the twins and Mrs. White in it. Usually the twins were running up and down the stairs and in and out of rooms and Mrs. White was yelling at them for something or other.

Jean plopped down on her floor bed, and Tamar sat next to her, pushing her braids behind her as if readying herself for action. Matasha stood, unsure where to place herself.

"We wanted to talk to you about something," said Jean.

Uh-oh, thought Matasha.

"We've made up a list of everything we think is wrong with you and everything we think is right with you. Do you want to hear it?"

Matasha sat down on the floor. She didn't know quite what to say. "Which is longer?" she asked.

Jean and Tamar looked at each other. "The things that are wrong with you," Jean replied.

It occurred to Matasha what her mother would say about this situation. Her mother was often scattered and sometimes said exactly the wrong thing, but at other times she had advice that was truly valuable. There had been times before when Jean had turned on her—though never like this, never for more than a day or two—and Matasha, distraught, had gone to her mother and asked what she should do. She'd been younger, then; she'd wept as if the world were coming to an end, as if she were falling through space without stopping. And her mother stroked her back—a little fluttery-like and briskly, it was true—and said, in a way that Matasha knew she was serious and wasn't just telling her something she wouldn't tell herself: "When someone is cruel to you, you have to walk away."

"But she's my friend," Matasha would bawl.

"She's being a nasty little bug," her mother answered. "And you *walk away*."

Right now her mother would say it again: *Walk away*.

But what if the list contained things Matasha really needed to know? What if they were things everyone saw besides her?

She would need to fix them, or else she might become the next Molly Jentel. Once that happened, there was no coming back.

"Why don't you just read me the first thing on the bad list," said Matasha. "Then I'll decide."

Jean pursed her lips but nodded. Tamar was apparently the keeper of the lists; she pulled two sheets of loose-leaf paper out of her knapsack. From where she was sitting Matasha could see the big gray pencil marks, but she couldn't read what they said.

"One," said Jean. "You act like you are smarter than everyone else, which is really annoying, and besides it's untrue."

"That's not fair," Matasha said. "I don't act like anything. I act like myself." She thought: *This isn't so bad.*

"Two. You take everything too seriously."

"What do you mean? What things?"

Jean didn't have time for answers. She continued:

"Three. Your clothes are weird. You wear high-waters and stupid shirts with appliqués."

Appliqués were stupid? Why hadn't anyone ever told her? Matasha loved the striped shirt they must be talking about, the one with the big brown bunny on the front. It was cute! And she did *not* wear high-waters. Just because she didn't want her jeans catching under her sneakers, trailing on the sidewalk to gather up the cigarette butts and dirt . . .

"Four. No one likes you."

Matasha was going to cry. It was going to come any second. But instead she barked out: "That's not a *thing.* That's not something *wrong* with me. That's your *opinion.*"

Jean was startled. Tamar smiled idiotically. *Tamar doesn't even care whether any of this is true*, thought Matasha. *She just agrees to anything.*

"Are the next things on your list facts, or just opinions?" demanded Matasha.

Jean gathered herself. "You're so weird," she spat out. "*'Are the next things on your list facts or just opinions?'*" she mimicked.

Matasha folded her arms. She watched Jean and waited for an answer to her question. To her wonder, she wasn't going to cry. She felt she could wait a long time.

Jean glanced at the list again. She opened her mouth. She closed it. She sneered. "Let's go get some cookies," she said to Tamar. "She's hopeless."

"I'm full," said Tamar cheerfully.

"Well, I want some!" shouted Jean.

"Everything okay down there?" called Mr. White from the top floor.

Jean stuck her head out the door. "YEAH, Dad. Everything's fine! We're just going to get some cookies!"

Her father came out on the landing. "No cookies, Jean. It's too close to dinnertime. Your mother made moussaka."

"Okay, okay." Jean came back into the bedroom.

"I want you to go home," she told Matasha.

"I want to go home too." Matasha went downstairs and got her coat and knapsack. She knew, as she pulled on her hat and mittens, that she wouldn't ever be back in this house again. She wished she could go upstairs and say goodbye to Mr. White, but it seemed too awkward.

Tamar appeared on the steps. "I ride the same bus as you," she said.

Matasha supposed this was Tamar's way of saying that she wanted to come along. She didn't think Tamar was expressing any kind of solidarity with her. Tamar just didn't want to walk to the bus stop by herself, because of Martin Kimmel and all. Well, let Mr. White take her.

"I'm going home alone," said Matasha firmly. Because, numb as she was right now, by the time she got on the bus she would be weeping fully. And by the time she got off the bus she would be raging, yanking leaves from the hedges lining the apartment buildings, kicking pebbles, loudly whispering all the curse words she knew. And if Tamar thought she was going to be privy to any of this, she was out of her mind.

Matasha swung her knapsack over her shoulder. "Bye," she said to Tamar. She trudged out onto the street. She was walking by herself where Jean's mom wouldn't let Jean walk by herself. At 4:00 p.m., though, the street seemed tranquil and unforbidding, just the same as it had for all the many years that Jean and she had walked along or played on it.

But in her distraction, lost in her angry and grieving thoughts, Matasha took a wrong turn somewhere and ended up on an unfamiliar street. She stopped, stunned. How had she gotten here? Where was the stop? She headed onto a side street, certain that it would bring her back to the one she was supposed to be on. But that street let onto another that was completely strange to her also. Matasha began to panic. She didn't know where she was, and Martin Kimmel had been taken near here, and Jean's mother would never have let Jean be alone like this. She tried one more turn but suspected she was getting farther and farther away from her stop. Where was she? If she kept moving, she would only get more lost, but she couldn't just stand still. It would get dark before long. Where was her apartment from here? How would she get there?

She put her hands to her face and cried into her mittens, hating herself for crying—why did she cry so much? That was probably on Jean's list too: *Five: you cry all the time.* She was sobbing loudly and openly now, sure that she would never find her way home, when an older woman stopped, handed her a handkerchief, and walked her to where she needed to go. Which turned out to be only a couple of blocks away.

PART TWO

PART TWO

1.

Matasha's mother hadn't said anything about An or the adoption since the afternoon they'd looked at An's picture. Something told Matasha the plans weren't moving forward anymore. Or maybe her mother was just tied up with other things. Maybe it was still going to happen. One day Matasha decided to see if she could sleuth out some information about it. And that was how she came across the letter from the man in Switzerland.

In the Waxes' apartment there was a room called the sewing room. No sewing went on here; the sewing machine and supplies were all in Sunset's room. The sewing room was just the name—never explained—of the room where Matasha's mother had her office. She paid bills and wrote letters here, and when she'd been in school, it was where she'd done her classwork. There were two bracketed metal bookshelves hammered into the wall, a desk with drawers, and a radio that Mrs. Wax kept tuned to the classical station. On the desktop was her IBM Selectric typewriter. The room also held a daybed that Mrs. Wax had bought while she was in school. When Matasha had asked her mother why she needed a bed in her office, Mrs. Wax said, "Sometimes I just want to be all alone when I rest." And indeed Matasha had sometimes caught her mother taking a nap in the middle of the day, fully clothed and with her heels on, and at other times her mother had her eyes closed but was awake, holding a burning cigarette. Matasha knew she was awake because if she stood watching long enough, her mother would bring the cigarette to her lips and inhale. The sewing room was the only place she smoked. Matasha knew not to bother her mother about anything at such times. When she returned, half an hour later, her mother would be at the desk again, the smell of smoke clinging to the air.

Sometimes Matasha explored the room when her mother was out. There were books on the shelves that interested her, some left over from college and art history school and some not: one with pictures of curious little Japanese figures called "netsuke"; one with the paintings of Roy Lichtenstein, which looked like comic strips; *The Joys of Yiddish*. Matasha also liked checking out her mother's office supplies. There was a neat device called an "embosser" that looked like a stapler; Mrs. Wax used it to stamp the family's return address in raised letters on the flaps of envelopes. In a drawer there was her typewriter eraser, a stick with a pink rubber wheel on one end and a whisk on the other for sweeping away the gray bits after you'd scrubbed an error. There were boxes of pristine typing paper in the bottom drawer, full of promise: onionskin for everyday typing, heavier and watermarked for correspondence. There was delightfully flimsy blue airmail stationery, because her mother had friends she wrote to in other countries. More oddly, there was a tiny doll no bigger than Matasha's thumb, made of straw and string— something from a trip abroad? Matasha always checked to see which kinds of stamps her mother had most recently bought, President Eisenhower (he'd been president in the fifties) or the jet airplane. There was a shoelace that never got used, a dime that never got spent.

But Matasha wasn't just poking around on this particular February day. She was wondering if she might find anything to reveal what her mother was thinking about the adoption. It was a good bet that her mother kept papers related to the adoption in the desk drawers. So she checked. And there they were, in the middle drawer. Some were the papers relating to An that Matasha had already seen, with An's photo clipped to the front. The papers relating to Qui, plus Qui's photo, were still there, underneath. Matasha looked at Qui's photo and nodded to herself: they'd made the right decision. Although once again she felt guilty: If the Waxes hadn't taken her, did that mean no one had? What happened to the children that nobody said yes to? Or did that never happen? Matasha told herself it didn't happen.

Between the An papers and the Qui papers was a large manila envelope with the name of the placement agency on it. Matasha turned it over and saw that it was unsealed. She lifted the flap—why shouldn't she? It wasn't like the adoption was a secret—and then hesitated. You weren't supposed to read other people's mail, even if you more or less knew what was inside. Removing papers from an envelope felt different from reading papers that were just lying in a stack. Maybe both were a little wrong, but the envelope felt wronger.

Matasha got up and closed the door. She supposed this was a tip-off that she was up to something, but it made her feel less exposed. If Sunset came along, she'd have time to stuff the envelope back in the desk. She sat on the carpet close to the drawer and drew out the papers. She would need to keep everything in the proper order. The top pages were straightforward: her father's name, her mother's name, their jobs, their birth dates, their social security numbers. There was her own name, her age and birth date, her grade in school. Then there were forms from her parents' doctors and Dr. Andrews, showing the dates everyone had received their vaccines and boosters. Another page described illnesses they'd all had; Matasha was interested to discover her father had had scarlet fever as a child, a fact she'd never known. She'd thought it was something people got only in the nineteenth century, and that they died from it, like Beth March. She looked to see if her mother had included anything about Matasha getting growth hormone shots, but as if to protect her daughter's dignity, she hadn't.

On the next page there was a series of questions.

Please describe some of the activities your family enjoys together.
What sort of vacations have you taken, and what did you do on them?
Describe the role of religious faith in your family.
What are your family's routines?
Please list members of your extended family and how often you spend time with them.
What cultural activities do members of your family enjoy?
What hobbies do members of your family enjoy?

Do any members of the family play a musical instrument? Proficiently, competently, as a beginner?

None of the answers had been filled in.

On the following page, next to a request for a family photo, Matasha's mother had attached a Polaroid showing the three of them at the Wisconsin inn they'd gone to for spring break last year. They'd tried cross-country skiing and had flailed around a good bit on the woodsy trail, getting their ski tips caught, sliding wildly when there was an incline ("Pizza slice! Pizza slice!" her mother had shouted, because the guy at the ski rental shop had said that to stop yourself, you should separate your heels so your skis made the shape of a pizza slice). Her father cried "Egad!" each time he fell. Her mother trudged on gamely. Overall, it had been a nice day, although the trail was longer than any of them had expected and toward the end they grew tired and sore and impatient to get back. Matasha remembered how flushed she was at the end, her cheeks warm against the gusty wind, how satisfying the mug of hot chocolate back at the inn had been. Then, as they sat near the inn's fireplace, her mother had said something characteristic: "Well, we tried that. Now we never have to do it again." And her father, rather than clearing his throat, as Matasha expected—on some level she understood that whenever he did this, he was trying to dislodge his bafflement or unease—started laughing, a deep, warm sound with real delight in it.

"What?" her mother said, turning to him, as if suspecting she was being made fun of.

Her father shook his head, still laughing. "No, no, you're absolutely right, Jenine. We never have to do that again."

That was fine with Matasha. It had been fun, but a whole lot of work too. And now it was interesting to see that her mother had chosen the photo of them all fitted out in front of the rental hut just before they'd headed down the trail, looking game and optimistic and as if they frequently did this sort of thing together. As if they were some sort of hearty, outdoorsy, family-ish family.

Below the picture, the application made another request:

Please describe the members of your family, and your family life, in any way that you wish.

Followed by blank lines.

Matasha sighed. She would have liked to read what her mother would say about her. Would she say she was very small? Smart? Too serious? Too occupied with creepy thoughts? (Did her mother think what Jean thought?) Would she say she loved her? Matasha turned the sheet over, just in case. Nothing on the back either.

Matasha carefully placed the pages in order inside the envelope and opened the drawer to return it. At the back of the drawer lay a blue airmail envelope, not blank like the stack in the lower drawer but addressed to her mother. Curious, Matasha picked it up. It had the always-intriguing stamps of a foreign country on it. The return address read "SCHWEIZ." Matasha didn't know where that was, but her mother kept a dictionary by the desk, and Matasha, looking in the geographical section, found that "Schweiz" was the Swiss name for Switzerland. She instantly conjured up the map of Europe, Switzerland as a wiggly splotch bordered by France and Italy and Germany and Austria. Smooshed right up in the center of all of them, like the icing in the middle of a thumbprint cookie.

Normally, Matasha would have let the envelope be. It was not addressed to her. And what could be the appeal of a letter from some grown-up in Switzerland? But today she wanted to see what it said. Surely it would be boring. But maybe not.

The fragile paper, folded in three, crinkled in her hands as she opened it.

Darling Jenine:

"Darling"? Matasha skimmed ahead, looking for other interesting words. The handwriting, like the stamps, was immediately recognizable as foreign. What made handwriting foreign? Matasha wasn't sure, but somehow you could tell.

I can't understand why you wish to give Robert another chance. He devalues your projects, your ambitions. He has not half the wit or sophistication that you do. He will never understand you. Your soul is too expansive, you will never be happy with him.

Matasha stopped reading. She looked back at the date of the letter. July 30, 1975. Over six months ago. She and her parents had been in South Haven then, after Matasha's month at overnight camp. But the envelope was addressed to Chicago. Matasha recalled that while they'd been in Michigan, her mother had made occasional trips back to the city to take care of business things. And apparently to pick up mail.

I don't want to read this, she thought. But now she had to. She had started, and her mind would never let go of it now.

I am begging you once again to leave him. You and Matasha and I will find a new home just for us, in Zurich or Paris if you prefer.

This person knew about her, Matasha?

Or in London if the language barrier intimidates. Wherever you wish. As I have argued on my own behalf many times, I am an experienced father of daughters: my three lovely grown ones should attest to the good job I've done. (I give credit to Adèle too, of course.) I would be a good stepfather to Matasha. Naturally I don't wish to separate her from her biological father. There would be frequent visits to the US so she could spend time with him. She could spend each summer with him. As you know, money is not an issue.

Since I first saw you I knew we were meant to be together. I have waited all these years, respecting your wishes, but never giving up the conviction that time

*would unite us. And our recent days of intimacy have
assured me of . . .*

Matasha put the letter down. She purposely avoiding
looking for the name of whoever had written it. Trembling, she
folded it up and put it exactly where she'd found it. It wasn't
necessary to read every word. At least not right now. She'd come
back for it. She would read every word. Later, though. When she
felt stronger. Just not now.

2.

It was nice at first to walk into Margaret E. Marvin Elementary after you'd battled the cold and winds off the lake, but the building was overheated in the winter, and sometimes by the end of the day the children stumbled around sleepy and stupefied. This was one of those days. Matasha had butterflies from the moment she'd awakened, wishing as she often did lately that she could go to her locker without having to be near Jean and worry what Jean might say or do. She wished she could just pretend that Jean had never existed, that everything to do with their friendship could be cleanly erased. At the same time she was trying not to think too much about the terrible letter she'd found, which talked about her father as if he were a bad person and addressed her mother with words no one but her father should say. Probably nobody at Margaret E. Marvin had ever run into anything so shameful before; anyway, even if she had been willing to talk about it, she had nobody to talk to. The thought of the letter sat like a stone in her belly all day. At lunch period, she stood in the cafeteria line, and every single item of food behind the steamed glass looked repellent. She finally bought a package of Hostess Ho Hos, and enjoyed it a little.

Just to cap it off, there was art class today. All the excess heat in the building traveled upward and concentrated in the art room, and when Matasha entered, it was unbearable. She was a bit late to class; she always dragged her feet going, but today she'd dragged even more than usual. Miss Fillmore claimed there were no failures in art class, but then she made it clear with her voice and face whenever you had in fact failed. Even gym was enjoyable by comparison. Matasha wasn't strong but she was fast, so while she got low scores whenever they had to do things like pull-ups, she compensated when they had relay races and timed sprints. The worst part about failing in art was that she could never understand why what she was making wasn't very good, even when she could see that it wasn't.

"Yikes, it's *stifling*," she said as she walked in, searching out the stool where she usually sat, at the end of a row so that fewer kids would look at her work and ask questions about it.

There were titters in the room. Matasha looked around, confused. What was funny?

A girl named Eleanor Barry gave a guffaw. "Every single kid who walked into class said, 'It's so hot in here!' Then you said, 'It's *stifling*!'"

"You always have to use a bigger word," said Jennifer Stegner.

What was the use? Matasha felt defeated. It was just the word that had occurred to her in the moment, the one that most explained things.

"A big vocabulary is a lovely thing to have," interjected Miss Fillmore, apparently hoping to prevent things from moving in an unpleasant direction.

Yeah, right, thought Matasha. *You don't care about vocabulary. You're an art teacher. You care about collages and those stupid decoupage things we had to do a couple of weeks ago. And why can't you teach us how to draw properly?*

She dropped onto her stool, stared at the crayons that were laid out at each seat. If she'd gone to school in the nineteenth century, someone would have taught her how to draw by now. In novels, nineteenth-century girls always knew how to draw. Why had they gotten rid of that?

But now, and for the first time today, she was in luck. She'd forgotten that they were going to be working on one of the few art projects she liked. At the last class they'd covered a large piece of paper with blocks of crayon color, any way they wanted to, and then painted over the crayon with a special kind of black paint. Today, now that the paint had dried, they'd use sharpened wooden sticks to scratch out pictures. The beautiful color would rise from beneath the paint, and it was always a surprise to see which colors turned up where. All this was neat although Matasha still hated her clumsy designs. Once again the square house with four windows and a chimney that didn't look like any house she knew. The winding lane leading to the front door that was like a swollen piece of pasta. Forget trying to make a dog or cat. Elliot Gleason, opposite, was meticulously scratching out a race car and its helmeted driver. It looked pretty good. Matasha watched Allison Rodgers make a big moon face as large as her paper. Matasha wished she'd thought of that, but of course she couldn't copy Allison. She decided to make a leaf. She'd gotten a bit of a sense of how to draw a leaf shape from watching Jean. She scratched out an elongated oval that was pointy at the top. It came out kind of lopsided, like a deflated balloon. She drew in the veins but got overenthusiastic, and soon the shape was so crosshatched that it didn't look like a leaf at all. Disgusted, she was tempted to take her stick and scribble all over the thing, just make garbage out of it, but that would aggravate Miss Fillmore and land her with an even worse grade than usual. She managed to stay in the B range for art; it would be too shameful to get a C. You had to *try* to end up with a C in art. On the other hand, she could argue that scribbling all over your art piece *was* art. She could reference the crossed-out-face picture in her own home. Matasha checked out Allison Rodgers's drawing again. The moon now had huge eyes with lashes and was smoking a pipe. It looked quite terrific. Matasha sighed and scratched the word "LEAF" at the bottom of her drawing. At least now Miss Fillmore wouldn't ask what it was. Whatever anyone thought it looked like, whatever it might actually look like, with a word Matasha could insist on what it really was. "LEAF."

After art, Mr. Evinrude saw her in the hallway and stopped to mention the Little Sisters project again. Matasha froze. The truth was she hadn't given it a minute's thought since he'd brought it up. He said that they had a nice group of kids involved and that Camille Janklow and Kay Bledsoe were the president and vice president of the new Margaret E. Marvin Little Sisters club. That did it—there was no way Matasha was going to join in. She stared at the ground and stammered out something about being very busy.

When the day was finally over, Matasha paused at the middle-high construction site on the way home and watched the workers. There were more upright grids now, both at the perimeter of the site and within; she wondered how they got turned into real walls. Other than that, though, there once again didn't seem to be a lot of forward movement. Probably there had been too much snow. It was hard to believe there would be classrooms and lockers and an auditorium with seats by September.

3.

On weekends Matasha usually woke up before her parents, but that Saturday morning the door to their bedroom was open and she saw no sign of them inside. When Matasha was younger she'd whiled away the morning's dullness by watching TV cartoons; these days she listened to her records on low volume. Around 10:00 a.m. her mother and father would emerge from their bedroom, her father looking rumpled in his green bathrobe, her mother already freshly showered and with her hair pulled back in a neat bun. Later, her father would go to the office and her mother would do whatever.

Today her father was downstairs squeezing orange halves in the electric juicer. There was a wonderful citrus smell in the air. "Hi!" he said. "Do you want some juice?"

"Great!"

Mr. Wax smiled. "That's what I like about you, Matasha. You don't say 'Sure' or 'Okay.' You say 'Great!'"

"Where's Mom?" Matasha settled herself into one of the bar stools.

"I don't know."

"There is *nothing* going on in this house," Matasha complained. "I guess I'm supposed to just sit around all day."

"You love sitting around all day." Mr. Wax slid a glass of

squeezed juice over to her. "The last thing anyone can ever do is get you out of the house. So what's the problem?"

"I don't know," admitted Matasha. "I guess I'm just grumpy."

"Fine, be grumpy."

"Don't you even know when Mom's coming home?" Some Saturdays her mother was around and might be coaxed into a movie, other times she was busy with her business. Lately, with no Jean in her life, Matasha cared more about her mother being around.

"I have no idea."

"Well, can't you stay home then? Let's do something. Let's go out and take pictures." Mr. Wax had a real camera, a Leica, and sometimes they went out together looking for things to photograph. Mr. Wax had promised to get Matasha a good camera to replace her Instamatic when she turned fourteen.

"You know I have to go to the office. I'll take you tomorrow."

"Tomorrow's going to be yucky. The papers said so. Sleet."

"It will have to be tomorrow, I'm afraid."

"How can you not know when Mom is coming home? Didn't she say anything?"

Mr. Wax didn't reply for several moments. Finally, he said, "I don't know where your mother is, and I don't know when she's coming home. She didn't come home last night."

Matasha didn't reply for a bit either. She swallowed. Then she said quietly, "Is she dead?"

"No! She's not dead. She's gone somewhere. And I'm not going to take the bait and worry about it."

"Daddy! How do you know? Don't you think you better call the police? What if something did happen?"

"I know your mother. She's done this before."

"She has? When?"

Mr. Wax hesitated again. "Over the summer, while you were at camp. Before that, it was a few years ago. You were so little, there was no reason for you to know. She left for about three days, and then she came back. And there was once before then. I don't ask her where she goes, and she doesn't tell. She needs to do it for some reason. Your mother is a little crazy, frankly."

"Mommy is *not* crazy," said Matasha angrily.

"Fine. But she leaves. She is a married woman and a mother and she leaves." Her father rolled his empty juice glass in his hands; it made Matasha nervous. What if he dropped it? Even more nervous-making was the thought of the letter she'd found in her mother's drawer, which she'd successfully put out of her head for days now. Did SCHWEIZ have something to do with all this? Should she tell her father about it? He was standing now, putting his glass in the sink. He opened the briefcase that was perched on the counter.

"What if she went far away?" Matasha asked in a trembly voice. "What if she got on a plane or something?"

"She didn't get on a plane," said her father. "You know what she does, Matasha? She gets a hotel room, and she *thinks*. When she gets really angry and fed up, you know what she tells me? That she has no room to think. In this big apartment, with her husband at work and her daughter at school all day! So she gets a hotel room and she thinks for two or three days and then she comes back, with her mind all freshened up, and she's happy, or *happier*, for a little while again." He clapped his briefcase closed. "And I can't do a damn thing about it. Excuse my French."

"Why can't she think?" asked Matasha desperately.

"I don't know. I guess the walls here talk."

Matasha didn't know what he meant. She wanted to keep him from going to the office. She put out her hand and held on to his sweater.

"Sunset's here," said her father. "You don't need to worry. I asked her to stay."

Matasha followed her father to the door. "I won't be back until after dinner," he said. He bent down and gave her a kiss. It was eight thirty in the morning. Then he squatted next to her. "I want to tell you one thing," he said. "I want you to keep this in mind. This crazy idea your mother has about adopting a Vietnamese baby—"

"Girl," interrupted Matasha. "Not a baby."

"Girl," said Mr. Wax. "You help your mother get that idea right out of her head. You think she's fit to take care of another child? Disappearing like this, whenever she wants to? Do you think your mother really knows how to deal with another girl, a girl who's lost her parents and has God knows what problems? Do you think so?"

Matasha wished her father weren't repeating himself so much, and that his voice weren't getting so loud. She got it—she wasn't stupid.

"No," she said miserably. "I don't think so."

"Well, then." He stood up. "Your mother gets carried away by her enthusiasms. But this one is serious. This isn't like adopting a pet dog. Which if she did, I'm sure that . . . well." He didn't finish his thought. He walked out the front door and pressed the elevator button.

"Bye, Matasha."

4.

Matasha read her bound collection of Wonder Woman comics. She watched *Fat Albert* and *American Bandstand* on TV. Sunset made her a tuna fish sandwich for lunch. She did some homework and listened to Bob Marley and Bruce Springsteen. She felt too low and jumpy to work on her Chicago Fire book, even though she was at an interesting part: Rachel discovers that Sam has stolen a loaf of bread, and she insists that he return it to the street vendor and apologize, and then work for the vendor for free for a month. She does this even though they are both extremely hungry and in need of the bread. Matasha planned for the vendor to become a friend who later supports them when the neighbors become threatening.

At 3:00 p.m. Matasha finally gave into temptation and phoned her father's office. The sun was already sinking in the sky; the grayish dark moved in through the tall windows. Soon the entire apartment would be dusky, even with the table lamps and overheads turned on. "Mommy's still not home," she told him.

"She'll be home," her father said. "I'm on the other line."

Matasha talked Sunset into playing a game of checkers with her, and then a game of Mastermind. She wanted to tell Sunset that she was frightened, but she was embarrassed and she was humiliated too. Did Sunset know her mother had disappeared?

She wasn't sure, and she didn't want to say anything. Talking about it would make it more true.

The phone rang in the kitchen. Normally Matasha thought of the phone as something to do with the adults, no concern of hers. Sunset would pick it up, or whoever it was would call back. But now she thought: *Mommy.* She ran to the kitchen.

"Hello?" she asked. Her voice came out high, a little strangled. No one said anything on the other end. There was noise, though, the noise of a big room with people talking loudly in the background. "Hello?" she asked again.

The noise continued. Matasha didn't hang up. She *knew*: it *was* her mother, and she was calling from an airport. There was the sound of a PA, a woman's voice asking for a Mr. Somebody.

"Mommy," breathed Matasha.

"Honey," said her mother.

"Where are you?" Matasha began to sob.

"I'm . . ." But she didn't continue.

"Don't go away, don't go away!" cried Matasha. She wept into the silent phone. She could hear the PA again, and people passing in the background, but her mother didn't speak.

"Please, Mommy, please! Don't hang up!" She could feel herself losing her mother, losing the connection. She was doing what she should never do around her mother: beg, plead, grow hysterical.

"I'll call you again," her mother said quietly. Then she hung up.

●

Matasha called her father. The phone rang and rang. He might have gone out for dinner, but in her feverishness Matasha imagined him also disappearing: getting on a plane, a train, or just magically vanishing. Sunset made no comment when Matasha didn't eat any of her spaghetti dinner. Afterward, Matasha called her father again and he answered. She started to explain, but he couldn't understand what she was telling him through her crying. She had to start again a few times.

"Did she say she was in an airport?"

"I could hear it, Daddy! I know!"

She knew he was taking off his glasses and putting them down by the phone and rubbing his forehead. These were things that didn't make any noise, and yet she had seen him do them so many times that she could hear them right now.

"Matasha, I am going to finish the work I have here and I'll be home around midnight. You go to bed soon."

"Are you going to get Mommy?"

"I don't know where she is. And you can't just go 'get' another person. She has to want to come back. She's a grown woman. She knows where we are."

Matasha didn't agree. Maybe sometimes you just had to go get someone. She wasn't sure how that was done, but maybe you got a private detective or something. Or you drove to the airport and asked people in uniforms if they'd seen a tallish slender woman with long dark hair and a big belt. You checked all the terminals.

"What if she doesn't call again?" Matasha meant: *What if she doesn't come back?*

"Matasha, you're a little young to have to learn this, but I guess there's no choice now. It's possible that she won't come back, isn't it? I mean, isn't it in the realm of possibility? Think about it."

It *was*? It was within the realm of possibility?

"What would we do?" she asked in a very small voice.

"We'd go on. We'd be all right. I want you to know that, Matasha. We would be all right."

It seemed she was expected to say something now, but she wasn't sure what. She gripped the phone for a long time while her father waited.

"Bye, Daddy," she said finally, quietly. "Come home soon."

It wasn't late, but Matasha washed her face and brushed her teeth. She felt as if she'd stayed up for three days and then run three miles. But no matter how much she would have loved to close her eyes and make the day go away, she had to do her shot. She always had to do her shot. She got a pouch out of the refrigerator, filled the syringe, injected a spot on her thigh, rinsed the syringe, and returned the pack to the fridge. Matasha couldn't say that the shots no longer hurt, but she was so used to the injections that sometimes she forgot to notice the pain. It was very strange. She might be thinking about math class or something that had happened on *Welcome Back, Kotter*, and only afterward would she realize the shot had hurt just the same as always. But since in the moment her mind had been elsewhere, it was as if it hurt only in retrospect.

She climbed into bed and pulled the covers up high. Her father was wrong. It wasn't possible, and they wouldn't be all right.

5.

When Matasha woke up, her flip clock read 10:13 a.m. She wasn't sure she'd ever slept so late before. At first she didn't remember what had happened, and then she did. She ran to her parents' bedroom—no mother there—then downstairs. No mother in the sewing room or the kitchen. Her father was working at a large desk that was in the same room as the family TV, his papers in piles around him, a bowl of pistachios at his side. Matasha crawled into his lap. He pushed back his swivel chair to make space.

"Did she come back?" asked Matasha, although the answer was pretty clear.

"No," he said. He stroked her hair. "You smell like flowers. Is that your shampoo?"

"I guess." The hours ahead loomed long and horrible. "What are we going to do today?" Outside, just as predicted, moisture was pouring down in thick gray sheets.

"How about we go play tennis at the Lake Shore Club?"

"Okay," said Matasha doubtfully. "No. What if Mommy comes home and we're not here?"

"Sunset will be here." This didn't seem entirely to address the question, but Matasha said, "All right." She found she really did want to play tennis. Her father said it was supposed to clear up by midafternoon and they could bring their cameras to the club in case.

"Does Sunset know about Mommy?" Matasha asked. Yes, her father said, she did.

Upstairs, getting into her tennis outfit, Matasha had an idea. She sat down and wrote a note to her mother. She would give it to Sunset in case her mother came home. Or, if her mother called, Sunset could read her the note.

The note said:

Dear Mommy,
I know you are having a rough time right now but I really really need you. I'm only eleven. If you could just wait until I am eighteen then I would be in college and out of the house and maybe we could think about your leaving then. I really love you and miss you and I can't imagine life without you. You are the greatest mom

Matasha paused at those last words and decided that her mother would not appreciate any exaggerations. She erased the last three words and wrote instead:

You are a great mom, even though sometimes your head is someplace else. I would be so lonely if you didn't continue to be my mom. I hope you'll reconsider all this. I'll really work with you to make this work out.

Love,
Matasha

She folded the note, put it in an envelope, sealed it thoroughly, wrote "FOR MOM" in big block letters outside, and gave it to Sunset with her instructions. She could feel her father watching her.

"Did Mommy call?" asked Matasha when they returned home. They'd played a set of tennis and had hamburgers at the club, and then, because it did clear up, they'd walked around the neighborhood taking photographs. Her father had let her use his Leica, helping her adjust the focus and aperture. The one hobby Mr. Wax allowed himself was photography. He used the laundry room as his darkroom, since it had no windows. He put the pans of developing fluid on the top of the washer and dryer. He had a special black light that he used to see what he was doing, a light that didn't expose the prints. Matasha sometimes watched him while he got the negatives to come up in the developing pans. It was wild, like watching ghosts turn into persons. Her father liked to take pictures of buildings. Matasha wondered at that. She preferred pictures of people, like the short, squat fellow with the cap pulled low on his brow and an enormous cigar sticking out of his mouth whom she'd once snapped on the corner of Diversey and Broadway. Her father had made a print of it that her mother got a frame for; Matasha kept it proudly in her room. She liked faces and she liked signs: signs on diners and shoeshine places, hardware stores and jewelry shops, with all their different kinds of letters, upright, slanted, boxy and skinny, script and plain print. Her father liked buildings—not houses, which were sufficiently interesting to Matasha (porches, windows, steps, and front doors), but apartment buildings and company buildings: long, smooth elongated rectangles, their narrow ends pointing into the sky. Straight sides, flat tops, zillions of identical windows. A gleam on their faces; her father liked to catch that gleam.

They'd taken photographs until their hands grew numb from fiddling with the dials, and then Mr. Wax hailed them a taxi home.

"No, dear one, your mother didn't call," Sunset said. "All right, Mr. Wax, I'll see you on Tuesday." Because she had stayed over the weekend, she needed to go home and catch up on things. Mr. Wax told Matasha that she had permission to order in pizza for dinner tomorrow night. Tonight, as usual, he went to pick up Chinese. Matasha used up about twenty napkins eating her spareribs, and couldn't understand how her father could make do with just one. They hadn't ordered lo mein; that was something only her mother ate.

"Tell me about one of your cases," Matasha said.

Mr. Wax cleared his throat. "I don't really have cases," he said.

"Yes, you have cases. What do you do all day?"

"I have clients, and I do the things they need me to do. But I don't have cases in the way I think you mean. I don't go in front of a judge and argue things."

"You do sometimes!"

"I do, but not often. And not in the way you think."

"Well, tell me what you *do* do. I want to know. For instance, what did you do yesterday?"

"Yesterday I drafted a merger agreement between two companies."

"What does that mean?"

"Oh, Matasha. It would be hard to explain, and I don't think you would find it very interesting."

"*Yes*, I would find it interesting."

"All right. Let's see. When two companies legally become one company, the liabilities—those are the debts—and assets of one become part of the other. So there's due diligence—research, I mean—that has to be done on the part of the acquiring company relating to the financial condition of the other company, and in this case there are issues around funding and stockholder arrangements. Does that answer your question?"

"Argghh, Daddy, don't you ever have to defend somebody who's done something wrong? Like the guy who kidnapped Martin Kimmel."

"Martin Kimmel?"

"Martin Kimmel! You know, the boy who was kidnapped from the park last summer."

Her father considered. "It rings a faint bell. They found the kidnapper?"

"No. But when they do."

"I'm not a criminal lawyer, honey. I work with businesses. I think you know that."

"But businesses do things wrong too. And they sue each other, right? So don't you have cases? Cases in court!"

"Well, last year I helped a company defend themselves against another company that claimed it stole its design for a toaster."

"That sounds interesting." Matasha felt more hopeful. "What else?"

Mr. Wax scraped the leftover ribs back into the takeout container. "I don't know, Matasha. That's the best example I could come up with. I'm very limited. I do one thing very well and I don't do and am not interested in much of anything else. Why don't we talk about something new. What are you studying at school?"

Matasha tried to tell him about *The Hobbit*, which they were just finishing in English class. They had an assignment to act out a scene. Matasha picked the one where Bilbo confronts Gollum in the cave and answers his riddles. She was going to act out both parts. She imitated Gollum's lisp for her father, but she could tell his mind was wandering.

"How about some popcorn for dessert?" he asked.

"Yeah!"

Her father got the popper from the pantry closet. Matasha measured out the kernels, and her father poured in the corn oil. She kept watch as the popper slowly heated and the smell of the hot oil began to waft into the room. The process always seemed to take a long time. Eventually there would be that first, lone pop and then, after a pause, one or two more, and finally there would be the frenzy of popping, noisy and abundant. Then, too soon, it would end. Her father unplugged the machine and lifted the plastic lid to let the steam escape. He tipped the contents into a large metal bowl, dropped in a pat of butter and shook it around, then sprinkled salt over the top and shook it up again.

"Voilà," he said.

They stood at the counter eating greedy fistfuls out of the bowl.

"Do you think Mommy's in a hotel right now, thinking?" asked Matasha. She herself was skeptical. If that was what her mother wanted to do, why had she been in an airport? *Had* that been an airport? Matasha kept remembering the envelope with the Switzerland stamps on it, but she was still afraid to mention it. What would happen if she did?

"I don't know," said her father. "I'm trying not to think about it too much."

How could you not think about it? "Why?"

"Because it won't do any good. The thoughts in my mind are not going to make your mother return any faster. They'll just make me miserable, and keep me from getting my work done. And the last thing I want is for your mother to keep me from being able to work. That's what she wants."

"She doesn't want you to work?"

"No."

"That doesn't make sense, Daddy."

"That doesn't mean she doesn't want it," said her father. "In fact, that makes it all the more likely that she would want it."

"Don't you want her to come back?" The question surprised even Matasha. It came out of her mouth before she knew it.

Her father chewed and then swallowed a mouthful of popcorn. He had a large swallow—you could see his Adam's apple move. It was uncomfortably compelling; Matasha never got used to it. He dabbed his mustache with a napkin.

"I don't know," he said. He looked angry that she had asked, angry that he had to answer.

"Why, Daddy?" Matasha's heart was beating fast.

"It's kind of nice and quiet around here without her," he said.

Matasha began to cry.

He patted her head awkwardly. "Shh . . . shh . . ." he said. But Matasha wasn't going to be shushed. If he didn't want her to cry, then he shouldn't have said anything so mean.

"I just mean it's more simple," her father said. "It's a little bit of a break. Of course I want her to come back. Soon."

6.

In the middle of the night, the phone rang. Matasha half heard it, something far away and muffled. By the time she figured out what the sound was, she knew she had been hearing it for a while. She scrambled out of bed, her half-asleep legs wobbling, and ran to the landing to pick up.

"Hello?" she said. "Mommy?"

There was quiet on the other end, but a live quiet, the quiet of somebody's presence.

"Hi, Matasha."

"Mommy." Matasha didn't cry this time. She had been crying so much for two days that the tears seemed momentarily to have run out.

"I'm sorry for calling so late. I know you have school tomorrow."

Matasha pushed the receiver hard against her ear, as if by doing so she might be able to bring her mother closer. Was she correct that her mother's voice was shaky?

"It's okay."

Her mother didn't seem to know what to say next. After a long pause, she asked: "What was your homework this weekend?"

Matasha said she'd had some math, and that she'd finished

reading *The Hobbit*. "We're going to write play scenes from it."
Was this really what her mother wanted to talk about?

"Oh, *The Hobbit*'s a good one. You read that already, didn't
you?"

"Mm. But I liked reading it again."

"You know J. R. R. Tolkien invented an entire language
for the hobbits, something with a complete vocabulary and real
grammar. It's something you could learn if you wanted to."

"I know."

There was a pause. Matasha thought she heard street
noises in the background, a clattering of something like glass. It
sounded like daytime where her mother was.

"Mommy? Where are you calling from?"

"Not very close. But I wanted to talk to you."

"Okay. I'm talking." Matasha's stomach rumbled. She
yawned loudly, not able to help herself. She hoped her father
hadn't woken up, wasn't hearing any of this.

"When are you coming home?" Matasha had prepared
this sentence all weekend. She remembered a book she'd once
found at a school book sale. The book said that when you wanted
something, you should ask the other person not *if* you would get
it but *when*. You would be surprised, the book said, at how often
that made the other person feel that the *if* was already decided
and they couldn't change that.

"I'll call you again soon," said Matasha's mother.

"I can talk! I'm awake now."

"It's expensive, Matasha." Matasha knew that was a lie. Or

rather, her mother rarely cared whether things were expensive. Only her father did. She was shocked that her mother would use this excuse.

Matasha chewed on the inside of her cheek. "Just a little, Mom?" Her stomach rumbled again; she thought she might have to run to the bathroom. "Daddy promises things will be better if you come home." That was completely untrue; he had never said such a thing. But maybe one lie generated another.

"He did?" Matasha could hear her mother grow still and intent.

"Love?" said a voice in the background. A man's voice. A low, gravelly voice, with some sort of warning in it.

"Sweetheart," her mother said to her. "I'm going to go now."

Instinct made Matasha know not to beg. "All right."

"I'll call you again soon. In the night, okay? I knew you'd hear. I knew you'd pick up."

Quietly, Matasha put down the receiver. No sound from her parents' room. Her mother would call again; she'd said so. What choice did Matasha have but to believe her?

7.

The next day, as soon as she got home from school, Matasha went to look in her mother's office for the letter from Switzerland. With Sunset gone, she didn't even have to sneak.

She'd had a feeling about it, and she was right: the letter was no longer there.

She racked her brains, trying to remember the name of the city that had been on the return address. Why hadn't she written it down? She hadn't guessed that it might be so important, that it was a fact she would later *need* . . . She thought it started with *S*. It was something German-sounding. She simply couldn't conjure it up. She got out the atlas her father had given her in fifth grade and peered at all the town names in small print scattered throughout the little, mountainous country. She especially looked for *S*. Sargans. Sempach. No, no. Then she found a name that struck her with a special ping. Küssnacht. That was it. It didn't start with *S*; she must have been remembering the *s*'s in the middle. But that was it.

On Tuesday, after classes, she went to the school library to find a book on Switzerland. The card catalogue listed one, but it had nothing on the town of Küssnacht. Matasha did learn, however, that Switzerland was originally called Helvetia, that the Swiss produced most of the chocolate in the world, and that the wristwatch was a Swiss invention. She got absorbed enough to forget what she was doing—trying to find out something about her mother—and when she remembered, she felt uneasy and put the book guiltily away. She went down to the ground-floor pay phone and called Sunset to tell her she was going to take the CTA to the main public library downtown and that she'd be home later. There was a library branch near school, but Matasha knew she needed the big one. Sunset said, "All right, dear one," and Matasha decided that after the library she'd stop at Marshall Field's and buy Sunset some of the Frango mints she loved.

The main library was a dazzling building with a wide central staircase, elaborately painted walls, and a huge domed ceiling. It was even nicer than the Art Institute. She'd been to the library only a few times before, with her mother, but she asked the CTA driver which stop she should get off at and he told her. She knew it was right on Michigan Avenue, on the same bus line she took to her piano lesson when her mother didn't drive her. (What would happen with her piano lesson this week?) She told herself not to be nervous, that she knew how to get home just fine.

A lady behind a large desk told her she needed the reference librarian on the second floor. The reference librarian smiled as Matasha approached, that smile that made Matasha know that she was amused by Matasha's small size, thought it hilarious that such a little creature could actually walk and talk and wanted to research something! She swallowed her anger. She had something important to do.

As it turned out, the librarian was helpful. She led Matasha to the section that had books on Switzerland and German Swiss culture. She asked Matasha if she knew how to use an index, and Matasha said thank you very much, she did. She checked for the town of Küssnacht in book after book, and found a few mentions. It was practically in the middle of the country, on Lake Lucerne, in an area called Schwyz—which looked sort of like "SCHWEIZ"—that was known for its cherry blossoms. Küssnacht went back to the Middle Ages, and there was a lot of skiing there. It had an unemployment rate of 2.1 percent. Most of the people who lived there were Catholic.

Matasha planned eventually to present all this information and more to her father like a real detective. Somehow she would know when the time was right. Her father would be grateful and impressed. What would happen after that was a little fuzzier, but she pictured her father getting on a plane. He'd go to Küssnacht and straighten things out, and Matasha's mother would return with him. Things would go back to the way they'd been before, with her mother chewing the skin on the side of her thumb and walking around with that furrowed look, as if she'd forgotten something important.

The librarian poked her head back in. "Are you writing a report?" she asked.

"Yes," Matasha told her.

At five o'clock, Matasha put the books back on the shelf, put her loose-leaf notebook and pencils away, and went to catch the bus. It was dusk and starting to snow lightly. She pictured her mother walking down a street lined with cherry blossoms, walking in a park with the man who had called her "love." She remembered that it would be midnight in Switzerland now—so, no park-walking probably. Also it was February: no cherry blossoms. Soon her mother would be sleeping. Her mother looked very peaceful when she slept. When Matasha was little and had a nightmare, she would come into her parents' bedroom, and her mother, who slept nearer the door, would be lying on her side, a slight smile on her face in sleep. The smile reassured Matasha. If her own dreams were bad, her mother's were apparently good, and if Matasha got into bed next to her, she might have good ones too. She shook her mother, waking her, then clambered into the bed between her parents. Her father grumbled a bit in his sleep and turned over. Her mother protested ("Watch out . . . not so rough . . .") and let her stay for only a little while before sending her back to her own bed. But it was usually all right by then. In the morning Matasha could never recall what she had dreamed that had frightened her so.

She walked the short distance to Marshall Field's, a building in which she had spent so much time in her life, shopping for school and camp clothes, for winter coats, looking through the books in its bookshop, waiting while her mother picked out a new soup tureen or a watch, getting to buy candy in the sweetshop when her grandma Nan came to visit, although it had been a while since that had happened. She had gotten lost in the store more than once and learned that you could look at the floor and it would tell you, in bronze letters set into the tiles, which street outside you were closest to. Whenever she got lost, she was supposed to go to the Washington Street door and wait for her mother. Now, she went into the sweetshop and bought a box of Frango mints for Sunset; luckily she had enough money with her. It was four dollars, over three times her weekly allowance.

The bus home was hot and stuffy, and Matasha dozed off and went two stops too far. She ran to the front in a hurry, calling, "Stop, please! Stop, please!" When she'd nearly reached the alley to her building, she realized she'd left the bag with the Frango mints on the bus seat. She almost sat right down on the street in despair. Sunset would have been so happy! She would have hugged her and called her "sugar," which was a rare elevation of "dear one" that she used when particularly pleased. And of course she would have let Matasha have several pieces herself. Passing into the apartment foyer, she could smell dinner—spaghetti again. Matasha sat down at the table with the newspaper and picked her way through her iceberg lettuce salad. She choked down the glass of warmish milk. She told Sunset about the Frango mints and Sunset said, "You did? That was sweet of you." For some reason Matasha decided that Sunset didn't really believe her, so she insisted, several times, that she really *had* bought the mints, she wasn't making it up, she *had* bought them, really, and had just left them on the bus, until Sunset looked puzzled and stopped thanking her and walked off to clean up. Matasha went upstairs and took a long, hot bath to make herself feel better.

8.

A week went by. Two weeks. Four.

9.

Matasha wandered into the laundry room to talk to Sunset. The laundry room smelled tropical when Sunset was busy with the laundry, and after you'd been in it you got a pleasant shock of coolness walking back out into the kitchen. Matasha leaned in the doorway and watched Sunset folding her socks and shirts and—this always embarrassed Matasha—her father's white underpants.

"Hello there," said Sunset. "What are you up to?"

"Nothing," said Matasha. "I'm just roaming around."

"Roaming around? What are you roaming for?"

"I don't know. Because I can't think of anything else to do."

"Nothing else to do, in this whole big house? With your whole big closet full of games and toys?"

"Well, there's no one to play with," said Matasha. "You have to play games with another person." She was immensely tempted to ask Sunset to play Clue or Masterpiece or Careers, but she knew Sunset had too much to do.

"Maybe I should make cookies," said Matasha.

"We don't have any cookie dough. I'm making a list to call into the store tomorrow and I will put that on it."

"I can make them the old-fashioned way," said Matasha. "With flour and sugar and chocolate chips."

"I don't think we have chocolate chips either."

"What is WRONG with this house?" cried Matasha. "There is NO FOOD anywhere!" It was true. Ever since her mother had left, the shelves in the pantry and refrigerator, never heavily stocked, were nearly empty. Her mother had each week noted what they needed and called it in to Landauer's, the local supermarket that delivered. They got eggs and bread and cans of frozen orange juice, which Sunset whipped into fresh in the blender; they got meat and buns and Lender's frozen bagels and the fish Mrs. Wax once in a while had Sunset make for Matasha and that Matasha would never touch. After Mrs. Wax left, the supplies dwindled until Sunset told Mr. Wax they needed such and such and perhaps she should call in a grocery order, and since then she'd taken over and done the weekly telephone shopping. But Matasha's mother had always ordered at least something in the way of cookies or chips and ice cream, and Sunset, for whatever reason, did not put these automatically on her list. Now Matasha told Sunset that she would like the chocolate chips and also Chips Ahoy cookies and Pringles and Triscuits and two kinds of ice cream, chocolate and Neapolitan, which was the flavor with three strips: one chocolate, one vanilla, and one strawberry. Honestly, Matasha ate around the vanilla. But her father liked vanilla, so it was all right.

"You're going to eat all that?" asked Sunset.

"Yes," said Matasha. "And right now I'm going to make some plain cookies. Some plain boring cookies without the chocolate chips."

"There you go," said Sunset approvingly. Matasha went to

get the flour and sugar out of the pantry, and there she saw a box of Trix cereal with the rabbit on it and stopped, rebuked. For she had not fed Mr. Bunny today, nor yesterday, nor—could it be?—the day before. She had simply entirely forgotten about him once again.

How long had it been, really, truly, since she had remembered to go out to feed him? She didn't know. She put on her coat and her snow boots, unlocked the back door, and walked through the chilly back hallway to the fire escape. There was a metal door to the escape that required a good tug to unstick it from its frame. It was windy enough that she pushed a metal chair between the door and the frame in case a gust pushed the door closed behind her. She wondered if her mother and father had ever sat out here at the table when they'd first moved in. Maybe they had, on hot summer evenings long ago, before Matasha was born. Back when maybe they enjoyed each other and did romantic things like sit outside in the twilight and watch the sky or whatever it was grown-ups did.

Matasha called Mr. Bunny's name softly, tentatively. His cage was mounded with snow, and his food bowl was under a snow hillock. She lifted his hutch, afraid to find a still, frozen body. But there he was, hunched on his paws, breathing. Matasha brought inside his food bowl, dumped the snow into the sink, dried it, and filled it high with pellets from next to the fire escape door. She ran warm sink water over his water bottle until it thawed and then she ran new water, not too cold, into it and refastened it to the side of the cage. She crouched down and offered Mr. Bunny an apology, adding some criticism of her parents: "They are messed up. But it's almost spring. It'll warm up pretty soon."

Back in the kitchen, she dug out an old cookie recipe of her mother's—it was strange to think of a time when her mother might have written out recipes, in her neat, loopy handwriting—and made the cookies without the chips. They came out better than she'd expected. She ate a few and wished she could feed one to Mr. Bunny. Sunset took a couple and pronounced them very good. Matasha put two on a plate covered in plastic wrap with a note saying "DAD" on top, and left them in the kitchen for him.

10.

Dear Dottie:

Do you remember about Martin Kimmel? It seems like everyone has forgotten about him. Not his parents, of course. I wish someone would find him so I could stop thinking about him. I used to be sure I knew what had happened to him, but now I'm not. I'm still a little creeped out about the whole thing. But mostly I think it would be awful if everyone stopped caring about finding him.

The problem about writing you is there are so many different things that are bothering me. All the letters in your column have only one problem.

This had remained an obstacle in Matasha's mind when it came to writing Dottie a letter. As had difficulties in putting things into the right words. She'd done her best with the praying, but one night, staring up at the ceiling, she realized that the Supreme Being she was imagining hovering beyond it was not a bearded older man but Dottie Summers, in her gold skirt suit and pumps. Dottie was the one she really wanted to be listening. And so, at last, Matasha just spilled everything onto the page without worrying too much how it came out.

For one thing, my best friend since first grade is being really mean to me. She ignores me and then tells me what she hates about me. She's made friends with this other girl. I don't really have friends anymore.

I have to give myself growth hormone shots every day. I hate it.

My mom

How could Matasha explain about her mom, even to Dottie Summers? When she got to this part, she almost gave up on the letter again. What had happened with her mother was so shameful that she didn't even want to write it down. In the past weeks she had spent time in both the school library and the public library looking for books about divorcing parents or a mother leaving a family. There were only a few about kids going through a divorce and none at all about a mother leaving home. Maybe Matasha was the only person in the world this had ever happened to. Mothers weren't supposed to leave families, although every so often a father did. Maybe she was even weirder than she had previously thought.

My mom

If she didn't write, she wasn't going to get an answer. And she needed an answer.

My mom left one night and didn't come back. It's been

over a month. I've decided that if six weeks go by and she doesn't come back she might not come back at all.

What will I do if my mother doesn't come back? I don't think I could live if that happens. And what if other people find out?

Sincerely,

Too Many Troubles

She drew a circle at the bottom of the letter and put the letter *D* inside. She got an envelope and a stamp from her mother's desk, and the next morning she dropped the letter in a mailbox on the way to the bus stop.

11.

Matasha's father did not mention her mother. He started working at home on Saturdays so that Sunset did not need to be there, but Sunset still stayed through Friday night, and she returned Sunday nights now instead of Monday mornings. She told Matasha that her grandniece was going to start helping out some days and staying over some nights because she, Sunset, was getting too old to work such long hours. Also, sometimes Matasha needed to get to a doctor's appointment—like with Dr. Karnow, who needed to see her every other month—and Sunset didn't drive. Sunset reminded Matasha that she'd already met the grandniece, Ellen, at her parents' Russian party in the fall. She said Matasha would like Ellen. She didn't say anything to Matasha about her mother, about these changes having anything to do with her absence, and Matasha was grateful for that. She didn't want to talk about it with anyone. Not with Sunset, and certainly not with anyone who didn't know: her teachers, the neighbors, other kids. Maybe her mother would come back before long and it would be as if it had never happened. And there would have been no need for anyone to know.

She still hadn't told her father about the town of Küssnacht and what she'd learned at the public library. The truth was that none of it helped. She'd had some sort of idea that she'd find her mother in those books, and of course she hadn't, just facts about chocolate, flags, and religion. And by the time she'd replaced the books on the shelf, she'd begun to be afraid that even telling her father the name of the town might be a problem. On the surface, he didn't seem to be curious about what was going on with her mother. On the other hand, Matasha sensed that he was angry. What if she told him about the letter and he exploded in a fury? "Küssnacht?!" he might yell. "She went to Küssnacht?!" Maybe he knew something about that town. Maybe he even knew the man who had called her mother "love." Maybe he would get on a plane and when he found her mother he would yell at her and divorce her. Maybe he would get into a fight with the Love Man and get hurt, although it was hard to imagine her father fighting anyone.

And then there was the part of the letter where the Love Man said to her mother that maybe Matasha would come to live with them, all the way over in Switzerland. Matasha didn't want to live in Switzerland. She couldn't for a single minute imagine living in Switzerland. Although it wasn't so wonderful living in Chicago right now, with no friends and the black snow high on the sides of the roads and the late March wind still so cold that her fingers were numb by the time she got to school. And injections every night and the visits to Dr. Karnow—he took blood every time, something she forced herself to endure by squeezing her eyes closed and balling one hand into a fist that she shoved underneath her bottom, trying to think of nothing as the needle went in—and the long Saturdays feeling more bored than ever. Last month Dr. Karnow said she'd grown three-quarters of an inch since she started the injections in November, which was something but not as good as he had expected.

But she still had her classes at school and her homework and the school library and the Dewey decimal system. She still had strawberry yogurt and chocolate chip cookies and Hostess Ho Hos. She still had *The Once and Future King* and *The Hobbit* to reread and Bob Marley and the Top 40 radio station, WCFL. And sometimes she remembered to go take care of Mr. Bunny. Spring was officially here; it would start getting nicer out. On the whole things would have to be a lot worse to make her want to go to Switzerland.

12.

Matasha had a cold. She'd gone into the third-floor bathroom to get some toilet paper to blow her nose and saw Camille and Glenda sitting on the countertop, swinging their legs. "I heard your mother doesn't live with you anymore," Camille said.

Matasha was stunned. How could Camille possibly know? Matasha hadn't told anyone. She knew her father wouldn't have told anyone either. At least she didn't think so. She decided to brazen it out.

"That's not true," she said.

"Sure it's true. My mom and dad said. My mom said your mom hasn't been at the symphony with them for a month. She hasn't been playing tennis at the club."

"She's been traveling," said Matasha. Her nose was running; she licked the sweet mucus from above her lip. Then she darted into a stall to get some paper.

"Nope," said Camille. "Your mom left you. My dad said."

"Your dad," said Matasha, wrapping the toilet paper around her hand as she emerged, "is a lying shit." She could hear her own loud internal gasp—like the gasp of a very shocked classroom teacher. She had never said that word aloud to another child, although she had hissed it once after banging her thumb with a hammer.

"Oh. My. God," said Glenda. "Ohmygod, Camille. Matasha is, like, *deranged*."

Camille was quiet for a moment. "You're in really big trouble," she said, and Matasha knew that she was.

"Did you know," asked Camille, "that my dad once dated your mom? She was crazy, he said. That's why he didn't marry her. There is something really wrong with your mom. And that's why there's something wrong with you."

"That's why he didn't marry her?" asked Matasha. "I thought it was because he loved your mom." It didn't come off with quite the bang she'd hoped for. It was a little too hard to parse. Camille looked baffled, then contemptuous.

"You're in really big trouble," she repeated.

Matasha tried to write a letter to her mother. At first she wrote about what was going on at school, but that depressed her so much she crumpled up the page and started a new one. She didn't want to write down that she had no friends and that Camille and her buddies had started to harass and torment her on the way to school and in the hallways. She thought of writing about doing a timed sprint in gym in under eight seconds. That was faster than some of the good athletes in the class had been able to do, and she had been proud. A few of the girls, the ones who weren't busy hating and being mean to her, had even applauded for her. Even several of the boys did. The boys didn't seem as clued in to the new hating-Matasha rule. But explaining all that just made her feel tired.

Should she write about her father? What was there to say? Also, if she wrote about him, her mother might read between the lines and realize that he never said anything about her and didn't seem to miss her.

Finally, she wrote a couple of sentences about an author who had been on the Johnny Carson show recently. Her name was Gail Bakersfield and her current novel had so far sold, Johnny Carson said, three hundred thousand copies. Matasha was surprised to see a woman author on the show. She couldn't remember that happening before. She didn't particularly like the woman, who wore a lot of makeup and had grand, fake gestures. What she wrote about didn't sound compelling either: rich people who took a lot of pills. Matasha wasn't interested in reading about that. She was sure that she wouldn't be interested in reading about it even if she were grown up. Still, it was something to think about: a rich lady writer sitting on Johnny Carson's couch. This was something that felt worth telling her mother about, but once it sat all alone on the page, with so little else around it, nothing about school or her father, it felt odd, funny. So she put the letter in her Messy Drawer without finishing it.

Besides, she didn't have an address to send it to.

Every morning, over her cereal, Matasha turned to Dottie Summers's column to see if her letter was there. It never was. She left for school, rode the bus hoping to see neither Camille nor Tamar, and walked past the construction site, where things were picking up again. The exterior walls for the first and second floors were in place, and later, when she came home, there were always a lot of trucks parked on the street nearby, unloading materials.

Cranes deposited mysterious things into openings on the top floors. At lunch Matasha sat with Gina Wilkins and Wendy Urquhart and their friends as always, and didn't interact with them much otherwise.

Her mother did not call back. Matasha counted out the days on the calendar since the last call, but she already knew the number. Forty-two. Now she told herself that perhaps six weeks wasn't the real deadline, but if her mother didn't call back after two months, she would know she was probably not coming back.

If she misses me, thought Matasha, *doesn't she want to hear my voice?*

She must not miss me.

On the way to school Camille and her friends worked up a litany.

"Do you know why Matasha's mother left? It's because Matasha smells."

"Do you know why Matasha's mother left? It's because she thinks Matasha is *bo-ring*."

"Do you know why Matasha's mother left? It's because she doesn't love her."

Matasha pictured their words as large stones. Each one hit her and threatened to crush her. But she found that if she didn't cry she could keep on walking, and all those crushing things would somehow not crush her. She kept on walking. Each thing they said made her feel as if she might die from shame, and yet she didn't die. She kept walking to school, and when she got there she was still alive. Her hands worked, and her head.

In the stairwell one day, out of nowhere, Camille grabbed

Matasha by the collar and yanked and called her a slut. Matasha wasn't 100 percent sure what a slut was but she knew it was very bad and she turned and brought up her fist and punched Camille right in the face. She didn't even remember her brain deciding to do it. It just happened when she felt that yank against her neck. Camille put her hand to her cheek and stared. Matasha stood square against her, her hands balled into fists, ready to swing again if she had to. She could feel the heat and energy coursing through her veins. Camille cried, "You're *dead!*" and ran down to the next floor. Camille didn't touch her after that, although the taunts continued.

Something interesting happened. Now that Camille was busy dreaming up ways to make Matasha miserable, Jean stopped being so unkind. Matasha thought she even caught Jean looking dismayed at some of the things Camille did. Once Camille and three others—Kay, Glenda, and a very large fifth grader named Mamie O'Court—came up to Matasha at her locker and made a circle around her. Silently they stepped closer and closer, forcing Matasha against the opening. It suddenly occurred to Matasha that they might force her inside, bang the door shut, and lock the combination lock.

"Hey, Matasha," said Jean. "Do you have your math book? Can I look at it?" She stepped between Matasha and Camille's crowd. Camille fell back, and the others did likewise. Jean talked to her about the day's math homework, and did she get how Mr. Evinrude did the last problem? The air went breathable again. Camille and her friends dispersed down the hallway, and Jean turned back to her locker without a word.

13.

The locker incident scared Matasha enough that she finally told her father what was going on. His lips tightened and he became very stiff.

"That is unacceptable," he said. "This is going to have to stop."

Matasha was glad to hear it, but she wondered how her father was going to make it stop. Would he call the principal? The principal couldn't follow Camille all the time into the stairwells and watch her at the lockers. Her father did know Camille's father, though. Maybe that would help.

The next morning Ellen told Matasha that she was driving her to school. Matasha was ready at the usual time, but since they didn't have to leave until later, she sat around watching the clock and feeling uneasy. She liked driving with Ellen, though. Ellen drove more sedately than either her mother or her father, and she sometimes told stories along the way about her childhood with her five brothers. Today they were quiet, and Matasha rested her head against the window and thought about how she wanted to look like Ellen when she got older. Ellen was nineteen and sort of a hippie. She had long brown hair that she kept either down or in pigtails, and she wore skirts made out of jeans that had been cut open and then patched with big quilted triangles of colorful fabric front and back. She wore earrings made out of feathers. Matasha was back to thinking about getting her ears pierced. When they arrived at school, Ellen said she'd be there again at 2:45 to pick her up.

During lunch, Matasha was called into the principal's office. Dr. Daisey asked Matasha to tell him about anything that had been going on recently involving other children teasing her or attacking her. Matasha looked at the floor and felt tears well up for the first time in a while. The kids at school knew about her mother; the principal knew about her mother; everyone knew.

She told Dr. Daisey what she needed to through her tears, hating him while she was doing it.

"I don't want you to worry anymore," Dr. Daisey told her. "We're going to make sure that anyone who tries to bother you will be punished." Then he told her he had something for her. He opened a drawer and pulled out a picture book with the title *Maybe Yes, Maybe No*.

Oh, God, a picture book, thought Matasha. *Come on, Dr. Daisey.*

"I know, it looks like a little kid's book," said the principal. "But the pictures are very beautiful. They're watercolors. And the story is a very old Chinese folktale. I read this book myself at times; I find it very useful. And I give copies to students I think will understand it." Matasha took the book from his hands. Dr. Daisey fished around a little more in the drawer and found a dusty green Tootsie Pop. "Take that too. But, er, save it until you get home," he said.

She thanked him and got to math class only a few minutes late. Mr. Evinrude nodded at her, as if he knew the reason for her tardiness. Matasha slunk down in her seat without even glancing at Jean and Tamar to see whether they were talking together, what they were up to.

Mr. Evinrude was teaching about ratios. Matasha didn't even watch the board. She stuck the Chinese book in her lap and opened to the front page. Her head down, she read silently:

Once upon a time there was a Chinese farmer whose horse ran away. His neighbors came by to tell him how sorry they were. "How will you be able to plow your fields?" they asked. "How unfortunate."

Mr. Evinrude didn't say anything.

14.

Matasha's father cleared his throat. The previous night he'd come in as usual after she'd gone to bed, but this morning he was up early and sat opposite her as she ate her cereal.

"How was school yesterday?" he asked.

"It was okay. Dr. Daisey talked to me. He said he'd make sure nobody was going to bother me anymore. Nobody did bother me. He gave me a book."

"A book?"

Matasha was sorry she'd mentioned it. Too hard to explain. "Just a book to look at."

Her father cleared his throat again. "Do you want to take the bus to school this morning, or do you want Ellen to take you?"

Matasha wanted to be driven, but how was that going to work every day? Ellen came only a couple of times a week. "Ellen," she said. Her father looked worried. "But then I'll start taking the bus again tomorrow." Her father smiled. "That's my girl," he said.

They both went back to reading the newspaper. The minute she'd gotten downstairs she'd checked as always for her letter in Dottie Summers's column. But today there was a letter from someone who had recently moved from the country to the city and was disgusted by the impoliteness of city people, and another from a woman who felt her husband didn't bathe often enough. Since Matasha knew her father preferred the news and business sections, she left those for him and turned to the arts pages. There was a boring review of a book on World War II. After a while, she said to her father, "I guess An isn't going to come live with us."

Her father looked up. "No, she's not."

"We were going to have four people in the family and now we're only two. That's not even a family."

"Don't say that, Matasha. Two is still a family. We're still a family."

"We're not, Daddy. Face it. We're a father and a daughter. That's it."

"Are you sure you don't want to become a lawyer one day?"

"I'm sure. It's too dry."

He sighed.

"I still want a sister," Matasha said.

"Now, you know that can't be."

"I don't know," she said stubbornly, although she knew she was arguing against reason. "She could go to school with me. I would have someone to be with on weekends. Mommy doesn't have to be here. I'll take care of her."

"It was a crazy idea, Matasha. It always was. Even if your mother had stayed."

"It *wasn't*. Not if you really wanted it."

"Well, isn't that the point? I didn't want it."

Matasha was quiet. "What will happen to An?"

"She's probably already been taken by another family."

"What if she hasn't? What if they run out of families?"

Her father frowned. "I don't know, Matasha."

"Maybe we were her only chance," whispered Matasha, but she mumbled it so that her father couldn't hear. Aloud, she said, "Did she know that she was supposed to come to us?"

Mr. Wax thought. "Probably not. I don't think they would have told her anything until the arrangement was more definite."

"Can we find out where she went, and write to her?"

"I don't think that would be such a good idea, Matasha. She'll need to settle down into her new family. It will be confusing enough as it is. I think it's best if we just put all this behind us, and give it up."

You give up too easily, Matasha wanted to say. If you cared about something, you had to fight for it. Her father didn't even care enough about her mother to fight to get her back. Of course, he probably had no idea where she was, and Matasha did. Again, she was tempted to tell him what she knew—what she thought she knew. Again she pulled back: she didn't want him, too, to leave for Switzerland. Still, there was something wrong with her father's attitude. *Somehow*, Matasha was convinced, he could find a way to fight successfully for her mother's return. Could let her mother know he was willing to do just that. That that was exactly what her mother was waiting for.

After that morning, Matasha took the bus again to school. Camille kept her distance, mostly. Sometimes, she said nasty things under her breath, and occasionally she huddled with her friends looking pointedly at Matasha and laughing. She rightly guessed that Matasha wouldn't go to anyone about this: it would be too much Matasha's word against hers. But Matasha felt Camille was wary now, careful. And Matasha was wary too. She remembered the way her veins had streamed with a strange exhilaration when Camille had grabbed her in the stairwell, how when her fist had shot out to punch Camille, the thought passing through her mind was that she might well get stomped to death but that she didn't mind. Looking back, she was impressed with herself, as she might be impressed with a heroine in a book, but she was frightened also. Because she also remembered that she'd been ready to kill Camille. Not kill her the way kids talked about all the time—"I could kill her"—not even "kill" as a hyperbolic way of saying "really hurt her physically." But "kill" as in *kill*. She'd felt she had it in her to smash Camille's head against the wall, bash and bash until it gave way and despicable Camille became a puddle of blood and brains. This was *in* her, this willingness. She couldn't entirely trust herself any longer. She would have to watch herself.

So she regarded Camille carefully, too, on the bus when they rode together, on the walk to and from school, in gym, in the hallways. Not just because she feared Camille's tongue and presence. But because if Camille did anything more to make her really angry, she no longer knew what her own strong will might do.

15.

Once upon a time there was a Chinese farmer whose horse ran away. His neighbors came by to tell him how sorry they were. "How will you be able to plow your fields?" they asked. "How unfortunate."

"Maybe yes, maybe no," the farmer said.

The next day the horse came back bringing seven wild horses with it. The farmer's neighbors came by to congratulate him. "You have eight horses now!" they marveled. "You are a wealthy man! How lucky!"

"Maybe yes, maybe no," the farmer said.

The following day the farmer's son tried to ride one of the wild horses and it threw him and he broke his leg. The farmer's neighbors came by. "You won't be able to do all the farm work on your own," they said. "How unfortunate."

"Maybe yes, maybe no," the farmer said.

The following day government officials arrived in the village because war had broken out in the land. They demanded that all the young men join the army. They did not take the farmer's son with them because of his broken leg. The farmer's neighbors came by. "So many of our sons will die in this war," they cried. "How fortunate you are!"

Matasha got it. Dr. Daisey was trying to say that you never knew how things would turn out. Everything that was awful now might lead to something good later, something better than if the misfortune had never happened. Matasha couldn't deny that this was possible, but it also seemed like the kind of thing that grown-ups were dying to tell you when you were upset. That way they didn't have to think too hard about the truth, which was that things were absolutely horrible for you *right now*, that you needed change right away and not at some maybe-time in the future.

16.

Some problems that appeared in Dottie Summers's column:

- A woman afraid that her fourteen-year-old daughter had tried marijuana.
- A woman who hadn't been on vacation in thirteen years and felt her husband should be paying for them to take one.
- A grandfather concerned that his son was spoiling the grandchildren.
- A woman arguing that the proper way to hang a toilet paper roll was with the sheets dispensing from the top. Many letters over the next weeks argued against or agreed with this statement. The issue seemed to generate a lot of emotion.

There were dandelions in the park, expanses of bright yellow. The sixth graders went out at recess.

A letter arrived for Matasha. It had foreign stamps on it.

Dear Matasha:
It's been two months since I spoke to you. I bet a lot has happened to you during this time. A lot has happened to me. I'm sorry I didn't call but I was trying to sort

things out. Maybe when you get older you will know what I mean by that. I was afraid to call because all calling did was confuse me and make me cry. I know it must have been hard on you not to hear from me.

I'm living in Switzerland now, in a town called Gersau, which is a little town in the Alps close to a larger one called Küssnacht. Gersau is very pretty, with quaint old houses and a beautiful old church and farms. I'm happy here, or at least as happy as your mother is capable of being. When you're older you may understand that comment also. Actually, I hope that you won't.

I miss city life but we are not that far from Zurich, which is quite a big city, and I go regularly to the opera and ballet. The theater not so much because my German is not good. I never was good with languages. We might move to Zurich or Paris at some point but not just yet.

I guess I just said "we." The other part of the "we" is Alban. If you can believe this I met him on a trip to Europe with my girlfriends before your father and I ever knew each other. Some years ago he found out where I lived and began to write me. He has three grown children and has been divorced for a long time.

I do love your father, or at least I did. I can't live with him anymore though. His head is in his work. There's no room there for me, not really. I have to live with someone who hears me when I speak and listens not just to what I say but to what I am feeling and needing. Your father is a good man, and he tries, but he can't do these things for me. I think he does them better with you. He has always had a special connection to you. When you were a baby you were the one thing that could bring him out of himself. He cares about you, even if he sometimes has trouble showing it. He is also more steady than I am. I think he is the better parent for you.

Now, even though I just said this, I want to make a suggestion. You don't know Alban, but oddly enough he knows you. I have been writing to him about you for years. He has seen you grow up through pictures. We would like you to come live with us during the summers. Would you consider that? I don't want you to grow up without me. I know I'm the one who left but it doesn't mean I don't care about you. [Something here was x-ed out and although Matasha spent long minutes turning the paper over and trying to read under the ink marks, she couldn't.] *Can you believe I was talking about adopting a Vietnamese boat child? It just goes to show you how addled I'd become.* [The next words were also x-ed out, but less thoroughly, and this time Matasha could read what they'd said. They said, "I was grasping at."] *I am better now. I need to be here. But I don't want to lose you. I don't want to force you though either. You think about it, and do what is best for you. Talk to your father about*

it of course. He is very angry at me and probably won't
want you to come. But you think about it by yourself
and try to feel what you really want. Then let me know.
   Love,
   Mom

She'd written a phone number at the bottom.

Matasha put the letter in her Messy Drawer. She was going to think about it. She didn't want to ask her father about it just yet.

17.

"Matasha!" called Sunset. "The phone is for you!"

Matasha sped to the landing. She hadn't heard the ring over her record player. She'd been jumping around her room strumming an invisible guitar to Springsteen's "She's the One." She had to put her hand over her heart to slow it before picking up the receiver.

"I got it!" she screamed down to Sunset.

It wasn't her mother. It was Helen Lake, asking about history. All the sixth graders had to write a ten-page final paper about a major development in Chicago's history. They had to choose their topic this week so they could start researching. Matasha had already asked Mrs. L'Enfant if her Chicago Fire novel could fulfill the assignment—she was nearly done with it. In the last scenes, a new school is built to replace the temporary lean-to, and Rachel's mother becomes the new teacher after the sadistic teacher is found out and fired. Mrs. L'Enfant had said no, but that if she turned it in, she would give her extra credit.

Helen wanted to know what topic Matasha had decided on. Matasha planned to write about the redirection of the Chicago River.

"That's a good one," said Helen morosely. "Do you think I could write about that too? I can't think of any good ones."

Matasha didn't want Helen to write about the same topic.

Helen was very smart, once she got going, but she was lazy in her way. She would moon about, saying she didn't know what to do for this or that school assignment, then at the last minute she'd write something that blew everyone else out of the water. She put together facts and ideas that occurred to nobody else. She read books Matasha had only vaguely heard of. Once in the hallway Matasha saw her reading Freud's *Interpretation of Dreams*. She'd heard of Freud and was proud she knew that the correct way to pronounce the name was "Froid." But she didn't know much more than that. Helen said it was an amazing book, all about what was going on in your mind when you were asleep. Matasha realized her mother had the same book at home, and she spent some time looking at it later that day. Much of it was impenetrable, but she enjoyed reading the actual dreams. Her mother had always said that dreams mattered, but you had to know *how* they mattered.

"What about the Columbian Exposition?" Matasha suggested.

Helen sighed. "Yeah. Maybe. No. Hey, do you want to come over after school tomorrow?"

Matasha felt fluttery: flattered and anxious. "Sure," she said.

"Dinah, my cat, had kittens last week, five of them. You could see them."

"Wow!" cried Matasha. "Sure!"

Helen lived walking distance from school. The sun was out the next afternoon and it was genuinely, deliciously warm. They walked with their faces turned up to the sky, and a man passing said pleasantly, "Girls, you're going to bump into something."

As soon as they arrived, Helen led Matasha into the laundry room. The mother cat was lying on her side behind a large steam pipe, her nipples pink and sticking out, while two kittens fed on her and three more lay in a heap just beside. One was gray, one calico, one black and white. It was too hard to see the last two.

"They still don't have their eyes open. Mostly they just lie there all day in a big pile keeping each other warm."

Matasha couldn't believe how tiny the kittens were, how fragile. They were wet-looking, not fluffy or particularly cute. But they were fascinating.

"Why are they in the laundry room?"

"Dinah picked out the place. I guess because it's sheltered back here, and warm. When the dryer's going, it gets really toasty."

"When will they open their eyes?"

"Another couple of days. Mom said we could keep one this year. Last year we had to give them all away, because my brother was tormenting them. Chasing them all the time and throwing them up in the air. Do you want one?"

"I'd *love* one," Matasha said. "I already have a rabbit, though." Her stomach pinched as it always did when she thought of Mr. Bunny. "I'll have to ask my father."

"My father" hung in the air, trumpeting loudly the absence of the normal phrase, "my mother." Helen didn't say anything about it. "I hope you can take one," she said.

They couldn't hold or even get too close to the kittens;

they were way too new, and it would upset Dinah. The girls got a snack and then played Mastermind in Helen's room. Matasha was delighted that Helen also loved Mastermind and didn't care if Matasha took five minutes sussing out her next move. Later they went back to the kittens and Matasha concluded that the black-and-white one was definitely the cutest. She decided it was a girl even though Helen said that until the kittens got older and they could start handling them, they wouldn't be able to tell. Helen told her more about how the kittens would grow. They were still totally deaf as well as blind, but later their ears would start to poke up (they lay flat now), and that would mean they could hear. They would get little teeth and begin to clean themselves rather than have Dinah lick them clean. The best was around six weeks when they started to run around. Last year, the kittens' favorite toy was the vacuum cleaner. They ran up and down it like maniacs. "First Dinah has to teach them to walk, though. She picks each one up by its scruff and takes them out into the foyer and sits with them until they get going."

"Oh, my God," breathed Matasha. "I wish I could see it."

"I'll invite you back when they get started. It's funny too. They keep wobbling and falling down."

That night Matasha left a note for her father:

Dear Daddy:
Today I went to Helen Lake's house and her cat just had five kittens. She said I can have one when they get to be eight weeks old. May I please take one? There is a black-and-white one that I am so in love with.

I've already named it Peanuts. PLEASE, Daddy.
I know you don't like pets. I would do all the work.
I'm learning from Helen how you have to take care
of them. Cats are very clean, they bathe themselves
all the time. THEY DO NOT SMELL. PLEASE,
Daddy. Let me know.
> *Love,*
> *your daughter,*
> *Matasha*

When she woke up, her father was still sleeping. Matasha returned home from school to this note on her bed.

Dear Matasha:
I will think about it. There is another decision we have
to talk about, isn't there?
> *Love,*
> *Daddy*

18.

On Sunday morning Matasha helped her father with his matzoh brei, which was sort of like scrambled eggs with matzoh in it. You crumbled matzoh sheets into a mix of eggs and milk, poking at the bits to get them completely soaked through, then fried them up in a pan. Matasha set the table and poured the orange juice while her father cooked. They sat in silence, eating and gazing out at the gleaming lake and the smoke puffs rising from the nearby rooftops.

Her father cleared his throat. *Oh, no*, thought Matasha.

"Can I get the kitten?" Matasha asked.

"I want to talk to you about this summer first. Have you done any thinking about it?"

Matasha wanted to know how her father knew about the invitation to Switzerland.

"Your mother wrote to me. She said she was writing to you too. Were you surprised to know she was in Switzerland?"

Matasha hesitated. "Yes," she lied. She hated lying. It felt like washing her hands in slime.

"I suspected she was there," her father said. "At first I thought she'd gone to a hotel, but after a few days I began to guess."

"How did you guess Switzerland?"

"I know your mother pretty well. Even though she would say I don't."

"I don't think I want to go," said Matasha. In truth she'd been unable to give it any thought. The minute she'd closed her Messy Drawer, she'd allowed herself to put that off. Things were going reasonably well now, what with having Helen to hang out with—Matasha had been to her house again and seen the kittens with their eyes open—and Camille and Jean staying out of her hair. In saying she didn't want to go to Switzerland, she was really just trying on the idea to hear how it sounded.

She thought her father might be pleased at her statement, but he didn't smile. And in the next moment she became afraid. If she didn't go, when would she next see her mother?

"Actually," Matasha said, "I think I do want to go." Her father didn't look any more pleased by this.

"Daddy, stop looking at me."

Her father looked at his watch.

Matasha's stomach was jumping around. "How would I get to Switzerland? Would I have to fly over there all by myself?" It seemed very far. What if she got on the wrong plane? What if no one was there to get her when she arrived?

"I don't see how it could be any other way," Mr. Wax said.

"Why can't Mom come here?" Matasha started to cry. She cried a lot less often these days, but sometimes the spring just started up again. "Why does she have to make everything so hard?" She cried more. Mr. Wax watched her uncomfortably. Matasha began to hate him for sitting there so uselessly.

"Just HUG me, Daddy," she hissed at him.

He held out his arms and she came over. He pulled her in awkwardly. *Hopeless*, she thought. *Just hopeless.* But it was better than having him sit across the table while she cried all alone.

Matasha knew she would end up going to visit her mother, though she didn't see how it could actually happen. The plane, the strange town, this Alban . . . it was just unimaginable.

"*I want a kitten!*" she raged.

The throat clearing again. "Well, one thing relates to the other," said her father. "I believe you, Matasha, when you say you'll take complete charge of the kitten. But how is that going to work if you go away for the summer? Who will take care of the kitten then?"

Matasha leapt up. "You mean I can't have Peanuts if I go visit Mommy?"

"I'm afraid so, Matasha. If you go, Sunset won't be here most of the week, there's no need for her. There will be no one to take care of the cat."

"I can't BELIEVE it!" screamed Matasha. "I HAVE to have Peanuts. I have to!"

Mr. Wax pushed his chair back from the table. He was going to do what he always did: move in the opposite direction from any unreasonable emotion.

"You can't not let me have Peanuts just because I'm going to Switzerland. It's not fair! It's not fair!" Matasha swiped her plate off the table and it fell to the floor, shattering into several large pieces. The sound of its shattering was immensely satisfying. She ran to the window and punched it hard, but it didn't break.

Thwarted, she wasn't sure what else to do. She planted her feet and opened her mouth and screamed as loudly as she could.

Then she stopped. She was panting. Her face was wet. Already a new sensation was creeping in: she felt silly. Her father was looking at her in appalled bewilderment. She turned and went upstairs. Quietly she closed her door and lay on her bed. She prayed her father would not come in. Then, as the minutes passed and nothing happened, she wished he would come in. Finally she felt more alone than she had ever felt in her entire life. After that, mercifully, she fell asleep and didn't wake up until the middle of the afternoon.

Though she was mortified and wanted to forget the whole incident, Matasha knew the next step was up to her. If she left it to her father, he would simply ignore everything that had happened and never bring it up again. Nothing would happen with the kitten. A ticket would show up for Switzerland, and Matasha would have to go.

She thought about it for the rest of the day and the next one. In the evening, she wrote another letter to her father:

Dear Daddy:

I am writing you the most serious letter I have ever written you in my life. I'm really begging you to listen.

I am sorry about the way I acted. I won't do that again. But having a kitten is really, really important to me. It just is. I will take good care of Peanuts. Over the summer Sunset can take care of her on the days she is here. The litter box only needs to be changed once a week (that's what Helen told me) and Sunset can do that, right? I'll talk to her about it. The rest of the week ALL YOU HAVE TO DO is change Peanuts's water bowl and give her food in the morning and when you get home. Cats get dry food and canned food. It's so easy. Daddy, you can do this for me. You really can. Then I'll be back from the summer and I'll take over COMPLETELY.

This is my proposal. When Peanuts is eight weeks old I'll bring her home for a week. You see if you like her. I'll show you about her water and food. If after a week you still think it's a bad idea I'll give her back to Helen. Give Peanuts/me a chance, Daddy. Okay?

> *Love,*
> *Matasha*

In the morning:

Dear Matasha:
Okay. We'll try that.
> *Love,*
> *Daddy*

Sunset harrumphed when she heard they were getting another pet. "First the photography chemicals and now a litter box in the laundry room?" she asked. "Your laundry isn't going to smell nice anymore."

"Just wait and see. Maybe it won't be that bad." "Just wait and see" was Matasha's new favorite advice, to other people and to herself. It covered so many situations. But to soften up Sunset, she promised to change Peanuts's litter box twice a week instead of once. Sunset seemed skeptical she would follow through, so Matasha made a note to herself and taped it to the wall next to her bed: "Be grown up about this. You really have to DO it." In the meantime, every time she read the note it reminded her to go visit Mr. Bunny. She wished she could boast to someone that he was getting fed and petted every day now, but nobody, not her mother or father or Sunset, seemed to care very much what happened with Mr. Bunny.

19.

Matasha saw in the movies section of the *Tribune* that the movie *2001: A Space Odyssey* was playing at the Argosy Theater downtown. A couple of years ago her mother had taken her to a Charlie Chaplin film there, *The Gold Rush*, which Matasha had loved. Charlie Chaplin had been so delirious with hunger that he'd eaten his shoes, after doing a little dance with them in which he hallucinated that they were potatoes. She'd loved the theater too: massive, with carved pillars, a big domed ceiling, and deep-red velvet seats. Her mother said it had been built in the 1890s and used to have vaudeville shows and Ziegfeld Follies–type performances with dancers in feathers and sequins. It was the height of elegance to go there, although these days it was shabby—her mother's words. Matasha couldn't see the shabbiness: the spaciousness and rich colors were positively royal to her.

And her mother had once told her that *2001* was a masterpiece, an astonishing film that she must one day see.

Matasha mentioned the showing to Helen, who unlike Jean got a spark in her eye at the idea of doing something unfamiliar, and one Saturday Matasha took the bus to Helen's and then the two of them together took another bus to the Argosy.

Matasha bought Junior Mints and Helen bought malted milk balls and the movie was very odd, interesting in some parts and dull in others. Matasha liked the part where the astronaut disabled the computer, HAL, and his voice got slower and slower and deeper and deeper as he wound down like a toy. It was spooky. Helen liked the part with the apes best. One of the things she thought she might like to be when she got older was a biologist, or maybe a vet. She also thought about being a psychologist. Her mother was one, and saw patients in their home. Sometimes Helen thought she could be an animal psychologist.

There was a small crowd at the exit, and as they gained the street, Matasha saw something bizarre right in front of her—a man's hand sliding into a woman's brown suede purse. The purse was hanging at the woman's side, behind her elbow, and either she had left its zipper open or the man had opened it a moment before; whichever it was, the woman couldn't see or apparently feel the hand that was now emerging from the purse with a slim wallet.

"Hey!" cried Matasha, deeply offended. And then she did something that astonished her. She reached out and plucked the wallet from the man's hand. Later she realized it had been like the newspaper reports of people who jumped down to rescue people who'd fallen onto the El tracks: "I did it before I even thought about it." The thief, a small man for a grown-up, began to her even greater surprise to stammer an apology. "Mistake," he said beseechingly. He actually held out his palms. "Mistake—!"

The woman had turned at the commotion. She saw her wallet in Matasha's hand and froze, confused. Matasha handed it to her and the woman, utterly bewildered, murmured, "Thank you," and hurried away. The thief was already zigzagging through the milling patrons into the open street. In a moment both he and the woman were gone, as if zapped into different story lines.

Matasha looked at Helen. Helen looked at Matasha. Helen started laughing.

"You're crazy!" she cried. "What if that guy had a gun?"

"He didn't have a *gun*," said Matasha, disgusted. Somehow in the moment she hadn't felt any danger, just outrage.

"You're crazy!" Helen repeated, delighted. "You did such a good thing! Let's go get ice cream."

And that did seem the proper response to the event: to treat themselves. They got off at a stop near school where there was a Baskin-Robbins, and Matasha had rocky road and Helen had mint chip, and they traded bites, which Jean never wanted to do, she said you got each other's spit. When they were done with the ice cream, Helen asked, as Matasha had hoped she would, if Matasha wanted to come back to her place and see her kitten. Matasha was fizzy with anticipation. "They're getting active now," Helen promised, and indeed they were.

Dinah had the kittens out in the living room. Helen said she'd moved their home base to the liquor closet there, maybe so she didn't have to keep sharing space with Evelyn, the housekeeper. The kittens were wobbling around and falling down under her watchful eye.

"I still think yours should be called Peanut," said Helen. "She's only one."

"No," said Matasha definitively. "Peanuts."

"All right," agreed Helen.

Helen's mother appeared and stood watching the cats with them.

"Are you done seeing patients today?" asked Helen.

"All done," said her mother. Mrs. Lake was slender and wore a man's tailored shirt untucked over a narrow skirt. She'd taken off her shoes and was in bare feet. Matasha hadn't met her before. Mrs. Lake's therapy office had a different entrance, around the corner, and Helen said the patients went in and out all day and she never saw them. That was to protect their privacy.

"Are you the friend who's going to take the black-and-white?" asked Mrs. Lake. Matasha thrilled to the word "friend." She liked how naturally it came off Mrs. Lake's tongue, like there was no question about it. Matasha answered that she was, and Mrs. Lake said she was pleased to meet her. Did Matasha want to stay for dinner with the family?

Matasha was dying to stay, but Saturday night was now restaurant night with her father, so she said no thank you. She and her father always ate at a particular place near the apartment, and he let her order anything she wanted, including steak, plus dessert. Sometimes instead of having dessert they went out afterward for ice cream, and Matasha thought her father ate ice cream like a kid, with obvious pleasure, licking up the drips on the side of the cone instead of wiping them with a napkin the way many adults did. If they had ice cream tonight, that would make two ice creams in one day.

Over these dinners Matasha and her father often talked about stories Matasha had read in the newspaper, or about different kinds of cameras and photographic processes and how they worked. There was going to be a presidential election in November, and sometimes they talked about why her father was planning to vote for Gerald Ford. They decided what they were going to do the next day. Twice now they had gone bowling. Tomorrow, maybe it would be warm enough to get their bikes out of storage and go for a ride along the lake.

As Matasha walked down Helen's front stairs to get her coat, Helen's little brother zipped past and squirted her with his water gun. "Hey!" she said.

"Stop acting out!" yelled Helen at his back. "It's developmental," she told Matasha apologetically. "Although my parents also give him too much freedom. He needs boundaries."

"Okay," said Matasha, drying her cheek with her sleeve. Helen used a lot of language that came from her mother and from the psychology books she read. Matasha was trying to keep up. She thought some of the things Helen knew might be helpful in figuring out what was going on with her own baffling family.

20.

Matasha's father took her downtown and bought her a large suitcase for her trip. She showed him the department at Marshall Field's where she and her mother did camp shopping, and she got several pairs of shorts and tops, two bathing suits, and two sundresses. Her father was less attentive than her mother to the shopping and also more patient. He did work while she browsed and tried things on, so she took as long as she wanted. They stopped in the shoe department and Matasha bought sneakers and flip-flops. Matasha needed all new things because she'd grown. During her April visit, Dr. Karnow said she'd gained another whole inch. Matasha had figured as much because her pants seemed short (they really were turning into high-waters) and her toes were cramped in her shoes. She wasn't eager to go to her annual physical when she turned twelve, but she knew she ought to and that her father might not know to schedule it. So she reminded him, and she got to see him in the middle of the day, looking businesslike and significant walking into Dr. Andrews's waiting room with his briefcase and suit. She took a taxi, the first time she'd done so by herself, and met him there. She copied what she'd seen her mother do innumerable times— walk out into the street and wave—and it worked. When the doctor came in, he seemed to have completely forgotten what had happened the last time they'd seen each other, or at least he wasn't letting on. He spoke to her pleasantly and asked her to get on the scale.

"Four feet five and three-quarter inches," he said. "That's marvelous. You're responding well to the treatment, Matasha. Any aches or pains in your legs or anywhere else? No? Great." And Matasha weighed in at sixty-eight pounds. Her father went out of the room when Matasha got into her paper gown to be examined.

"Guess what?" said Dr. Andrews, after checking the straightness of her spine and listening to her heart and testing her reflexes. "No shots this year. Here you are probably a champ at shots now and I don't have any shots to give you." He smiled.

21.

In the middle of May, just days after Matasha's twelfth birthday, there was a sad surprise: Mr. Bunny died. He had made it through the entire winter, through days of his water bottle being frozen and of no food, and through the last snow squalls of April. But even though Matasha had been remembering to feed him every day, and there was finally some sun and warmth, Mr. Bunny had given out. Matasha went out to the fire escape one afternoon and thought Mr. Bunny was sleeping when she lifted his hutch, although normally at her approach he would wake and raise his head expectantly. She put out her hand to pet him and right away knew something was wrong: he was too still. Bracing herself, she lifted him up, and his legs hung stiffly beneath him, not pedaling anxiously as usual. She put him back down quickly, thinking: *I've touched something dead!* She ran inside to the sink and thrust her hands under the faucet, washed them for a long time, and then told Sunset what had happened. Sunset sighed.

"What do we do?" Matasha cried.

"We're going to go out and wrap him up, and then we'll ask your daddy," said Sunset.

"He won't know what to do." Matasha was quite confident of that. "We need to bury him!"

"Dear one, I don't know about burying. Where would we bury him?"

Matasha thought of the park. But the association with Martin Kimmel, who might after all be in the ground there somewhere, gave her the shivers. She didn't expect that her father was going to be willing to drive her outside the city to dig a grave. Where would that even be? And anyway, that would have to wait until Sunday, and what would they do with Mr. Bunny's poor body until then?

"I expect," said Sunset, "we can bring him down to the incinerator."

Matasha put her face in her hands.

"It's clean," said Sunset. "And he can't feel anything now. He'll just go like smoke back into the sky, into heaven, like all of us do eventually."

Matasha didn't quite get the logic—how exactly did everyone end up as smoke in heaven?—but she recognized, as she often did lately, that she had only so many options. "All right," she said.

Sunset found an old sheet, and they went together onto the fire escape. There was a humid breeze, and in the wind off the lake, Matasha got a whiff of summer. She was startled to realize that Sunset wanted nothing to do with touching Mr. Bunny. So she folded the sheet in half and scooped him up, and then she sat with the fire escape slats pressing uncomfortably into her bottom, cradling him in her lap and crying.

"He never did anything to anybody," she cried. "He was just a nice bunny. He didn't have a very good life."

"Now, Matasha. If you hadn't had him, he would have been some rabbit off in the woods, running away from the foxes and dogs all day. He would have been scared and hungry all the time."

"He probably was scared and hungry all the time *here*."

Sunset made a sound in her throat but didn't say anything.

"The Waxes are terrible people," Matasha said fiercely. "We're not even a family. We can't take care of anything." She wrapped another layer of sheet around Mr. Bunny and hugged the bundle closer. She wasn't frightened or repelled by him anymore. She just felt very sad. She felt, somehow, that Mr. Bunny was very sad, too, even though he was dead. He had not had a particularly good life and he had deserved better.

"Okay," she said finally and reached out a hand so Sunset could help her up.

Jim, the garage man, wasn't with the cars, so they walked down to the basement and knocked on his apartment door. They explained what had happened, and he took the bundle from them without surprise or questions. Matasha wondered if other pets in the building had found their way eventually to this door.

"I'll take care of it," he promised, and Matasha and Sunset returned upstairs, where Sunset suggested they watch *The Edge of Night* together. Matasha said fine even though it was the kind of show where, if you hadn't been watching for a long time, you had no idea what was going on. Sunset explained as they went: this woman had had an affair with that man's brother; this college student was on drugs; this man had been embezzling money from his employer.

The soap ended and Sunset stood up to start dinner, making her groaning noise.

"What's for dinner?" Matasha asked. She'd had hamburgers or spaghetti three days already this week, so it would probably be tacos out of the box.

It was tacos out of the box.

In bed that night, Matasha began to worry that she would have a nightmare about Mr. Bunny. She had touched him when he was dead, and that seemed to make it likely. Helen Lake had tried to explain to her that all dreams were about getting something you wanted. This made no sense, since some dreams were nightmares: about your parents dying or about being chased by a monster or drowning in the ocean. Or even about realizing you'd gone to school in your nightgown: nobody wanted to do that. Helen said Freud had talked about that very dream, the nightgown one. He said it was a wish to go back to the time when you were very little and nobody minded if you ran around without your clothes on. Matasha didn't think she'd ever run around without her clothes on. Had Helen? Oh, sure, Helen said. Matasha argued with Helen: she was upset in those sorts of dreams, not happy. Helen said it had all seemed more convincing when she'd read it in Freud's book.

If she had dreams about Mr. Bunny, Helen might say they were because she wanted him back, and she did want him back, but not back *dead*. She didn't want him chasing her with evil in his eyes and long fangs, or turning up in that white sheet they'd wrapped him in. She didn't want to come out to his cage and find him again, not moving. She didn't want . . . but then she was, in fact, asleep, and she didn't dream of him, though months later, she did, and it wasn't scary. In those dreams, Mr. Bunny somehow lived out in the suburbs in someone's backyard where she could visit him every so often, and the person who owned him left his cage door open so he could come in and out and run around the yard as he pleased. But that was when she and Helen were separated for the summer, and so it was a while before they got around to continuing the conversation about whether dreams were wishes or fears or some combination of both or maybe just meaningless movies that turned up when you went to sleep.

22.

Jean now made conversation with Matasha whenever they found themselves together at their lockers. She wasn't hanging around with Tamar that much anymore; perhaps she'd finally admitted to herself how dull that was. Her tone, as she made some comment about gym or math, suggested that nothing had happened between them, nothing that needed talking about. Matasha wished she could see it that way, but she couldn't, and she could never answer in a similarly offhand tone. Something had happened, and Matasha would never feel the same way again. If Jean would only say to her: "Look, I was horrible and mean and I apologize and I want to make it up to you," maybe they could be friends again. She missed Jean enormously. But not this way, not by pretending. And Matasha couldn't bring herself to tell Jean this. It wasn't something you could say. Having to ask for an apology canceled out its value. Matasha remembered her father saying of her mother, "You can't just go *get* somebody. They have to want to come home." It wasn't exactly the same, but it sort of was. So she said, "Yeah, Mr. Evinrude didn't make any sense today," or whatever was called for, and swallowed down the bad taste in her throat and tried to straighten her expression.

She didn't talk to Jean about it when, at the end of May, they found Martin Kimmel. He was alive after all, to everyone's great surprise. What had happened was this: Martin Kimmel had an uncle who was part of a very strict religious sect. Martin's father had grown up in the sect too. The brother, whose name was Gerhard, was upset that Martin's father no longer belonged to the sect; Martin and his parents didn't go to church at all. Gerhard believed that they would all go to hell. That was what he told the papers after his arrest. Gerhard had moved to Chicago without telling the family, in order to observe them and learn Martin's schedule. He had decided that Martin's parents were a lost cause but Martin was a child and he could still save him. He came to the park day after day, waiting for a time when the woman who took care of Martin was distracted and no other eyes were on the boy. Finally he had gone up to Martin as he stood at the water fountain and introduced himself as his uncle. And since Martin had seen pictures of his uncle, he walked off trustingly with him, and was whisked away to a kind of religious commune in northern Minnesota that called itself the People of the Restoration and forbade most contact with the outside world.

When the police found Martin, he was thin and suffering from a chronic cough and bronchitis. (The community did not visit doctors or use prescription medications.) However, he didn't seem unhappy. He reported that he'd been homesick at first but that his uncle had told him his parents had arranged this extended visit and that eventually they would come up and see him. In the meantime he'd been indoctrinated into the various practices of the community, which included four hours of prayer a day, fasting two days a week, and laboring at the farm the sect owned and through which they fed themselves. He received an hour of school a day, mostly Bible study, and had forgotten a good deal of his math and geography. There were only a very few other children in the community; most of its members were older people or childless.

Matasha was thunderstruck. In all of her imaginings about Martin, this outcome had never occurred to her. First of all, he was alive! This was thrilling: sometimes you thought the worst— the worst seemed like the most likely result—and yet it didn't happen. Second, what a story! Maybe when Matasha finished her Chicago Fire novel she would set a new one at an extreme religious commune. It might be hard to get good information about how a place like that worked, though.

Luckily, the newspapers and TV stayed interested in the story for a while. They ran updates about how Martin was adjusting to life back home with his mother and father. Something odd happened. Martin became more distressed the longer he was with them. He told his parents they were going to hell and that he wanted to return to the farm, which had already been shut down and the residents scattered following revelations of tax dodging and child labor. Martin's mother reported that her son was afraid of her.

"We're trying to figure out, slowly, what Martin was told about me," she said on TV. "It's going to be a long road back to normalcy."

Not long after the news came out, Matasha told Helen how she used to think Martin Kimmel was buried under the new middle-high school. Helen was tickled. "What made you think *that*?" she asked. Matasha admitted she had no idea. "Well, it could have happened," said Helen judiciously. Matasha didn't tell her about the time she and Jean had gone down into the construction pit—she didn't think she would ever tell anyone about that.

They were in Helen's living room with the kittens. One of the grays was scrambling after the calico, falling and righting himself again and again. They had ranged far from their mother, who was curled on the window seat, blinking at the three kittens who had decided to stay within her orbit. They were a roiling ring, swiping at each other's tails, leaping up and rolling over, separating and coming together again. Matasha watched Peanuts's black head appear and disappear in the scrum. She wanted to grab and kiss that head a million times. After she and Helen had enjoyed this entertainment for a while, Helen thrust in her hands and grabbed Peanuts in a way Matasha was still trying to learn. Helen put her hand under the kitten's bottom to quiet him and brought him to Matasha's lap. Peanuts had turned out to be a him, once Helen and her parents were able to check. This had required a day or two of disappointment and adjustment, but now Matasha felt Peanuts had been always and obviously a boy. She kept her hand firmly but gently on his bottom as Helen had taught her and felt him begin to settle and then purr. She stroked him over and over, feeling him fuse deeper with the motion of her hand, the heat of her lap. She closed her eyes, absorbing the perfect moment.

"What are you going to do in Switzerland?" Helen asked. Matasha wasn't exactly sure. In a phone call, her mother had said they were going to hike in the mountains and spend time sailing on Lake Lucerne. Matasha found it hard to believe that her

mother was going to spend any real time on a boat or hiking—
these sounded more like things that, like the cross-country skiing,
she would try once and then say she never had to do again—but
then it turned out that Alban owned a boat, so maybe there was
going to be a lot of sailing after all. There was a club where the
boat was kept and where Matasha would meet other kids, some
from other parts of the world. Matasha wasn't crazy about this
and told her mother she wouldn't need to go to the club, she was
going to bring plenty of books with her. Her mother paused and
said she wanted Matasha to *try* to make friends but that if no one
suited her, she could do what she wanted. She added that the
club was famous for serving a treat Matasha would love: melted
chocolate on a waffle. That did sound good.

Matasha did not let her father know how frightened she
was to get on a plane by herself and go halfway around the
world to a place where she wouldn't have Peanuts or Helen or
Sunset or him, no one except her mother and some strange man
who might be awful. She wouldn't even have her Chicago Fire
book; she'd finished it and turned it in to Mrs. L'Enfant. She'd
decided the religious commune book would be too hard to
write, so she still needed a new idea. Helen said that since she'd
been so interested in the Martin Kimmel case, maybe she should
write a mystery novel, and Matasha was intrigued. It would be
a challenge. She'd have to come up with a crime and then work
backward to think of all kinds of clues as well as irrelevant details
that would mislead the reader. Perhaps she could get started on
it during the plane ride. *Plenty of paper*, she reminded herself.
The idea of bringing a big stack of blank pages was comforting,

stabilizing somehow, as she planned her trip.

Helen rummaged in her knapsack and brought out a book, yet another one Matasha had never heard of, this one called *The Presentation of Self in Everyday Life*, which sounded beyond boring to Matasha, but Helen said it was great, all about how no matter what you were doing, you were always playing a part. People were always saying you should be yourself, but there was really no such thing. Whether you knew it or not, you were always trying to be some kind of role: a student or a daughter or a sister, a smart person or a bubblehead. Did Matasha know that the original meaning of the word "person" was "mask"?

Matasha didn't know. This seemed awesome in some way she didn't have time to sort out.

"I just want to be normal when I grow up," she said. "That's all."

"You probably won't be. Nearly every human being has one or more significant neuroses."

"That's so depressing," said Matasha, who wasn't entirely sure what neuroses were.

"I don't know," said Helen. "I think it's kind of neat."

While Helen read, Matasha dreamed over the kitten, imagining the type of food she would feed him—tuna fish could be a treat, couldn't it?—and how Peanuts would sleep in her bed all night. When Matasha gave herself her shot, Peanuts would wait on her pillow, sadly recognizing what Matasha had to do, and cuddling with her afterward. Peanuts would tell Matasha that this was all going to be worth it in the end, that she'd grow up to be a nice, small woman and not some big monster. Peanuts would promise her she wouldn't get cancer from the shots. Peanuts would say that after spending the summer with Matasha, her mother would decide to return to Chicago with her, but then Matasha would tell Peanuts that he couldn't actually know something like that.

When it was time to go home, Matasha gently lifted a limp and sleepy Peanuts to the floor, where he shook himself, stretched, and then trotted away toward his siblings, who were batting at a pencil stub that someone had dropped.

"You're going to be so excited next Friday!" Helen informed her. Next Friday was when Peanuts would be eight weeks old and Matasha could adopt him.

When the day arrived, Helen and Matasha brought Peanuts to Matasha's house in a boot box, lined with newspaper, that Helen had gotten from home. Sunset had to smile when she saw him. How could you not? He was plump and fluffy, with a soft wet nose. His eye color had turned from baby blue (Helen said that all kittens had blue eyes at first) to gray. His head and body were black, but his chest, his paws, and the area just around his nose and mouth were snow white. He let out a tiny meow when he laid eyes on Sunset, as if acknowledging her authority.

"All right," said Sunset. "Let's see what the little devil does."

Matasha sat on the kitchen floor and lifted Peanuts out of the box. He took a few careful steps and meowed again, clearly feeling out of his element. Then he trotted forward and slipped on Sunset's well-waxed tiles. Matasha didn't mean to laugh at him, but he looked so silly and sorry. She put him in her lap and consoled him until he was vibrating steadily.

"Want to hold him?" she asked, lifting him toward Sunset.

"Oh, no you don't." Sunset put her hands up like a policeman going *Stop.*

"I'm so jealous," said Helen. "I wish we could keep him. You picked the best one."

Matasha beamed.

That night she tried to stay awake until her father got home. He wasn't back by ten thirty, so she set her alarm clock for midnight. She took Peanuts to bed with her, but while she was asleep, he crawled off and went somewhere. At midnight she got up and found him under her bed. She swiped him up before he was too awake to dash off. Downstairs, the light was on in the kitchen. Mr. Wax was having some orange juice and an apple.

"Matasha!" he said, surprised.

"Daddy, did you see Peanuts?"

"Why, did he get lost?"

"No! I just want you to see him."

Peanuts was still sleepy, his eyes irritable slits. Matasha held him against her chest and let her father pet him.

"Did you ever have pets growing up, Dad?"

"Are you kidding? Grandma Nan wouldn't have stood for it in a million years. She had to have everything in the house just shipshape."

"That's sad."

"Mm. Don't you think you should get back to bed now? Maybe Peanuts wants to go to sleep."

"No, Peanuts wanted to meet you."

"Uh-huh. Well, I'm glad to meet Peanuts also."

23.

The trial week with Peanuts went by, and Mr. Wax didn't say anything. Sunset seemed to accept his presence and even brought him a green ball of yarn to play with. The yarn made him bananas; he batted it, jumped on it, chased it, rolled over and under it. He was a little creature with loads of energy. Fearful of ruining a good thing, Matasha didn't bring up the trial deadline with her father. As time passed, she figured that Peanuts was staying for good. Every few days Helen came over to see him and to hang out. Helen did things with other kids, too, though, and wasn't always available. It wasn't like with Jean, where Matasha had known she was Jean's best friend and vice versa, where they were always each other's first choice for being together. With Helen, Matasha had to share, and this was new and not always welcome. And there were other differences she'd had to acknowledge. A few times Matasha tried to play Helen the types of records she and Jean had listened to so avidly together, but Helen wasn't interested. She had the same lousy taste in music as everybody else. So mostly they visited Peanuts or played board games or read together on Matasha's bed, Helen folded into lotus position with her back against the wall, Matasha sprawled any which way. Right now Helen was reading Studs Terkel's *Working*, which was just a bunch of people talking about the jobs they did. Matasha had borrowed it to read a few chapters and found it surprisingly fascinating. Helen said she could have her copy when she was done. She brought Matasha her *Jane Eyre* as a substitute. They didn't even hear when Sunset called them down for dinner.

And sometimes Matasha walked to Helen's house after school. It would never feel like Jean's house, messy and old-fashioned and warm, but it had its points. All the furniture was colorful and squishy and comfortable, and there were bowls of candy—jawbreakers, Hershey's Kisses, candy corns—just lying around. And of course, there was the kitten Helen had gotten to keep, the gray she'd named Homer, and the mother cat, Dinah. Once, during the week, Matasha stayed for dinner. Even though the Lakes had a housekeeper, Mrs. Lake joined the kids for dinners before going back to see more patients. At that meal she gave Matasha a postcard of sailboats on the brilliant blue water of Lake Lucerne. Matasha taped it to the wall by her bed alongside the reminder about the care of Peanuts, which she had never really needed: she never forgot to do what she was supposed to for him. She had determined after the first two days that he would learn to sleep in the bed with her, so she brought him there every night and eventually he did stop hiding underneath. She woke with him by her head or nested in the crook of her arm, and when she roused herself, he got up too and stretched a luxurious stretch, his little black back humped up and his paws kneading the bed quilt, as he got ready for his day.

24.

On Class Day at Margaret E. Marvin Elementary School, each student got a certificate saying that he or she had met the requirements for his or her grade and was hereby promoted to the next one. There was a speech by Dr. Daisey and class prizes for academic performance and citizenship and art. Everyone dressed up and parents attended. For the sixth graders, it was a special occasion, as they would be graduating to the middle school. Mrs. Andretti, the music teacher, had the class learn a special song to perform, something about the waving wheat and flowing rivers of the Midwest. It had such a tuneless melody that everyone had trouble singing the right notes, and during rehearsals Mrs. Andretti had had to struggle to keep everyone cooperative as she banged out the dramatic parts on her grand piano.

The sixth graders sang their song on the stage and then took their seats in the auditorium. Then Dr. Daisey talked for a long time about the new middle-high school and how it would be ready for move-in by Labor Day, although the pool and the science lab were behind schedule and it would be "a little bit of an adventure" working around the construction in the fall. Each middle school and high school grade, the principal reminded the parents, would be taking in twenty new students; this was a long-hoped-for expansion made possible by the new space. "This is a new era for the Margaret E. Marvin School. We can make our superb educational opportunities available to a broader range of students. Due to the generosity of parents and alumni, we are increasing our financial aid offerings. We are actively seeking out high-performing students from less privileged neighborhoods and school districts. We want Margaret E. Marvin to better reflect the diversity of this great city."

Matasha was wearing one of her new sundresses and a pair of cork-heeled sandals instead of Mary Janes, which felt grown up to her. The class sat in alphabetical order, and Matasha was very aware of Jean's presence next to her. She seemed huddled and small and unhappy. Jean always complained about Class Day because she hated dressing up and because even though a good number of prizes were handed out, she never won anything. Matasha didn't feel sorry for her. If Jean wanted to win the art prize, then she shouldn't hide her art all the time. Matasha's father was sitting in the back rows with the other parents, or at least she hoped so. She couldn't see him. It was the first time he'd come to a Class Day; normally, because it was on a workday, only her mother came. Matasha had been nervous that even with her mother gone he wouldn't show up, but when he'd mentioned the date and she'd expressed some surprise that he had it on his calendar, he'd seemed hurt. Matasha usually won the academic record award, and it would be depressing if that happened and her father missed it. But he had asked for the exact time and said he would be there. She hadn't seen him come in and hoped that he had not been late.

The principal stopped talking about the new construction and financial aid and began to announce the class prizes. They started with the first graders, so there was a long wait. Matasha thought it possible that she wouldn't win the academic record award this year. Helen was much smarter than she was, smarter than anyone else around: that was obvious. On the other hand she was careless about turning in her assignments. If she lost interest in something, she just didn't bother to do the work. So maybe Matasha would win after all.

They finally got to the sixth graders. Helen won for best history paper. After not even having a topic, she'd decided to write about the history of Black neighborhoods in Chicago, and a dazzled Mrs. L'Enfant had read out portions from the paper in class. Camille Janklow and Kay Bledsoe got a special award for their work with Mr. Evinrude's Little Sisters project; they'd raised money for it through a car wash and some bake sales. Matasha couldn't believe it when Dr. Daisey praised Camille and Kay for "leadership and furthering good works at the Margaret E. Marvin School." Then she got so busy thinking about Jean and how annoyed she would be if Matasha was called up for the academic record award that she didn't hear when her name actually was called. Jean hissed at her to *go up*, and Matasha snapped back to attention. She climbed the stage stairs and shook Dr. Daisey's hand and took the small silver plate with her name engraved on it. The citizenship prize went to Gina Wilkins and Elliott Gleason for "class behavior, collegiality, and representing the values embodied by Margaret E. Marvin." Jennifer Stegner received the art prize. Then Dr. Daisey said that for the first time they were going to award a second art prize. The prize had always been for the visual arts, but this year they had decided to bestow it as well for an outstanding work of creative writing, *Before and after the Flames*, by Matasha Wax. And Matasha got up a second time, warm-faced and thrilled, to accept a second silver plate from Dr. Daisey.

After the gym award and the music award, everyone sang the school song, which, like the song the sixth graders had learned, was rather tuneless and bombastic, and then the auditorium was allowed to slowly empty, the youngest students first. As they waited in the crush, Jean grumbled that maybe one of these years she would win an award for going the most years without winning an award. She didn't congratulate Matasha on her two prizes, but Matasha didn't detect any real hostility either. Outside the auditorium, Matasha spotted her father; he waved.

It was only noon, but school was over: for the day and for the year. Mr. Wax put his arm around his daughter. "Well, congratulations," he said. "You've had a big day." He seemed genuinely proud. "I can't believe I got it for my book," Matasha said, a little bewildered. Just then Mrs. L'Enfant came by and congratulated Matasha as well. "I hope you don't mind that I shared your book with the prize committee," she said. "It was something special." Matasha, tongue-tied, hoped that her father and Mrs. L'Enfant would strike up a conversation, but nothing happened and after a minute Mrs. L'Enfant told Matasha to have a good summer and drifted away.

Some of the sixth-grade girls were hugging in that showy way that seemed to have gotten popular this year. A few were even crying, as if they wouldn't be seeing each other in three months, or more likely sooner. Helen and Matasha inspected each other's prize plates. Helen had promised Matasha that she'd come visit Peanuts sometimes while Matasha was in Switzerland. Helen and her family would be spending a month in Vermont, but while she was home she could do it. She'd even change his litter box. Mr. Wax had agreed that Helen could come over when Sunset was around.

"Sunset will be so happy," Matasha said now.

"I want to see Peanuts as much as I can," Helen said. She was still in mourning for the kittens they'd had to give away. She'd said that maybe she wouldn't want Dinah to have kittens again; it was too hard when they left. Matasha felt a pang herself: she was going to miss a good chunk of Peanuts's kittenhood.

"Cats get really crazy if you leave them alone too much," Helen said. "They act like they don't want anybody to bother them, but they need the cuddling."

"Maybe you'll mail me a picture," said Matasha, not too hopefully. She had already given Helen her mailing address but suspected that she would be a lackadaisical correspondent.

"Yeah!" said Helen. "I can do that." She sighed. "I wish I could go to Switzerland."

"You wouldn't want your parents to split up just so you could go."

"That's true. Do you think your mom will look different?"

"Different?" The thought had never occurred to Matasha.

"Sadness changes the way people look. So does happiness. Do you think your mom is more sad now or more happy?"

"Happier, I guess," said Matasha, thinking of the way her mother sounded on the phone during their occasional calls. "Or the same. Actually, I think she's probably the same."

"Well, maybe she won't look any different then."

"I'll teach you some German in my letters. I'm probably going to learn some German."

"Neat! It will help me read Freud."

"Do I have to go home now?" Matasha asked her father, who was hovering on the fringes of this conversation, jingling the change in his pocket. She was hoping for something to extend the day and keep afloat its strange buoyancy.

"I have to go back to the office, Matasha."

"I know. Can I come with you?"

"I'm going to be busy. What would you do with yourself?"

"I'm twelve. I know how to read and everything. I have a book with me." She had Studs Terkel's *Working*, which Helen had finished with. "If I get hungry, I can go out to State Street and get myself something to eat."

"Big girl," he said. "All right."

She spent the afternoon reading in one of the leather chairs outside her father's office, blinking up at the lawyers and secretaries when they came by and oohed and aahed over how big she'd gotten and how pretty she was (*Liars*, Matasha thought) and how long it had been since they'd seen her. One guessed that she was going into fifth grade, and she gave him a look and set him straight. A secretary brought her tea and cookies, and another on her lunch break bought her a copy of *Teen Beat* magazine, which was very nice of her even though Matasha loathed *Teen Beat*. The day's excitement kept her from getting hungry. At seven o'clock her father announced that they were heading out to a restaurant called Carmelo's. The table held a lit candle, and Matasha felt uneasy, as if her mother should be sitting in the seat she occupied, although she knew her mother never met her father for dinner during his workweek. Matasha ordered something she'd never tried before, baked ziti, because her father said it was good here, and it was good. But as usual she left two-thirds of it on her plate. She might be growing, but she still couldn't ever finish her food.

Her father paid the bill after scrutinizing it carefully and adding up the figures twice, and then he said it really was time for her to go home. Matasha agreed. He put her in a cab, and she watched as the familiar streets flew by in the dimming light. She felt like someone much older looking back at herself when she was young and riding in a cab at night was still new: the streetlamps coming on, the lake disappearing into shadow. When she arrived home, she immediately showed Sunset her two silver plates.

"Well, that's beautiful," said Sunset. "That's just beautiful. Your daddy must be so proud of you. And you're going to write your mother about it, aren't you?"

"I'm going to be there next week."

"Yes, you are going to write her. Tonight."

Matasha argued that the letter wouldn't even get to her mother before she did, but Sunset said it didn't matter, she needed to write while it was still fresh in her mind. Matasha wondered when Sunset had become such a stickler for letter writing. She'd never seen Sunset write a letter in her life.

"So what are you going to do with your BIG, WHOLE summer?" Matasha spread her hands wide.

"Well, I am going to pay attention to my garden," said Sunset. "I am going to raise a prize-winning crop of beans. I am going to take care of my sunflowers and my roses. I am going to enjoy being sixty-four years old and spending less time on my feet. I am going to *kneel* in that garden, and I am going to love sticking my hands in all that dirt. And then I am going to come here twice a week and keep this place nice for your father. Not that you can see a pin out of place when he has been around."

Matasha bounced up and down on Sunset's bed. "I'm excited, I'm excited," she called out.

"What are you so excited about?" Sunset asked with mock disapproval.

"I don't know!" cried Matasha. And she didn't. It wasn't a good feeling, and it wasn't a bad feeling. Or maybe it was a little bit of a bad feeling. The excitement felt speedy, like a car out of control. She wished it would slow down, but she was hypnotized by the motion. It was going to be this way, Matasha suspected, for a long time.

25.

Matasha asked her father to cut out and save all of Dottie Summers's columns while she was in Switzerland, and he said he'd try. She emphasized that it was *very, very important*, without telling him that she was still waiting for a reply to her letter. If she missed even one column, she might miss Dottie's answer. But she was starting to think that Dottie never was going to answer. Developments had made the part about Martin Kimmel irrelevant, for one thing. Her mother had turned up, and Matasha did now have a friend. Of course, Dottie Summers couldn't know all those parts. Even though some of the things she'd written about weren't so urgent anymore, Matasha was still eager to see what Dottie had to say. "Watch the newspaper," Dottie had told her. She had pretty much promised to answer.

The letter appeared the Monday after Class Day. Matasha was startled when she saw it, not just because she'd largely given up hope of seeing it but because it read like this:

Dear Dottie Summers:
I'm a teenager, and everything in my life has gone
wrong. I don't have friends anymore. My (former)
best friend since first grade is being really mean to me.
She ignores me and then tells me what she hates about
me. My mom left the house one night and didn't come

back. It's been over a month. I've decided that if six
weeks go by and she doesn't come back she might not
come back at all.

I don't want other people to find out about my
mom. What if they do? And what if my mother doesn't
come back?

Sincerely,
Too Many Troubles

What had Dottie done to her letter? Just for starters, what was that line about being a teenager? Matasha hadn't written her age in the letter, so why had Dottie made something up? Matasha understood why Dottie had taken out the part about Martin Kimmel. But why wasn't there anything about the shots? Practically the whole letter had been rewritten. Matasha had not said, "Everything in my life has gone wrong." She could have said it, but she hadn't. Those were not her words! What was wrong with *her* words? She'd written that she didn't *really* have friends anymore. That was because she did sit with Gina Wilkins and Wendy Urquhart at lunch; they were still nice to her. She'd said "really" completely on purpose, to show that these were not deep, true friends. By taking out that word, Dottie had made Matasha sound more pathetic than she was. And for no reason that Matasha could see, she'd changed the order of her sentences about her mom. What was the point of that?

Matasha was angry and troubled. She'd trusted Dottie Summers. It had never occurred to her that Dottie monkeyed with the letters people wrote her. Did she do this all the time?

Here was Dottie's answer:

Dear Too Many Troubles:

Your mother did a terrible thing. Unfortunately, you can't control what she will or will not do in the future. Nor can you prevent other people from eventually finding out. Your family situation is none of their business, though. If they bring it up, that's exactly what you should tell them.

As for your "friend," stop talking to that skunk. Join an after-school club or start spending more time at your church. Do some volunteer work. You will quickly find new friends and your ex-friend will become a distant memory.

Sincerely,

Dottie

That was it? That was all that Dottie Summers had to say? Matasha had expected Dottie's advice to her to be uniquely understanding. She'd believed that Dottie would say the single right thing that could make her feel better. But all she'd offered was the most obvious, shallow advice, advice that could be given by someone who was barely listening to you. Dottie should know that it wasn't so easy to stand up to nasty people or stop talking to the person who had been your friend forever. What if you hated after-school clubs? And what was this about a church? Dottie was Jewish!

And she had rewritten Matasha's letter!

And replied to it so late that it didn't matter anyhow.

Still, Matasha cut out the column and put it in an envelope with the copy she'd made of the letter she'd sent Dottie. She pushed the envelope to the back of her Messy Drawer. One of these years she was going to have to go through everything in there and decide what to get rid of.

In the next days, Matasha finished getting ready for her trip. She already had a passport. Mr. Wax had Ellen pick up a cooler bag for her to transport her growth hormone in. The stewardesses would put it in the plane's refrigerator while they were in flight. Matasha begged Sunset to try to love Peanuts a little while she was away. She and her father went over her American Express traveler's checks; he showed her how to countersign them and warned her to be very careful with them as they were the same as real money. Sunset gave her a large book of crossword puzzles, and Matasha had *Working*, a horror novel called *Audrey Rose*, and *Wuthering Heights*, which Helen said she should read now that she'd read *Jane Eyre*. She had her Instamatic camera, several boxes of flashcubes for the camera, and a three-hundred-sheet package of loose-leaf paper for starting her novel about a sister and brother, orphans who struggle to survive during the Great Depression. When she'd gotten down to trying to write the murder mystery, she found she couldn't do it. Once she came up with her victim, all she could think of was Martin Kimmel and the terrible things she'd once feared might have happened to him, and it made the murder feel too real. Reading *Working* had given her the idea for a Depression story, since a lot of the people in the book talked about the Depression. In her own book, the sister and brother become motherless as babies; their wealthy father dies of a heart attack upon discovering he's lost all their money in the crash of 1929. The sister, who is sixteen, finds work washing clothes to support the two of them. Matasha hadn't yet thought up any of their further adventures.

Her flight was in the evening. By the time she arrived in Zurich, it would be morning there. For once her father didn't run late—"You don't fool around with the airport," he said. They went up to the desk at the gate, and her father explained that Matasha was traveling as an unaccompanied minor. The woman behind the desk cooed at her and asked how old was she, nine? Then she gave her a pin shaped like a pair of wings. While they waited for Matasha to board, her father marked up papers from his briefcase and Matasha companionably read the comics from the *Sun-Times*. Then he hugged her goodbye—a real, tight hug—and told her to have fun, and that he'd call once a week on Sundays.

On the plane Matasha had a window seat, which was what she'd hoped for. On flights she never got tired of looking out at the thick layer of white clouds beneath her: how incredible that she was higher up than she could see when she gazed up at the sky from the ground. Helen would probably have some interesting and unexpected comment to make about that, maybe about how altitude affected people's behavior. A husband and wife sat in the seats next to hers, and there were two other rows beyond theirs, one in the plane's center and one on the far side. Matasha had never been in such a large plane before. The husband and wife spoke a foreign language to each other and left her alone. But before takeoff a stewardess leaned over and said, "You're the girl traveling by herself, aren't you?" and told her her name was Marsha and she would look out for her, that Matasha should just press the call button if she needed anything. Marsha was young and pretty and had a blue-and-red scarf tied around her neck. Matasha and Marsha, the stewardess said, their names were similar, weren't they?

Matasha had a plan for the plane flight: she was going to start a diary. She was traveling to a foreign country for the first time in her life—sitting on the beach in the Dominican Republic and Mexico didn't count—and it seemed as if she should preserve some of her new experiences. The new experience of Switzerland. The new experience of being with her mother while her mother was with another man. Whatever new things would eventually happen in her friendship with Helen. In the fall, the new school building and all her new middle school teachers.

She had bought a three-ring binder and some dividers with tabs so she could separate the diary section of the binder from the novel-writing section. When the early flurry of takeoff was over and cabin conversation had settled to a low hum, she turned to the diary section. Her father had said she should try to get some sleep on the flight, but she wasn't tired yet. After describing the plane and where she was going, she wrote about leaving Peanuts behind and how Helen was going to help take care of him, and then she wrote about Helen, what she looked like and what she was like, and writing about Helen led to writing about Jean and a short explanation of the things that had happened with her this year, and writing about *that* led straight to writing about the visit they'd made to the construction pit. Matasha had avoided thinking about that too clearly for a while, and she didn't describe it now. Instead, she found herself putting down disjointed sentences and questions. "Why does Jean hate me?" she wrote. (Did Jean still hate her? She wasn't sure.) "Why did she get so mad?" She chewed on the end of her pencil and thought. She took the pencil out of her mouth and realized that it was Jean who always chewed on the ends of her pencils; she herself never did. She let a picture assemble and expand in her mind: the two of them down in the pit, with Jean's mother's trowels and discarded pop bottles and the big mounds of earth taller than they were. The earthmovers, dirty and yellow. Jean's face: scared. Matasha had been scared too. But she couldn't see her own face in the picture. Jean's was the one she saw: pale, big-eyed, and very frightened. She, Matasha, had made that happen to Jean. She'd made Jean go down in the pit when she hadn't really wanted to, and maybe that had been wrong. Why at the time had she thought it was so important? It seemed crazy now that she'd believed she somehow magically knew where Martin was and that she would be the one to find him. That seemed like something a little kid would think. Anyway, Martin was okay now—or sort of okay—and that was good, at least.

Matasha put down her pencil. There was more to think and write about Jean, but it eluded her. She would try again tomorrow. She thumbed the rest of the pages in the diary section.

It was a nice, thick, promising block of blank pages.

She thought about the conversation she'd had with Helen about whether her mother was happier or not happier than before she'd gone away. In her last phone call with her mother, going over some final details about Matasha's arrival, her mother had in fact sounded happy. Happy to be seeing her, excited about the places she wanted to show Matasha. She told Matasha: "Alban is a very kind man. He's not going to try to be your dad, okay? He knows you have a dad. He just wants you to be comfortable while you're here and get to know him. He doesn't expect anything, not even that you like him." Matasha thought that sounded pretty sensible of Alban, and not being expected to like him made her actually like him a little.

Until this conversation, she'd still believed her mother might return with her to Chicago at the end of the summer. She'd imagined she wouldn't want to be parted from Matasha anymore. Now she didn't think that was so. Now she resented her mother for being happier with Alban than with her father. What was so wrong with her father? What was so much better about Alban?

She looked down at her open diary. A diary, she was realizing, carried some of the same difficulties as a letter to Dear Dottie. What counted as a problem? How did you describe it?

As it happened, she still had some business to finish with Dottie. Off and on she'd thought about writing another letter to her, demanding to know why she had changed the first letter and why she hadn't given better advice. She would put the *D* inside the circle again so Dottie would definitely see it. She was still so disappointed in Dottie. Maybe if she confronted her, Dottie would be ashamed and admit that what she was doing was not nice and not even honest. It would make her change her ways. But something told Matasha that this wouldn't happen. Dottie had been writing her column forever, and she probably wouldn't care what some kid had to say about it.

Dottie likely wouldn't change if Matasha wrote her a letter. But after staring out at the darkening cloud carpet for a while and asking for a Pepsi when the drinks cart came by, Matasha wrote it anyway. She would get the right kind of stamp and mail it all the way from Switzerland. In her letter, Matasha explained that you shouldn't change somebody else's words without asking permission. You should include some extra advice in case someone couldn't follow your main advice. She wrote that people all over the United States read Dottie's column and depended on her and that she had a responsibility. Matasha wasn't nasty. She wasn't disrespectful. She just laid out the case, maybe the way her father laid out his cases, as accurately and persuasively as she could, and explained her side of the story. Because you know what? Dottie should hear what Matasha had to say, whether she would change her ways or not.

After she finished the letter and returned her binder to her knapsack, she felt the man next to her, the husband of the foreign couple, looking at her. She raised her head. He was smiling.

"Is this your first time going to Switzerland?" he asked. He had an accent but his English sounded perfect.

"Yes," said Matasha. She meant to leave it at that, maybe even turn away. She didn't like talking to people on airplanes.

Usually they turned out to be strange in one way or another. But this man seemed pleasant enough, and in recent weeks Matasha had been thinking that if she wanted to be a writer, she should probably push herself to talk to more different types of people. So she added: "I'm going to see my mother. She lives in Gersau." Matasha hoped she was pronouncing it right.

The man turned to his wife and they spoke rapidly in their language, presumably German. Then he turned back. "My wife is reminding me about Gersau. It's beautiful there. There is a very historic church. Well, Switzerland has many historic churches. Has your mother told you about the salty cheesecake?"

"The salty cheesecake?"

"Yes. That's a specialty of Gersau. You will ask for it in a restaurant and you will love it, I'm sure."

"Okay!" agreed Matasha.

"And the lake—well, it is Lake Lucerne. Famous. Beautiful. I hope you will do some sailing."

"We will," Matasha assured him. The man turned to his wife and translated for her. She said something to him.

"My wife is impressed that you are traveling so far all alone," the man explained. "She says, 'Good for you.'"

Yes, thought Matasha. *I am traveling all alone.*
Good for me.

Acknowledgments

Much gratitude to Karin Gottshall, Anne Horowitz, Hannah Ratner, Jonathan Ratner, Joanne Serling, Anna Stein, and Fiona Wonderlich, who helped me bring the best out of these pages, and to Elizabeth Clementson and Robert Lasner, who gave a home to my girl.